I0638342

AUSTIN BY MORNING
AUSTIN AFTER DARK BOOK 3
Alexa Padgett

Austin by Morning © 2020 Alexa Padgett

ISBN-978-1-945090-27-1

Edited by Sarah Allan and Charity Chimni
Cover Design by Covers by Combs

For Sarah. You made this book so much better. Thank you for your time, your thoughts, and your patience as I struggled to give both Kate and Rye the love they deserve.

CHAPTER ONE | Kate

The ringing cell phone startled me, and I knocked my empty mug off the desk in a mad scramble to find it.

"Aha!" I grabbed it. My burgeoning grin fell when I saw my brother Cam's number.

I answered, "Hello?" and slipped to the floor to pick up the mug.

The mug's handle stayed on the ground. Dammit. It was my favorite—from a diner in Chicago—and I used it pretty much every day.

"I need your help, Katie Rose."

I slammed my head into the edge of my wooden desk. I breathed out a curse and inched upward with care.

"I've asked you not to call me that, Cam," I said.

"Sorry. Old habits and all that."

"I'm twenty-six years old. You need to let go of the image of me as your baby sister." I closed my eyes and prayed for patience. "Let's start this conversation again. What do you need, Camden?"

"My guitar's banged up. Can't play it today." Camden's voice was sheepish, and I'd bet he hung his head. Not that he was a sheepish or head-hanging kind of guy. A country music superstar, Cam and his ego usually matched. But his wife and my boss, Jenna, made him that guitar, and he adored the instrument almost as much as he loved her.

Such shows of cuteness activated my gag reflex, but his love for Jenna was one of the reasons I hadn't completely quit talking to him.

"What did you do?" I asked.

"Didn't do a damn thing." His irritation crackled through the phone line. I sat up straight, tossing the pieces of my mug in the trash bin before I glared at my computer screen. I would have preferred to glare at Cam, but he was all the way across Austin.

Convenient for him.

"Fine," I said on a sigh. "What happened to your precious?"

"She's standing right here next to me, looking as sparkly as her wedding and engagement rings."

Yeah, my brother had it bad. I bit back a smile but didn't try to stop my eye roll.

"*Camden.*"

"A roadie dropped my guitar. After he took it out of the case." I gasped. "He took it out?"

"Wanted a closer look at the design Jenna made in the metal."

"Let me guess. He's no longer your roadie."

"He's working a different stage now," Cam replied, his voice dry.

One thing about my brother—he might be angry with the man responsible. No doubt he was livid, but he wouldn't want the guy to lose his job. Yet another reason I couldn't completely justify my anger toward my dear big brother. He was kind. Noble. Good to Jenna. No doubt he'd adopt a stray dog in the next couple of months because he really was a great man.

No. The real problem I struggled to get past these last few months was that Cam and his twin, Carter, went along with my mother to perpetuate the lie we were one big happy family.

The worst part in the situation wasn't the fact I was the only spawn of the no-account asshole our mother married. No, the *worst* part was that my family—the people who claimed to love me—wouldn't have told me the truth. Ever. If I hadn't overheard Cam and Carter talking…

That stuck deep in my chest and ripped at my heart each time I remembered the twisted mouth and shadowed eyes Mama turned my way when I asked her about the lie she kept pushing.

I shoved that memory away, just as I did with all thoughts of my mother.

Cam wouldn't let me take time to hide and lick my wounds. He said I'd work myself up into a fit of righteous anger.

Um… *Exactly.*

But Cam kept calling, kept dropping by and being sweet, which made staying angry with him difficult. Carter, Cam's twin, I'd pretty much forgiven since he wasn't even in town when my world imploded. Plus, he'd just gone through his own personal hell.

I had no such issue with my mama. We were *not* on speaking terms.

"I need you to bring me one of the other ones from the shop," Cam said, breaking me out of my reverie.

"Any one in particular? We can showcase the narrow-bodied mahogany or the bell-shaped Brazilian rosewood."

"Good. Yes, both of those. And Jenna said there's another one in the back she's been working on."

"You expect me to carry three guitars into South by Southwest by myself?" I scowled. "That's over fifty thou in equipment, Camden. I'm capable of handling myself, but that seems excessive."

"Right. Fine. Then bring the two you think would be best," he said, his voice filled with exasperation. "C'mon, Katie Ro... er, Kate, sorry. I *need* a good guitar. I don't want to borrow my opening act's instrument. He's already a nightmare to work with."

He used the wheedling voice. The one I'd never been able to resist. Fine. I didn't want to resist it or Cam. I loved my big brother, even if he had hurt me deeply, and I wanted him to have a successful performance.

I glanced down in mournful silence at the pile of paperwork on my desk, still in need of attention.

"I'll be there in an hour," I said.

"Thanks, darling. Honestly, you're the best."

"Too right. Now, be sure to play something I like."

"Right after all Jen's favorites," Cam promised.

"Bye." I hung up and stood. After a quick stretch, I pulled down my ruffle-fronted, white silk blouse, re-tucking the front into my purple A-line skirt. I had great legs, and I liked to show those suckers off.

I slid my feet into the sweet black Manolo Blahnik slingbacks—ninety percent off at last year's Nordstrom Rack sale, thank you very much. After I carefully placed both guitars in their cases and double-checked their latches, I went to the front and shut off some of the lighting. I flipped the sign to "closed" and ensured the door was indeed locked, which it always was. Jenna had some trouble with an old...well, not flame, more like jerk-wad from her past. Since then, we didn't unlock the door until we knew who was on the other side.

After shutting down the computer, I tossed the phone and charger into my purse. I dug out my car keys before I collected everything and headed out to my car. I only had to run back in once—and then one more time to double-check I'd set the alarm and locked the rear door.

I looked back in longing one more time at the small, unassuming shop. My refuge, my baby these days.

With a sigh, I put the key in the ignition and wished for the patience to deal with this newest round of awkward.

———— ★ ————

I managed to get a decent parking spot, no doubt because it was still days before the festival began. I gripped the guitar case handles tightly and hoped to see one of Cam's security guys hustling toward me. Normally, thanks to my brother's overprotectiveness, Jen and I shared security detail while at work.

Because Jenna left early to meet Cam at the venue, I'd spent the afternoon alone, which I'd enjoyed immensely until this moment when I had to carry two expensive guitars across a dark parking lot by myself.

I power-walked as fast as my stilettos permitted. Until I heard that voice.

I stopped at the very first note. His clear baritone licked over my skin and made me shake with a desperate need to hear—to feel—more of him.

I stood, trembling, shocked by my reaction.

My brother's voice regularly reaped international acclaim. I should be used to such beauty. With a small shake of my head, I gripped the handles of the guitar cases and strode with purpose toward Cam's trailer.

Until the unknown singer began the next verse. My chest tightened as he crooned the lyrics. Not straight-up country. It had more…soul, I guess, though I wasn't sure that was the correct word.

I hurried forward. A face. That voice deserved a face I hoped would be as sexy.

Almost in a trance, I barely acknowledged Chuck, my brother's head of security, as I ran—hard to do in my stilettos—toward the stage.

"Katie Rose! You're a lifesaver."

Cam stepped into my path and I skittered to a halt, trying to ignore my hitched breath and aching chest. Much as I wanted to throw the instruments at him, I couldn't. They were worth too much money.

"Who's singing?"

Cam's face settled into a scowl. "My opening act."

Jenna walked up behind him and slung an arm around his waist, pressing a kiss to his cheek.

"He's a nice man, Cam."

"Late. Demanding. Shouldn't I get to be the demanding one since I'm the headliner?"

"Demanding doesn't suit you. In this situation." Jenna smiled and Cam softened, just as he always did. Jenna turned to me with a beaming smile. "Thanks for doing this. I know it's out of your way."

I shrugged. "I think I got the best of the ones we discussed.

Where do you want them?" My body vibrated with the need to see the man singing, but I wouldn't leave until the instruments were secured.

"I'll use this one," Cam said, picking up a case. Jenna grabbed the handle of the other one and they turned in unison back toward his trailer.

"Come on in," Jenna called. "Cam's got great snacks."

The singing stopped. I cursed my brother.

"Just a sec." Now was my best opportunity. I peeked around the stage curtain and out at the man now scowling at his sound guy. At least I assumed he was the sound guy based on his headset and the conversation about too much bass coming through the speakers.

A musician I was not. But I sold Jenna's amazing designs and brought her more acclaim with each passing month. The Instagram profile for J. Olsen's proved my genius. People couldn't get enough of a beautiful young woman creating mega-star's instruments—or the mega-stars playing those guitars in personal settings. Everyone loved a glimpse into the inner lives of famous people, especially when that wasn't the norm.

The singer brushed long blond hair back from his face. He had a beard—full but not too long, a couple of inches, accentuating his jaw. His mustache covered part of his upper lip, causing me to shiver with distaste, but his lower lip was plump and pink. His nose appeared straight, if a tad long. A nice face, strong and masculine. At least what I could see of it.

He brushed his hair back again, then pulled a hair tie from the thick golden mane and shook it out in annoyance. He turned toward me and started the process of pulling all the pieces back.

Blue eyes. Of course. He looked like a Viking. Well, his beard was too short for a full-on *How to Train Your Dragon* kind of warrior, but he was tall, athletic, and very sexy.

I'd never dated a blond man. Never dated one with long hair, either. Never thought shoulder-length hair on a man would be attractive. I was wrong. *So* wrong.

I shifted, planning to follow Jenna and Cam. Or, better yet, escape to my car and forget my brother or this blond god, who was almost near enough to touch. Then he glanced up and his eyes latched onto mine.

I gasped, shocked at the physicality of that look.

His face smoothed out as he continued to stare at me—just my face. He didn't drop his eyes to check out the rest of me, yet I still felt the heat from his ice-blue eyes steal over my skin.

"Thought we'd lost you, Kate," Cam said. "Come on, I'd like to discuss some social media ideas with you."

I huffed out the breath I'd unwittingly held and shook my head at my brother, who placed his hand between my shoulder blades and led me away from the stage.

Good timing on Cam's part. If I stared at the singer much longer, I might have done something stupid—like fling myself at him. My cheeks flamed as logic returned.

Never had I yearned with such abandon. Sure, the man's voice spoke to me. Sure, he was attractive. So were many of the men I met through Cam.

I couldn't reconcile either of those with the deep-seated need swirling through my belly.

And, if there was one thing I hated, it was not being in control.

CHAPTER TWO | Rye

I scrubbed my hands over my cheeks and beard, willing my heart rate to return to normal.

All those auburn curls. A sassy pink mouth. That skirt flirting around her knees and just a hint of silky thigh. Holy hell.

Lust slammed through me harder than a two-hundred-fifty-pound linebacker and knocked me flat on my butt.

Camden Grace glanced back, a scowl surging across his face. Definite step-off vibe. Kate, he called her.

I wasn't sure how she fit into Cam's entourage, but he was protective of her. With me, the guy who showed up nearly an hour late and demanded to practice first. I understood Camden Grace's dislike. I deserved his enmity.

Just as I deserved the bad press surrounding my life the past few years—especially the comments that I wouldn't ever finish my next album. I glanced down at my scuffed sneakers and winced. I'd barely managed to leave the condo I'd rented for the month via one of those by-owner sites.

What I put on seemed so far down the list of details. Until now. I wanted to impress her. *Kate.*

I shoved my hands in my pockets and trudged back to the stool. With a sigh, I picked up the guitar.

"You ready for this next go?" I asked.

Time to get my head in the game.

The sound engineer nodded, so I started playing the song I wrote a few years ago. The one that took my life on a much different trajectory than I'd anticipated.

I sang the lyrics, still burning with Deirdre's eventual dismissal.

You promised me forever, but that turned out too soon
I wish in our time together we could get a re-do

People always assumed I was singing about a fictional woman who died too young.

I wasn't.

Before I wrote that song, Deirdre and I seemed to have everything going for us. We were in love, but life gobsmacked us, and Deirdre didn't cope well.

Or cope at all.

No, she didn't turn to booze or pills or any of that trite shit. No, my wife—correction, *ex*-wife as of last year—turned into a zombie from too little sleep and too much guilt. Which was why I needed to be smarter about this woman. Kate.

While I sang, I thought of how Kate's long auburn ringlets might gleam in the stage lights, and how she rocked a prim dress shirt and flirty skirt better than any woman I'd ever seen. Even Deirdre. But that didn't matter.

Didn't matter that I was interested—didn't matter that Kate was the first woman I'd wanted in years. None of that *could* matter.

I had a job to do—and I needed this gig to go well. I needed this show to smooth over my months-late last album. I'd cut out a couple of singles from the still unfinished EP, and the second of those songs was just now hitting the airwaves to positive feedback.

I needed this show, no matter how much I didn't want to be there, didn't want to be opening for a country music star. I needed this show to take the heat off my wallet and my son...and for me. Because I probably wouldn't ever get the chance to finish my album.

Still wasn't sure that the doctor we were in Austin to see could fix the expanding hole in Ike's vision, but I wouldn't give up trying—not like Deirdre had.

Ike deserved more. He deserved every chance to see, to read the books he loved. And, yeah, while it was *my* dream, he deserved to play catch with me.

We'd never had that, and he was running out of time to ever have the possibility of "normal sight", let alone a normal childhood.

Better to put pretty Kate from my head. No woman wanted to get involved with a man who had a special needs kid.

I'd learned that when my wife—*ex*-wife—walked out on us.

———— ★ ————

I finished my last song and looked over at the tech. He gave me the thumbs-up so I hopped off the stool, already glancing at my watch.

Two hours and fifty-three minutes. If I hurried, I might be able to read Ike a story and kiss him goodnight. My favorite part of the day. Well, after the big hugs I received, along with a yawned "good morning".

My kid was the rock star. I just wished he could believe that.

I snapped my guitar into its case and hurried backstage.

"Good work there," Cam said.

I stopped. Spun toward him. While I wasn't a huge fan of his genre of music, I respected the hell out of his following—and the fact he wrote his own songs.

"Thanks. I appreciate you letting me go on first."

Cam raised an eyebrow even as his mouth turned down. "Not like you gave me much of a choice."

Guilt built, causing my cheeks to flame. But I held his gaze. "I have somewhere I need to be."

Cam strolled closer. "You going to show up on Saturday?" he asked, his voice laced with something more menacing.

I dipped my head once.

"Cuz I don't work well with people who shirk their responsibilities."

I gripped my guitar case tighter. He had no idea about my responsibilities. But this little conversation made the likelihood of me seeing Ike awake tonight slim to none.

"You hear me?" Cam growled.

"Oh, I heard you. And the threat. All of it."

Cam's lips quirked up in acknowledgment of my unwillingness to back down. "Seems like you got a mighty big chip on your shoulder, Rye."

I shook my head. He didn't know the weight I carried on my shoulders. My son's future.

"I'll be here Saturday. I'll perform. I'll make sure the crowd's ready for you to hop up there and do your thing."

"Then, it's the fact I'm headlining and you're not? That's what's bothering you?"

Years ago, I had been all set to headline my own tour.

Sometimes, late at night, I still tasted that excitement. But then Ike came, two months early and with a slew of health problems. Thankfully, most corrected over the last five years. Except for his vision.

"Nope. That doesn't bother me." Of course it did. While my career made me enough money to support my son, I might never have the adulation or fame Cam had…or another woman to share it with.

Kate's wide gray eyes and glossy auburn curls flashed across my mind again, but I shut that down.

Cam continued to study me, eyes narrowed as if I were little better than a gnarly bug.

"I'm going to head out," I said.

Cam sighed. "Fine. Do what you do."

"I'm leaving now, too," a soft, feminine voice said.

Cam and I turned. The redhead. Kate. Up close, I decided the name suited her. Her skin was creamy with a warm rose in her cheeks offset by all that flaming hair.

"All right," Cam said, though he didn't sound happy. "Thanks for taking those photos for Jen and me. Getting those posts up is gonna help a lot."

"It's what she pays me to do," Kate quipped.

Cam's expression turned sad but he nodded, giving Kate a short one-armed hug.

Kate's eyes sought mine and that damn zing sizzled down my spine. "Can you walk me to my car?"

"Yeah. Sure."

Cam opened his mouth—probably to warn Kate not to go

anywhere with me—but snapped it shut when Kate stepped away, and Cam let his arm fall back to his side.

"Thanks," she said as we strode toward the exit. "It's not much fun being the third wheel."

"They seem close."

She didn't reply. We walked in silence.

"What are you doing for him?"

"Hmm? Oh, social media posts. Mainly Instagram, but we're on all the platforms, of course. I highlight Jenna's guitars and the musicians who play them. She and Cam asked me to start photographing tonight for a series of posts for Cam's performance this weekend at South by Southwest."

"Sounds interesting."

"I enjoy that part of my job."

"What else do you do?" I asked. I wanted to learn more about Kate. The woman fascinated me.

"I run Jenna's shop. I manage the books and her schedule. I manage each project so that she can focus on building those amazing instruments. And I guess you've figured out I handle all the communications and PR."

"Sounds like you're pretty integral to her success."

Kate tucked some strands of hair behind her ear. "I like to think so." Her voice was soft, a little unsure.

I liked that, too.

"I'm over here," she said, waving her hand down a row of cars. She hesitated for a moment, her eyes wide and searching. Then, her facial expression shuttered and she offered me a tight smile. "See ya."

Maybe I'd misinterpreted her earlier interest. Not that I'd planned to act on it. But still…what just happened? We'd been getting along great. In fact, I'd been moments away from ditching my rule on women and asking Kate to go out with me.

I watched her for another moment before I blew out a breath. Just as I was about to turn away, a roadie slunk toward her, his eyes zeroed in on those killer legs.

I strode forward, my heart pounding. Damn, he had her crowded against a car. Not touching her yet, but still enough to make me uncomfortable.

I made it to her side just as the man leaned in, pressing his hips to hers. In the next instant, Kate's knee slammed into his groin, and the roadie howled in pain. As the man fell forward, Kate slammed her fist into his throat.

"Do not touch me," she growled at him.

The roadie groaned. "I'm gonna press charges," he muttered, struggling to rise.

His face was still ashen. Good.

"Can't see why you would," I said, stepping protectively between the man and Kate. "Seeing as how you accosted her first."

The roadie staggered up, pulling a knife from his pocket. I cursed, low and vicious, as I dropped my guitar and seized the guy's wrist. I brought my arm up in an elbow jab across his throat before grasping my other hand and squeezing. The roadie gurgled and groaned.

People were yelling behind me but I didn't dare take my eyes off the knife. Just as I anticipated, the guy tried to lunge toward me. I stepped my foot between his, throwing him off balance and used his own weight to slam his wrist into the top of the car beside me.

From the corner of my eye, I saw Kate cringe. She darted forward and grabbed the guitar case, making sure I didn't fall over it. The yelling got louder, and I could make out the patter of running footsteps.

With a grunt and gritted teeth, I slammed the man's hand onto the edge of the car again. This time, the knife fell from his fingers. Voices and yells surrounded us. I glanced over, quick, to make sure Kate was okay. She clutched my guitar case to her chest, eyes wide and mouth gaping.

The air shifted, and I managed to duck just before the asshole's fist landed against my face.

Two huge men came up behind the roadie and grabbed his arms.

I stepped back, chest heaving.

Shit.

Thanks to this guy, I might well not get to see Ike tonight at all. And if the jerk-wad tried to press charges, I might not get to see my son in the morning, either.

CHAPTER THREE | Kate

I clenched my jaw to keep my teeth from chattering. The roadie had made lewd comments, but my fear didn't spike until he had pulled the knife. Then, it hit me like a tidal wave. Because the look in the guy's eyes told me he wasn't going to stop until he got what he wanted, damn the consequences.

And those proved pretty hefty because it was either my blood, Rye's blood, or my body. I didn't like any of those choices.

Somehow, Rye managed to knock the blade from the roadie's hand. But that hadn't stopped the man's violence. Unleashed, he was a mass of angry limbs and vile words.

Ones I wished I could unhear.

Sure, I'd managed to protect myself from his initial onslaught, but I wouldn't have remained unscathed if Rye hadn't been there.

Rye stepped away as Chuck and another member from my brother's security team wrapped the cursing roadie up in their powerful arms. One of them must have squeezed the air from him because he quit spewing his vulgarities.

Rye turned to face me. "Did he hurt you?" he asked, voice urgent.

I mumbled a negative. Rye stepped closer, concern still etched in his face, along with something else. His eyes flared with primal heat, and for a moment I felt…marked. No, that was the wrong word. I felt as though Rye just claimed me—and my body accepted.

Holy...*what* was happening inside me right now?

I wanted to screw my face up and bawl like a baby. I also wanted to throw myself into Rye's arms and kiss him until neither of us could think of anything but the other.

"Kate."

Just my name, but I gulped and shuddered at the wealth of emotion in it. Fear drained from my body, replaced by sizzling awareness.

I'd been attracted to men before. But this wasn't a run-of-the-mill pheromone connection. At least not one I'd ever experienced. Like the first moment I heard his voice, I thrilled inside.

I turned to face Rye and my breath stuttered from my lips. A Viking, I'd thought earlier when he was on stage with his guitar. Now, though, that I'd seen him fight, his muscles flex and his powerful body shield mine, I knew I'd been correct.

I'd read, years ago, that adrenaline and near-death experiences brought out strange responses. Apparently, my body had decided it was Rye's personal thank you note.

Whoa. I mentally slapped myself. Put on the brakes and fast. I, Kate Grace, was an independent woman. One who could—and did—take care of herself. Hadn't I told my mama, my brothers, I didn't need a man?

Except the roadie poked massive holes in my theory. No, after this experience, I needed to be aware I couldn't protect myself from real harm.

Conflicting thoughts and emotions swirled through me,

causing dizziness. I locked my knees and breathed, clutching Rye's guitar case to my chest.

"First Cam's guitar and now his sister?" Chuck growled. "Dude, you must have a death wish."

Rye touched my arm, just below my shoulder. I flinched and his mouth went flat.

"You okay?" he asked, concerned, as his gaze skated over my face and body.

My cheeks flushed and my breath quickened, which had nothing to do with fear and everything to do with this maddening attraction. The way I was drawn to him, the speed of my desire for a man I didn't know, irritated me. And…yet, I couldn't control it.

I wanted Rye. Still.

No, no, no! I would *not* give in to instant attraction. I liked to know the men I dated. Especially after the debacle in Chicago.

I slammed that thought to a halt and blinked through the haze that spread through my body like a fast-acting virus.

Rye was a man. A good looking one, sure, but just a man.

One I didn't want *because* my body demanded his attention.

Focus. He asked a question.

"What?" I asked. "Yes. Yes, of course."

"I'll take that from you," he said. When I stared up at him, he gestured. "My guitar."

"Right. Sure."

My fingers and arms didn't want to cooperate, but I managed to let go of the handle. When his fingers brushed over mine, his lips parted on a slight gasp.

Well, *hell*.

Whatever burned between us, this connection, rose sharply. His pupils dilated and his chest rose and fell. At least he sizzled with the same fierce desire.

"Rye." I wasn't sure if I said it or just thought it.

More people ran toward us, their shoes and boots slapping on the pavement. Rye eased back, moving his body away from mine so that his heat dissipated. I shivered.

His eyes shuddered and the muscles in his arms and neck strained as if he were fighting to separate himself from me mentally as well as physically.

"Kate!" Jenna called.

Rye's dismissal etched in my mind, I whirled toward my best friend and fell into her arms.

"What the hell happened out here?" Cam demanded.

"Rye s-saved me," I said. And hurt me when he pulled back just now. But my teeth chattered too hard to get the words out.

Cam's eyes flashed to the roadie, narrowing as he no doubt recognized the guy, and then moved to Rye's grim face.

"Thanks, man. For making sure Katie R—I mean, Kate, was safe."

"Yeah, no problem," Rye said. "I figured that's why your guys came running so fast—they were watching her with me."

Cam didn't even try to deny Rye's statement, and, much as Cam's overprotectiveness annoyed me sometimes, in that moment I was thankful he'd asked his guys to keep an eye on me. I began to frown as I realized why Cam had kept watch—he was worried Rye would make a pass. I let Cam see my scowl but he shrugged, not the least penitent.

"How's your guitar?" I asked as I managed to pull myself together and out of Jenna's arms. Cam wouldn't let the slimy roadie hurt me, and Rye had already taken on the guy. I was safe.

Rye winced. The once-strong case was now shredded through the bottom to the guitar inside. Jenna took it from his hands and opened it, clucking at the damaged bell.

"Guess him damaging my guitar wasn't an accident after all," Cam muttered, turning to glare at the roadie who was now handcuffed. I probably didn't want to know where those had come from.

"The police are on their way," Chuck said, arms crossed as he glared at the lanky young man. I shivered, thinking about what he'd whispered in my ear. How he'd thrust his growing erection into my stomach. I forced down a gag.

"I think it's salvageable," Jenna said. "If you want me to try, I will. But, I think you'll need to play another instrument for a couple of days."

"Kate brought two," Cam said. "Okay for Rye to play the wide-bell one?"

Jenna nodded. "Of course. Actually, you can have it, Rye."

Rye shoved his hands into his pockets and rocked back on his heels. "I wouldn't feel right taking one of your instruments. I know how long the waiting list is."

"Yeah, well, none of those musicians saved my best friend's life," Jenna returned. "It's yours." She raised her hand when Rye went to argue. "You'll hurt my feelings if you say no."

Rye turned toward me, a helpless expression on his face. It

made me soften toward him and my heart rate slowed a little, almost back to normal.

"Don't look at me," I said. "I'm thankful you were there. Jesus. He had a knife."

My knees gave out. Both Cam and Rye reached for me. Rye got there first, and he slid an arm around my waist, hauling me into his side with a murmured, "I got you."

He did, too. More, I thrilled at him to hold me.

Instant attraction. That's what my friend, Sana, would call it. Insta-lust. I'd scoffed at her before. Sure, I could be interested in someone, want to get to know them better, but never in my life had I wanted to claw off a man's clothes and press my naked skin to his.

I didn't like this new reality.

But I adored the rush.

None of my jumbled emotions made sense.

Somehow, the moment I was in his arms I could breathe, and my legs functioned. I wouldn't say I was miraculously cured, but…something about Rye made me feel more alive than I ever had before.

Cam hesitated before he stepped back. The twist of his lips told me how unhappy he was that Rye held me. Cam's response cooled my body's reaction to Rye.

Hurt as I was with Cam, I trusted my big brother's judgment and his love for me. Still, I rested against Rye's side, and Cam seemed to swallow down the bitter pill of irritation with difficulty.

Then, Cam raised his head, eyes narrowing at the gathering crowd of festival workers and curious folks from the street. Many had raised phones.

"Let's go back to my trailer. The police are going to need a statement, and I'd rather not give the tabloids and websites more fodder than they've already managed to get."

Rye kept his arm around my waist, his fingers firm on my ribs and his side pressed to mine, almost as if he didn't want to let go of me either. That made me giddy. Or maybe that was the adrenaline dump from the attack.

Rye's faintly woody, clean smell drew me closer, and he absorbed my weight, rearranging my curves along his harder planes as if he not just wanted me there but needed the connection, too. We moved in sync back into the fairgrounds and to Cam's large trailer. Jenna continued to clutch Rye's guitar while Cam clutched Jenna.

As soon as we were inside and Cam rounded on us, taking in our close connection, Rye let go. I collapsed onto the nearest chair as I caught sight of Rye's grimace. So much for thinking he liked touching me.

I was delusional. More than likely, Rye was a nice man who happened to get sucked into a bad situation. Or, he was an asshole like Cam thought. An asshole who didn't want a woman hurt.

Rye glanced at his watch, teeth biting into his plump lower lip, and pulled out his phone. "I need to make a call."

Jenna and Cam wore matching confused expressions as Rye stepped out of the trailer.

"See what I mean?" Cam grumbled. "He's not the easiest musician to work with."

"We don't know anything about him, really," Jenna said.

She frowned a little but then seemed to shake it off and focused on Cam. "He saved Kate, so I think we need to give him some leeway here."

Cam nodded, even as he pulled Jenna closer to his side to kiss her.

"Lovey-dovey later," I said, my tone sardonic. "I need a shot of something."

"Cam has some good tequila," Jenna offered with a sympathetic look. Cam couldn't help it—he had to touch Jenna to remind himself she was his and she was safe. But Jenna remembered—all too well—what it was like to be the odd-girl-out.

And how very much that position hurt.

CHAPTER FOUR | Rye

Stepping outside gave me a chance to breathe.

Holy hell. My desire to break that roadie into tiny pieces made little sense. My need to protect Kate, to ensure not just her continued wellbeing, but her happiness. That was insane.

Caveman behavior.

From the moment I'd caught her staring at me, every one of my senses lit to high alert. My body zinged with desire.

I knew passion—Deirdre and I had enjoyed each other's bodies with the intensity of young love. Then, Ike came too early and everything we'd built together fell apart.

But, even when I lived with Deirdre, I could focus on something else. Like my music or my son. The moment I was near Kate, she absorbed *all* my attention. Like a fucking black hole.

Right. My lack of focus was why I needed to steer clear of her.

I dialed my phone and pressed it to my ear.

"Something's come up here, and I won't be back for a while," I said to the babysitter, Beatrice, who I'd hired to stay with Ike while I was involved with this festival.

"I'm here, Mr. Lawson. You just do what you need to."

"Can I talk to him?" I asked.

"Sure thing," she said, and I could hear her handing the phone to Ike.

"Daddy," Ike squealed.

"Hey, bud. So…I'm going to be later than I hoped. I can't tuck you in."

"Aw."

Ike sounded a little disappointed but not in full meltdown mode. I'd chosen Beatrice as his caretaker because Ike liked her better than the three other candidates he and I interacted with. So far, she'd been a steady influence that helped reduce Ike's tantrums. While a normally happy child, his life had turned upside down in the past month, and he'd been more prone to big emotions.

"That's why I called. So I could to talk to you before you went to sleep. To let you know how much I love you."

"You're not going to be home to read me a story?"

I heard the pout in Ike's voice, and my heart squeezed. "Of course I have time to read you a book. We'll do it now. Over the phone. You want to grab your favorite?"

"Yep," he chirped.

I waited. Cam stepped out of his trailer and turned that hot glare on me. At my last words, he stopped moving but continued to hover about five feet from me.

I closed my eyes and tipped my head back against the metal side of the trailer. I'd been trying to avoid this very moment.

Thankfully, I had five of Ike's favorite books memorized. I recited the lines about the pigeon and a bus as Ike turned the pages. At the end of the third "book" we read together, Ike yawned.

"I love you, Daddy," he mumbled into the phone.

"I love you, too, son. Get some good sleep. I'll be home as soon as I can."

I spoke to Beatrice for a moment to let her know I might not return for a few more hours.

"I set up the extra room, just in case," I said.

"I saw that, and I'll probably head that way if it gets to be past my bedtime."

"I'm really sorry about keeping you longer." I shoved a hand into my already disheveled hair and closed my eyes.

When I opened them, Cam's facial features had settled into a semblance of neutrality.

"He's a sweet child, Mr. Lawson. And you're a caring father. This time with you two brings me great joy."

Well, we'd see about how much she liked the job in another week or two when my hours remained inconsistent and Ike became irritable. I hated to let down my son, but I hadn't come up with a better alternative yet for earning a living. One I could stomach, anyway.

"Thanks, Beatrice. I appreciate all you're doing for him—and for me."

Cam tilted his head. Sure, I might be able to play the sympathy card with Cam—being a single father might get him to cut me some slack, but I didn't like to play games. Any kind of game.

Still, I needed this gig—needed the paycheck and exposure from this festival if I had any hope of proving to my ex I could cover Ike's medical costs without help from her father.

Because Deirdre's parents continued to block the very treatment I wanted for our son. And as long as Ike remained on Deirdre's health insurance, a necessity since her father owned a mid-sized transit company and I was a solo performer, I had no chance of winning the argument.

"Sorry about that," I said to Cam. "I needed to touch base with…" I hesitated.

Cam narrowed his eyes, studying me as one would a strange specimen that might be benign or eat his face.

"Kate's worried about you," he said. "She wanted to make sure you weren't hurt."

My turn to suck in a breath. Being so close to Kate caused my good sense to malfunction—to yearn.

"I'm fine," I managed to say. "Maybe it would be better—"

"Cops are here," Chuck said, striding into the halo of yellow light. "Let's get this statement done so that sack of foulness can rot in the modern version of hell."

This, at least, all three of us agreed on.

CHAPTER FIVE | Kate

The police questioning would have been worse if Rye hadn't witnessed the entire scene—and if my brother wasn't the hottest name in country music.

The good ole boy officer who strutted into Cam's trailer seemed to think the only reason that roadie came after me was because I asked for it. My fists clenched in my lap as I showed them the bruises on my arms from where the guy grabbed me.

Thankfully, the police officer's partner didn't share his Neanderthal ideology, because Cam was close to going off on the guy. Chuck, always implacable, wore a deep scowl that turned blacker with each of Officer Wayne's comments.

Rye's composure broke first. He slammed his hand down on the coffee table.

"She did *not* flaunt herself. She did not smile at the guy. She didn't invite him out for a drink or bend over provocatively. What is this—the fricking eighteen hundreds?"

"Rye—" I began.

"No," Rye snapped, turning toward me, his eyes blasting the fiery will of his Viking ancestors. Damn, I hoped he had Viking ancestors. That was now part of the fantasy.

"This guy's attitude is shit," Rye continued.

The officers both shifted in their seats while Cam leaned back, ankles crossed, a small smile playing on his lips. Even Chuck's eyes gleamed with approval.

Great. My brother was falling under Rye's alpha male spell.

"He shouldn't be in this line of work if he views women this way," Rye said.

Rye turned back to the officer, who looked more confused than contrite. I remembered my father's saying: *Once a bull, always a bull.*

"She was walking to her car when the man crowded her against the vehicle and then ground his pelvis into her. I walked up just after she kneed him in the crotch and that's when things got ugly."

"He pulled a knife," Cam said, leaning forward, his face a mask of neutrality that belied his gritted teeth. "He was going to cut my baby sister, and you're sitting here feeling sorry the guy's got sore balls?"

Jenna laid her hand on his rock-hard forearm. I thought it was a placating gesture until she spoke.

"That's my sister-in-law, my right-hand lady, and all-around wonderful woman. Stop slut-shaming her and put the jackass who tried to hurt her in jail."

At Jenna's words, Cam, Rye, and Chuck nodded. Officer Wayne slammed his mouth shut, his face mottled an unattractive orange. Sure, Rye and Cam could talk to him like that, but he didn't like hearing Jenna call him out.

"We hear what you're saying, Mr. and Mrs. Grace, Mr. Lawson," Officer Fein said. "And we do intend to do something."

"That better include jail time," Cam grumbled. "A goddamn bucket of it."

"We'll do our jobs, which is what we've been doing," Officer Wayne said. He showed off his pen and pad. "Asking questions, getting answers to see if her story jibes with his."

Chuck stood up. He was a large man, with an intimidating presence. "Which is why, now that you have statements from Kate, Rye, and me, all of whom saw his provocation firsthand, you're leaving this trailer to go out and talk to the other bodyguards who were with me as we ran toward Rye and the sack of…" Chuck cleared his throat. "And you'll make sure you're investigating properly. I'll call to check-in tomorrow morning to find out the details. Nine a.m. work okay for you?"

But Chuck wasn't asking, and the officers were out of the space before they could open their mouths again.

Cam ran both hands through his hair. "I need to get on stage and you need to get on home," he said to Rye.

Rye dipped his head. "Appreciate that."

"Will you walk Kate out again? I'll have Lyle go, too, this time."

Whatever they spoke about outside had caused Cam to warm up to Rye, which made me happy. Except now Rye wouldn't look at me, and he'd made a point to sit as far away from me as possible. I swallowed down the hurt caused by his choices, wishing I could shut off my libido with the same ease Rye had shown.

"Sure thing. I can use the backup getting your sister to her car," Rye said.

I stiffened again, which I only noticed because I'd finally begun to relax. "You don't have to," I said. "I don't want to take up any more of your evening."

Rye shot me a strange look—one I couldn't interpret. "It's not a problem. I'm just hoping for less drama this go-around."

"You and me both," I said.

I ignored Rye's burgeoning grin as I hugged Cam, who held me for a long moment. I soaked in the warmth of his embrace and how glad I was to have him looking out for me.

"Want Lyle to go home with you?" he asked in my ear. I was freaked out, but I shook my head. Cam decided not to argue, which I took to be a good sign. I thanked him before I hugged Jenna, who pressed a quick kiss to my cheek.

"Glad you're okay, lady," she said.

She thanked Rye again and handed him the guitar I'd brought in earlier. I loved that he accepted the case with reverence—maybe even a bit of fear. Jenna appreciated his reaction as well because she beamed at him.

"Oooh, I know, Kate," Jenna exclaimed. "You can add photos of Rye to our feed, too. That'll be so cool. Two artists here, using my instruments."

I glanced at Rye, who looked as shocked as I felt. But I didn't want to dim Jenna's obvious joy in her idea, so I just smiled—it felt more like a grimace—and told her of course.

"You can hang out here when Cam and Rye are on the grounds. That should give us lots of cool shots. You have such a great eye for these posts." Jenna's smile was genuine, and I felt a rush of affection for my sister-in-law.

"See you tomorrow," Jenna said. She bounced up and down like a kid on Christmas. "This is going to be amazing. I just know it."

"I'll let you know when I get home," I said, knowing Cam would worry if I didn't. Not that I intended to go home right away—I planned to finish the project I'd started earlier back before Cam called me.

Rye fell into step next to me as we headed out of the cluster of trailers set up for talent. Most were dark because many of the performers weren't yet in town. The path that led to the parking lot was well-lit, but cold inched up my spine. I glanced back, thankful Lyle trailed a couple of paces behind. He'd be ready for any issue. All Cam's guys were former military and current bad-asses.

"What did you do to sweet-talk Cam?" I asked, trying to take my mind off the last time I stood in this lot. "He seems to like you more now."

Nope. Didn't work. I halted, hovering on the edge of the lot, skin tingling at the thought of heading toward the scene of the crime.

Rye tossed me a look. "Not a thing." He ran his hand through those long locks. Not as blond as it had looked in the stage lights. More of a brown, especially near the roots, with sun-kissed highlights. Because even his hair was *perfect*.

"Come on," he said. He held out his hand as I glanced with apprehension toward the rows of cars. My breathing hitched.

"I'll be with you," he said, his voice soft.

The tip of my tongue touched my bottom lip as I stared at his large, slightly roughened palm. I laid my hand in his, not even trying to ignore the surge of sexual energy sliding up my arm, warming my chest and belly.

We reached my car. Rye let go of my hand as if it were a white-hot chunk of coal. "Well, thanks for walking me to my car," I said. "Twice."

Lyle stood off to the side, hands crossed in front of his legs in that traditional male pose, his attention roving around, pursuing threats better than a heat-seeking missile.

Rye faced me, and I felt sixteen, my heart beating fast as I hoped the boy I liked would kiss me.

"Glad I was there to help," he said. He flashed a glance at Lyle before he wrapped one of my ringlets around his forefinger. "Stay out of trouble, Katie Rose."

At my indignant gasp, his eyes lit up with mischief. He leaned in and kissed my cheek.

My lungs constricted at the feel of his beard brushing against my skin. His warm lips made contact, and my body came to full attention. My breasts throbbed and my stomach dipped. I inhaled his warm scent, causing my head to reel.

Then, Rye stepped back, turned on his heel and plunged into another row of parked cars.

I watched him walk away and touched my cheek.

"Kate?" Lyle said.

"Yeah," I said on a sigh. I cleared my throat. "I'm going."

I opened my car and climbed into the driver's seat. Lyle made to get in, but I brushed him off.

"Thanks, Lyle," I said. "You can go back to Cam."

"But—"

"It's fine." I started my car and put it in gear. "I'm tired."

He nodded and stepped back.

I drove through the lot. The exit—*this* exit, anyway—just happened to be in the same direction Rye took.

I found him walking between the rows of cars, head down

as if contemplating the weight of the world—or his shoelaces. Maybe he found both equally fascinating.

I clutched the steering wheel, heart fluttering as I considered my options. I braked and rolled down the window.

"Rye?" I called.

He whirled toward my car.

"You want to grab a drink?" I asked.

He studied me for so long that I felt my face flush as I prepared for his rejection.

"Sure," he said.

Surprise and warmth spread through me faster than a west Texas wildfire. He walked toward the passenger side and placed the guitar case in the back seat with care. He climbed into the passenger seat and shoved the chair back to accommodate his long legs.

"I'm a little worried about that guitar, though. Wouldn't want anything to happen to it."

Another wave of heat slammed through my veins and my breathing turned shallow, but I managed to sound normal when I said, "I know just the place."

CHAPTER SIX | Rye

Getting in the car with Kate was a mistake—one I didn't seem capable of correcting. Sure, she was gorgeous. But many women were. Her professional clothing covered her but remained a little flirty, which appealed to me more than it should.

She was also the younger sister of the man who could make or break this crucial period of my career. Forgetting Cam's weight with the label—and the wider music community—wouldn't be just self-defeating; it would be downright stupid. And I wasn't in a place in my life where I could act stupid.

Ike's only chance at a sight-filled future depended on me.

I should ask Kate to stop the car. To let me out. I should go home. But Ike was asleep, and Beatrice planned to stay the night.

It was a drink. *One* drink, I corrected. I'd get to know Kate a little better, probably not even like her as much as my body seemed to think it would, and then this yearning would dissipate.

She drove with the experience of a native, flicking her blinker and easing in between the late-evening traffic. I'd been so lost in my thoughts I didn't realize she drove into a residential building, one I recognized as my own, until she pulled into an assigned parking spot two rows over from mine. But she couldn't have known any of that. Which meant… Surprise and heat curled through my gut in equal measure. Oh, this was bad.

"You brought me to your place?" I asked.

"You were worried about the guitar," she said as if that explained everything. But I saw the flush working its way up her neck and the slight but telltale shaking of her hands as she dropped her keys into her purse. She slid from the car before I figured out what to say.

I exited, too, mainly because I didn't have a better plan.

"Grab the case," she said over her shoulder. She hiked the purse up her arm. "That way you don't have to worry about it getting stolen."

Even as alarm bells blared in my head, my body did as she'd instructed. Then, like a fool, or a man walking to the gallows, I followed her to an elevator.

The door pinged open, and she stepped into the car. Her eyes caught mine in the silver reflection on the back wall. My feet shuffled into the space before my brain had time to think. The sexual tension between us rocketed upward, and I swore I could smell her desire, which shouldn't be possible.

My breath hitched. *Mine*. I liked that. The need to imprint my scent, my kiss, my body and essence on and *in* her grew. I tugged at the hairs on my chin, shocked by my thoughts.

And still, even as my brain screamed at me, I followed her out of the elevator and to her door. She opened it, and we stepped inside. She flicked on the lights as I shut the door and set my guitar case on the tiled entry next to a bench where she placed her purse.

She turned toward me and my hands came up to rest on her hips. Her lips parted and her eyes widened. With want, with need, but also with fear.

Like I was the big bad wolf.

I might just be.

"B-beer?" she asked, her voice breathy.

This time, she spun away before the situation between us escalated. Like she might be second-guessing the attraction blossoming between us. She walked to her fridge and I tried—and failed—not to notice the smooth-as-silk swing of her hips.

She brought out two cans and popped the tops before grabbing a couple of glasses. Kate handed me one of the cans and a glass. I took them, our fingers brushing. Flickers of awareness sizzled up my arm.

She filled her glass with the golden liquid, pouring so there was a foamy head. I sat mine on the counter and did the same, thankful for something to do. Once the glass was full, I picked it up and stepped back away from her warm body and magnolia scent.

"What will these photos you plan to take entail?" I asked because I was worried about it, but also to break the sensual spell wrapping around me.

She blinked at me, her eyes refocusing on my face. I wondered what she'd been thinking.

"You playing your guitar, mainly."

"But that's not all, is it?"

"With many of the artists we showcase, we get some behind-the-scenes shots. Like, what you do to prepare for a concert. Fans love that because each of you artists have your own rituals—one your audience loves to learn about. Like for Cam…I've taken some shots of him at the ranch, on the swing with Jenna, and tonight, the two of them chilling in his trailer."

No way I'd let Kate into my place to take photos of Ike. I'd never, *ever* let him be subjected to ridicule. Plus, Deirdre's father would probably find some fault with my parenting and insist I bring Ike back to his cold, dreary mansion.

That place was hardly more conducive to an active little boy's wellbeing than a prison. Sure, Ike's eyes struggled to focus, but he loved to run, climb, and jump as much as the next kid.

That's why I wanted him to have the surgery—to give him the chance to do those normal little boy activities, as well as drive a car and catch a football one day.

"I'm not comfortable with you at my place," I said. "In fact, that's completely off-limits."

Kate's hand pulled back from her glass, her mouth snapping shut with an audible click. "This isn't going to work," she said.

I frowned, deciding my best course of action was to play dumb. Sweat trickled down my back. "What isn't?"

She faced me fully, shoulders squared and chin high. Even nervous, she exuded a confidence of her physical self and place in this world. That was damn sexy.

"I'm attracted to you," she said. Her expression remained neutral even as her hands fisted at her sides.

Thank every star in the sky I wasn't the only one fighting this insane drive. I opened my mouth to say so, but she pressed on before I could.

"But that doesn't mean I'm going to let you hurt my feelings. If you don't want me in your life, professionally or otherwise, then it would be best if you said so right now."

"There are parts of my life I don't share with anyone. Period."

My voice was even, but the sweating increased. Kate thought we were discussing a business deal, but I was telling her certain things—like my son—were private. I didn't want to have to come out and tell her about him. Cam knowing was more than enough for now.

She snorted. "Don't hold back on what you really think about me," she said.

While her tone remained brave, even defiant, hurt crept into her eyes, making me feel no better than a bug on the bottom of her shoe.

"You don't know what I think of you," I said. Even I heard the backpedaling in my tone.

She studied me for a long moment, those amazing gray eyes darkening with pain.

"Good thing I already decided I'm not going to act on my desire."

"Whoa, hold up. I never said I was going to have sex with you." I stepped back, needing space. "I need this gig, and I'm not going to piss off your brother."

Not that my dick wasn't on board with being her sex toy. Oh, it so was. But my father-in-law used my pride to wipe off his shoes, and I wasn't willing to make the same mistake with another woman.

"Well, considering you don't want me in your life, *period*, this was obviously a mistake," Kate said.

CHAPTER SEVEN | Kate

Shame washed through me at my confession that I'd considered following through on our stupid-hot attraction, but I kept my stance and stare firm even as my neck and face burned and prickled.

"I deserve a man who treats me with respect, not like I'm someone unworthy to even see his home. Not as someone who is only willing to hang out with me to further his relationship with my brother."

His eyebrows shot up, parts of them disappearing into the cascade of chin-length, honey-highlighted hair framing his strong, bearded jaw.

Instead of answering me, Rye lifted his glass, gave me a small salute, and tossed back a good portion of the beer.

"I shouldn't have come."

I leaned my hip against the counter, needing a break from my high heels. "Why's that?" I asked.

"Because you want to fuck—"

"I just said I wouldn't—"

"And I don't do that. I have too many responsibilities to get involved with a—" He stopped himself, but the implication was already out there.

Hurt seared through me, and I had to look away before he

saw. "I'll take you back to your car."

"You most certainly will not," he said.

I looked back at him, gaping, at his angry tone. His eyes flashed with that Viking fire.

"I'm not going anywhere with a woman who'd fuck me over."

My head snapped back around. "You know *nothing* about me," I barked.

Rye came in closer, anger flaring in his eyes. "You're right. I don't. But I do know your brother cares about you a helluva lot. And you're willing to make him angry with me—you're willing to use me to…what? Get even with him? He seemed like a great guy earlier, definitely one who worries about you."

I drew myself up and narrowed my eyes at him.

"I love my brothers, and I respect Cam's opinion." My nose tingled with unshed tears. "I love both of them more than you could ever know."

Even though both of them and my mother perpetuated a lie—just like the one my daddy told me years before when I caught him in a hot-and-heavy make-out session with a topless Linda Bennett behind the barn when I was seven.

"It'll be our secret, Katie Rose. You don't want to hurt your mama, now, do you?"

No, I hadn't. So I kept the secret, thinking up until recently that my father's lying and indiscretions stopped that afternoon. I'd been wrong, and my brothers and mother intentionally blocked me from the truth.

Rye shook his head. He headed toward the foyer and I scrambled to keep up, unwilling to let him walk out, thinking so little of me.

Except…what did it matter? I didn't need to explain myself, or my actions, to him.

I marched over to my purse and picked up my keys. I tossed them to Rye, who caught them easily in one hand.

"Then go. Just take my car and get out of here."

I bit the inside of my cheek to keep my lip from trembling. Our passion had shifted from sensual to anger, quite possibly because our fears got the better of us.

Rye cursed and brushed his hand over his beard, his pale blue eyes filled with contrition. "I'm sorry, Kate. What I said… That wasn't right."

"No, it wasn't," I snapped, unwilling to bend and let Rye take what little dignity remained. He'd hurt me—this man who barely knew me.

"And for the record, if you'd been listening, I said I *wasn't* going to sleep with you because I *liked* you too much. Past tense. So, thanks for rectifying that little issue."

I turned on my heel, sped back into the kitchen, and took a swig of my beer. I felt rather than heard him approach. His tread was light, almost as if he expected me to whip around and verbally attack him.

"I'm not letting this go…"

I faced him, not because of his words but because of the faint pleading note behind them.

"Why?" he asked, his tone softening.

Such a loaded question—one I could take any number of ways. Why did I brush off my brother tonight? Why was there such an obvious distance between us? Why did I bring Rye here, to my house?

I returned my stare to the foam in my beer. "They lied to me," I said. I'm not sure why I told him the truth. Not because he deserved it. Maybe because the only other people I saw regularly were in my brother's employ, or Jenna, and I couldn't express these feelings to them. One, it would be disloyal. And, two, just no. Close as Jenna and I were, we didn't agree on this issue. Or maybe it was because Rye was asking me for more information, for the connection we'd had and snapped in the course of the past couple of hours.

"People make mistakes," Rye said. His tone held a friendlier note, but I ignored it. Placating me now wasn't going to help.

"You don't get it," I said, my voice low as I struggled to suppress my anger—with Rye, but more with my family. "They were willing to keep lying to me about who I was to them."

My voice cracked as my eyes filled with tears. I blinked them back because I was *not* an emotional mess. I was a strong, independent woman who had been knocked down but always got back up.

Rye placed his large, warm hands on my shoulders and turned me back to face him.

"What do you mean?" he asked. His eyes were filled with pain...for me. But that made no sense. Why would Rye feel anything other than the contempt he'd just wielded with such brutal precision?

I cleared my throat as I considered the best way to proceed. With a tired sigh, I walked over and sank onto my favorite chair. Its vibrant purple twill cuddled me.

I'd left my beer in the other room. I looked at it with longing. Inanimate object that it was, it couldn't feel my pining and didn't affix itself to my hand.

Rye settled on the edge of my couch, his expression intent.

"Bottom lining it, my brothers pretended that we were all one big happy family when they knew for a fact my mother was keeping secrets—details about my parentage—from me."

Rye jingled my keys in his hand. "That's unfortunate," he said.

I laughed but it was humorless. I wrapped my arms around my middle. "Look. I get that my problems seem silly to you, but they're real to me." I inhaled sharply. "My father was a cheating son-of-a…." I licked my lips. "My father was a serial cheater. I didn't realize that until after he died, and I found out just how bad his relationship was with the rest of the family. Which they'd all kept from cute little Katie Rose because she was too fragile to handle the details."

The words poured out of me. The anger and hurt boiled as it spilled over, but they were a relief to spill—as if the poison had been building and eroding me from the inside these past months.

And it made even more stark the fact I didn't have a confidant that I needed. Trusting Rye with Cam's secrets—my family's secrets—might well prove stupid. I'd know if I read the details online somewhere. But I'd learned years before when Cam's fame skyrocketed not to trust my former college friends or colleagues—they were all willing to expose the Grace family's secrets. The desire to share gossip was a siren song most people couldn't resist.

Rye leaned his shoulders back against the couch cushion.

"That might well be worse than my history."

"It's not a race to the bottom," I said, tone dry.

His lips twisted in a sardonic half smile. But a thin layer of peace blanketed my emotions, soothing my heart.

"Good point," Rye said. "Just so you know, I get the importance of discretion."

I sucked my lower lip into my mouth. "Cam would appreciate that, I'm sure." I was so tired. The tears I'd been holding at bay pressed against my eyes.

"Please, take the car and skedaddle. That way you can have a clear conscience and happy thoughts about the perfection that is country music superstar Camden Grace."

I closed my eyes and brought my hands up to pat at my hair, a nervous gesture I'd never quite been able to break.

"These are from tonight?" Rye asked. His fingertips drifted over the angry swelling ballooning around my wrist where the roadie grabbed me. I started because I hadn't realized he'd risen from his place on the couch.

The concern in his eyes and the gentleness of his touch caused my heart to quiver.

"Please," I managed to choke out. "Don't pretend to care."

He stared into my eyes for a long moment that left me light-headed. I wanted him. Not just in my bed as I'd first considered, which so wasn't me. I never offered that invitation until the man and I were in a serious, committed relationship. If I'd been honest with myself, I wanted Rye in my life. Possibly as that serious and committed significant other.

But he'd already proven that he could slash my heart apart, so

I needed to kiss a chance of getting to know him well enough to fill the significant other role goodbye. He didn't like me anywhere near as much as I liked him, and his disdain was my own fault.

I stood, straightening my skirt and walked to my front door. I opened it. "Goodbye," I whispered.

His attention stayed focused on my face as he pressed my keys into my hand. "Actually, I'd appreciate that ride back to the venue," he said.

Rye collected his instrument as I tried to gauge his reaction, but I had no idea what he was thinking. Dejected, I led the way back down the hall.

We remained quiet the whole ride back to the festival grounds.

Rye pointed out his vehicle, his first words to me since we left my apartment.

"Goodbye," I said again, and I meant it. Tonight had been crazy—the roadie, my fierce attraction to Rye, his response to my revelations. Exhaustion weighed on me, and my lip started to quiver. I clamped my jaw shut. I didn't know Rye well enough to be sad we'd never cross paths again because I was never going to take those photos of Rye with Jenna's guitar.

But my interaction with Rye, the confusion and pain Rye managed to tug out of me so easily, showed I needed to fix the relationships that mattered—namely with my brothers.

My mother…*so* not ready to go there yet.

"I'm sorry they hurt you, Kate," Rye said, his voice soft but powerful in the small interior of my car.

I dipped my head but refused to glance his way. I could not give him more of me.

He leaned over and pressed a soft kiss to my cheek, near the corner of my mouth. His beard tickled my skin and my entire body zinged with fire. When my lips parted in shock, he pressed a soft kiss against the edge of my lips. Much as I wanted to moan and relax into his caress, I held tight to the steering wheel and kept my face forward, ignoring my pounding heart and my broken breath.

Oh, oh, oh. My mind spun on that word, in tandem to the pulse pounding in my neck.

He pulled back and went to open the car door.

"Rye?" I whispered.

He turned.

And this time, I kissed him.

CHAPTER EIGHT | Rye

A strangled groan came from my throat as Kate touched her lips to mine. The gliding, sliding perfection wasn't a mere kiss. It was *more*. So much more.

When she parted her lips, her taste exploded on my tongue and her soft, creamy skin nuzzled against my beard and cheek. My hand tangled in her curls, those tenacious strands wrapping around my fingers, burying my digits against her skull, drawing me closer.

She tasted like heaven. Sweet. Warm. Wet. Perfection.

I angled her head and stroked my tongue against hers a second time. She pressed her palms to the column of my neck and her chest to mine. At the feel of her breasts brushing against my shirt, perspiration stippled my skin.

I *craved* more of Kate. So, I deepened the kiss, drawing more of her taste into my mouth along with her tongue, as my free hand slid up and over her full breast.

She made a soft sound and pressed closer. Her hand trailed down my shirt, over my pectoral muscle and taut nipple and down the plane of my belly.

The car horn beeped long and loud.

We sprang apart. I stared, taking in her wet, swollen lips and half-closed eyes. I cursed. That shouldn't have happened.

I shouldn't want to dive back in, to delve into the secrets of her mouth, to taste her skin and the sweet flesh of her belly… and lower.

With another groaned curse, I got out and grabbed the guitar from the back. I began to close the door, intent on leaving, until I caught a glimpse of her hands once again clutching the steering wheel, white and trembling. Her head remained bowed low and her breath broke into ragged streams.

"Goodbye, Kate," I said.

She didn't reply.

Her lack of response was for the best. Even if my heart stuttered in disappointment. I exited her vehicle and entered mine.

Only after Kate drove away did I start my car and drive it to my home…which was located in the same condo building as her place, two floors lower.

CHAPTER NINE | Kate

My fingertips lingered on my cheek, still tingling from his beard, then trailed to my tender lips. I'd never been kissed so deeply, with such focus.

Unlike the few men before, Rye possessed my mouth and all my other senses.

That was the greatest irony—I didn't do casual kissing, let alone sex. Not just because of how my mama raised me, but because there had been few chances to date when my brothers were home, keeping an eye on me. Even when I started at UT, Carter's reputation seemed to loom large, the Sword of Damocles over my head, and few boys were willing to approach me because no one wanted to upset Carter Grace or his Army Ranger brother.

Anyway, the one experience with a boyfriend in college soured me toward relationships. And then I made that incredibly stupid blunder in Chicago.

I shook my head, unwilling to relive those last days there— hating how shame still wanted to suck me under. Instead, I focused on something more potent: Rye's kiss.

I swallowed, moaning softly at the taste of him still on my tongue. A hint of beer and a smooth, crisp flavor that was all Rye. My cheeks flushed and my belly quivered as I remembered the way his tongue slicked over mine.

I drove back toward my condo, but I had no interest in going home. Not while I was this keyed up. Instead, I turned at the next intersection and drove toward the shop. My phone rang and I answered it via Bluetooth.

"Hey, Cam," I said.

"Where you at?" he asked.

Right. I scrunched up my nose, annoyed I'd forgotten to call him when I arrived home. I nibbled my lip but winced at the tenderness there. "I…um…grabbed a quick bite, and now I'm driving home."

"All right." He lowered his voice. "Would you call me when you get there? Otherwise, I'll worry."

Some of the tightness in my chest eased at his words. I knew Cam loved me. I knew he wanted to protect me from the world, even as he struggled to let me make my own decisions.

"Yes, big brother," I said. And at the next light, I did as promised and went back toward my condo.

His breath caught a little when he said thanks, the only sign my words impacted him. Once inside my place for the second time that night, I texted Cam to let him know. He responded with a quick thank you and that he'd talk to me tomorrow. He would, too, because Cam was like the mother hen who kept tabs on all his chicks. Part of that need came from being an officer in the army, but part of it was based on his PTSD. The more in his life Cam could control, the less prone he was to falling apart.

Not that he let his emotions overwhelm him often, but when they did, the fallout was explosive. Jenna eased the worst of the savageness in him, totally unintentionally, which was probably why he craved her company so much.

I toed off my shoes and stared at the aborted drink I'd hoped to share with Rye—for a few moments there, I'd hoped to share much more than a beer. And I had…just not what I'd intended.

I snorted. Story of my life, really. Those I wanted to give myself to didn't want me. But Rye wasn't mine and *never* would be. If I were lucky, I wouldn't even have to see him again—not close enough to talk to, anyway. I could take photos of him from a distance, thanks to my new phone's excellent camera.

I picked up my tepid beer and chugged the remaining liquid, wishing the taste could wash away my stupidity. It didn't, and the sour taste of not learning from past mistakes clawed its way up the back of my throat. I snagged Rye's half-drunk beer, poured the rest into my glass, and took it to the living room where I flopped down on the couch. I turned on Netflix and found the cooking show where no one actually knew how to cook, trying not to see parallels with my love life.

I failed at relationships, just like the contestants on the show.

Eventually I fell asleep, probably thanks to the beer-only dinner. I woke too early, neck stiff and body throbbing with the need for release.

I rose and stretched, wincing at the tight muscles. I stripped as I headed toward the bathroom, hoping a hot shower would work its magic.

I fell back to sleep in my robe with my hair wrapped in a towel atop the thick, downy comforter. This time I dreamed of the sweet, mischievous look in Rye's eye when he kissed my cheek last night. Before I invited him to my place and my halfhearted attempt at seduction imploded.

One truth stood out to my dream-hazed mind: I wanted to see the sparkle in Rye's eyes again. And I wanted to be the one who brought it out.

Would I ever learn that love—relationships—only caused me heartache?

CHAPTER TEN | Rye

Just the memory of the kiss caused my entire body to tighten and warm. I'd known better than to give in to the urge, but I'd still indulged in Kate's mouth. Worse, I hadn't been able to stop myself.

And that caused both frustration and fear to spike, hard and hot, in my belly.

I debated which was better: Kate's magnolia scent or the smooth skin of her cheek. Or…no, I would not remember the soft inhalation she made, how her head began to turn toward me when I pressed my lips to her cheek as if she, like me, couldn't stop the need for more, closer contact.

Nope. The best moment was the sounds of want she issued as my lips moved over hers, just before my tongue invaded her mouth.

That kiss… *Hot* didn't seem strong enough to classify those moments. Nor did *steamy*.

I closed my eyes and clenched my jaw. Kate was like one of those sirens from that Greek myth—the mere idea of her made me want to jump in and grab her with both hands, even knowing starting anything with her was career suicide.

Remembering her effect on me would be paramount to successfully navigating the rest of this week—and what I hoped to achieve during this month in Austin.

I wanted my share of custody of Ike so I could give him the chance to rectify his vision. I'd find out the cost of his surgery tomorrow. Once I knew that, I'd be able to plan out my next step in my effort to petition the judge to be Ike's full-time caregiver—his stable parent who insisted on the proper medical care.

I needed to focus on the long-term goal. On my son.

Not on a sexy siren who just happened to be the sister of a man who could break me—and my dreams for Ike—to pieces.

I shoved the gear shift into park and stepped out of the car. With great care, I took the guitar case from the back seat—a J. Olsen creation could not ride in the trunk. This baby was now my most prized possession. Besides my son, of course.

I entered the three-bedroom condo and found it quiet and dark except for the under-cabinet lights in the kitchen.

"Beatrice?" I called.

No answer. I'd expected her to be asleep, so no real surprise there. I set the guitar case on my bed, then checked on Ike. His little arm covered in car pajamas rested on his covers but the rest of him was cocooned in the sheets. I bent and kissed his forehead, shocked as always by the rush of love I felt for him.

He was safe and secure, just where I expected him to be. That meant all was right in my world.

I walked out of his room and left the door open a crack. Beatrice's door was shut, so I left her alone. I grabbed a glass of water from the kitchen and turned on the bathroom light for Ike. Then, I took my glass to my bedroom and set it on the nightstand.

After a fortifying breath, I opened the guitar case.

Cam had said this one had a wide bell. He hadn't mentioned

the satin of the wood or the rich, gorgeous color.

The neck was a darker wood—something nearly black or stained that color. No, closer inspection proved it was a naturally dark wood. I'd bet money on it. I stroked my thumb down the length of the body, reveling in the velvety texture. My mouth went dry.

I hadn't done anything to deserve this beautiful instrument. Any man would have stepped in to make sure a woman wasn't hurt. Rather, any man *should*.

Because I'd been there at the right time, and because my instincts refused to let another man touch what my brain, certainly not the rational part, had already claimed as mine, I was now the proud owner of this guitar. I strummed out a G chord. Clear, rich. *Perfect.* I strummed another chord and then another.

I played my favorite song, delighting in the sound.

No wonder the biggest names in music insisted on a J. Olsen instrument. Nothing I'd played came close to the clarity of sound.

Unable to resist its resonance, I played all of my songs, ending with one of Cam's biggest hits.

"Holy wow," I whispered. "This is amazing."

I had to come up with something to do for them—Cam and Jenna—to thank them for this. And...I needed to be kinder to Kate because she was the reason I now had this amazing instrument.

CHAPTER ELEVEN | Kate

The worst part of not sleeping enough, besides the foggy mind and short temper, was looking like I hadn't slept. And, boy, did I have the bags under my eyes to prove it. With a disgusted grunt, I tossed my concealer onto the bathroom counter. I finished off my beauty routine with mascara and a little lip gloss. That was as good as today was going to get.

So, of course, I stopped by Gordough's on the way into work, thinking a delicious, fatty breakfast bread would improve my mood. Nope, but it did make my skirt waistband feel a bit tighter when I polished off the second donut and an extra-large latte before Jenna arrived. I shoved the box at her.

"Eat these. Now. Before I lose all willpower and go for number three."

Jenna's face turned a sickly shade of yellow and she pushed the box back into my hands, bolting for the bathroom.

With a sigh, I opened the box and waved it under Lyle's nose. The bodyguard snatched out a treat and I did the same. Some days deserved a bajillion calories. Like the day I understood why some seemingly random guy managed to snag all my attention and my body's awareness without trying, and left me alone after the most amazing kiss of my life.

Jenna came back out of the bathroom a little shaky and sank

into her chair. I handed her a bottle of sparkling water I kept in the fridge. Catering to wealthy performers meant I had a wide range of beverages in stock and tons of caterers and the best restaurants on speed dial.

"I don't know how I'm going to make it to this delivery today." She pressed her palm to her belly. "My stomach's full of surfing toads."

"Cam's snacks last night didn't sit too well, huh?"

Emotions flickered over Jenna's face before she nodded. "Something like that, I guess. Thanks for the water. It's helping."

"I'll take care of the delivery," I said. Already, I began to mentally shuffle my day to fit in the time it would take to drive to the client's house and back. Two, maybe three hours depending on where they were. I glanced at my to-do list and grimaced.

But no way I was letting Jenna go out like this. One, Cam would kill me. Two, I didn't want her to get sick on the drive.

"You sure?" she asked, relief stamped on her features.

"Of course. Just get me the details, and I'll run it over now." That way, I'd have time to finish my project from yesterday and the projections for the next quarter.

She leaned back in her chair and took a sip of water. She smacked her lips. "You, Kate, are an absolute godsend."

I raised an eyebrow.

"And don't think I didn't see how interested you were in Cam's opening act." Jenna's eyes lit up with amusement. "So, I guess it's a good thing I'm feeling too lousy to drop off his care kit."

My jaw clenched before I could control the reaction, but Jenna had already turned away to grab something from the large, hand-stitched leather tote she lugged everywhere with her.

Rye? I had to go see the guy I'd steamed up the windows with last night? The one I'd promised myself to avoid at all costs?

"Maybe you can grab some photos of him playing the guitar I made while you're there. You could add a whole series to show him prepping at home." Jenna turned back to face me, her face animated as the excitement of the idea took hold.

I stalked over to the donut box, pulled out the first one my fingers touched, and shoved a huge bite in my mouth. My taste buds might be screaming in ecstasy, but my brain was already setting up worst-case scenarios.

And there were too many to count.

CHAPTER TWELVE | Rye

I spent every morning with Ike. Period. This was our time—a sacred space I carved out of my day to ensure I connected with my son and he knew he was my priority. Beatrice had woken and headed back to her place. I wouldn't need her today—we had to head to the doctor's office later that afternoon and I could practice my setlist here while Ike played.

All those details and errands could wait until we had breakfast and snuggle time on the couch. If the rest of the world didn't like that, well, too bad.

At least that's what I would have said before I saw Kate standing at the small stoop in front of my door, tapping one of those torture-device high heels that made her legs extra-long and too sexy for words.

I whipped open the door before my brain caught up with my instincts. The fleeting thought of if she smelled as good today danced through my mind before I managed to tame both my head and my raging hormones.

I might have been able to avert my focus, to remind myself she was just one woman in a world of billions, if I hadn't caught the faint hint of sadness drifting off her just before she noticed me.

She straightened and pushed out a smile that, if I hadn't captured her expression a moment ago, I wouldn't have known was forced.

"Hi. Sorry to bother you so early, but Jenna wanted me to make sure you had some of her care products." She tilted her head, her lips pursed in that way my sister did when she was deciding just *how* annoyed she was with me. "You didn't mention last night you lived in my building."

I leaned a shoulder against the doorframe. "I didn't plan on seeing you again," I said. I winced at how harsh that sounded.

She tilted her head as her lashes fluttered. "Right."

She shoved the wrapped package into my hands, and I took a moment to appreciate the richness of the paper and the tight edges of the wrapping job. High-end, all the way. But that was J. Olsen's.

I felt a small hand on the back of my thigh and stiffened as Ike piped up from beside me.

"Hi," he said.

Kate paused in her act of turning away. Her smile warmed up to a beaming ray of sunshine as she took in my son leaning against my leg. She studied the thickness of his glasses before she moved on to the rest of his face. I began to relax.

"Hey there," Kate said. She stuck out her hand and bent at the knees to Ike's level. "I'm Kate."

"Ike's my name, and you're named after a princess."

Kate's smile grew even wider. "Aren't you a charmer, Ike." She winked at him, and I felt a zing in my chest. "Thanks for making my morning special."

Ike dropped her hand and she stood and stepped back, clearly preparing to leave. And why wouldn't she? I hadn't been kind to her—mainly because of how damn much I wanted her. Not that Kate asked me to kiss her last night. I'd started that brief but intense make-out session.

That's what irritated me the most. I could only blame myself for an ever-deepening pining for Kate Grace.

Before I could think it through, the words tumbled from my mouth. "Wait. Would you like to come in…have some coffee?" I settled my hand on Ike's shoulder, letting him know I was close and testing to see whether he was okay with me letting Kate into our morning. "You can tell me why today hasn't gone so great."

"Everything's peachy," she said with brave, false cheer.

I wanted to hug her to my chest and rock her while I petted her hair. I settled for simply saying, "Kate."

For a moment, something bleak and painful flashed through her eyes. Kate opened her mouth, and I could tell from the distant expression settling over her face that she intended to tell me no. But Ike stepped out from under my hand to grab Kate's. He tugged her fingertips.

"Come on," Ike said, his voice filled with excitement. I frowned, startled by his interest in this particular woman, even as I sighed with relief.

Ike had one of the best bullshit meters of anyone I'd ever met. He couldn't stand his grandfather, Quentin Keen, long before I realized that sadistic bastard was willing to bribe the local judge to make sure I didn't get custody of my own child. Punishment, sure, for knocking up his precious baby girl who'd seduced *me*.

But, the effort was wasted because his hope to get Deirdre to head on home and stick there was vain. Deirdre didn't like to be tied down, or motherhood, or any of the responsibilities that entailed, which was why my son had been raised by a sweet older lady named Mrs. Paula. At least he had been until she'd had a heart attack two weeks ago and good ole Quentin Keen was forced to admit he didn't want Ike in his house any more than Deirdre wanted to go home.

"Daddy's good to talk to. He knows how to make everything better. And his boo-boo kisses really work. Unlike my mom's."

I caught a glimpse of Kate's widened eyes before she stepped past me into the living area, her magnolia fragrance wrapping around me in a slow caress that left me hungering for more than her problems.

"What's wrong with your mom's?" Kate asked.

Ike shrugged. "She's not around so she can't kiss my boo-boos."

Kate's shoulders relaxed, and I realized she'd been fishing for information about me. I fought the smile that wanted to stretch across my face until I realized Kate must have been worried she'd kissed me when I was in a long-term, committed relationship.

No wonder she looked both relieved and close to fainting. Man, nothing about our interactions had been smooth or easy. More like a four-by-four off-road trek up the side of an active volcano.

"Um. I'm sure your dad is great and all, but I need to get back," she said, glancing over her shoulder.

I noticed she didn't pull away from Ike, though. He'd laced his small fingers between hers and he gripped her hand tightly. She let him tug her into the kitchen.

"My breakfast is going to be cold, so you gotta sit with me

while I eat it," Ike insisted.

"What are you having?" Kate asked.

"Cereal," Ike responded, his tone serious.

"I don't like it when the milk makes the flakes mushy," Kate said. She wrinkled her nose in that adorable way that I'd already come to decide was the cutest expression. "That's why I quit eating cereal."

"You don't eat cereal?" Ike asked. He let go of her hand and went to settle himself back in his chair. He nearly missed the seat and Kate made as if to catch him before she stuck her hands behind her back and shuffled away. The ache in my chest grew as I realized she didn't want Ike to know she'd been ready to catch him, and she hadn't wanted to overstep her place since Ike wasn't her kid. But when she glanced over, that small smile flitting across her lips, I drew a breath. Kate realized what Deirdre never did: Ike needed to prove his independence.

"Then, what do you eat?" Ike asked.

"An English muffin with cashew butter and sliced strawberries," Kate said, patting her hair. "Or an egg white omelet and a side of melon."

"Oh! We gots cantaloupe. I like it cuz it's sweet and orange. Orange is my favorite color. I can see it best."

"I like orange, too," Kate said with a grin. "I even attended a university where the main color is orange."

I set the package she'd given me on the cluttered countertop and finished fixing Ike's bowl of bran flakes. I put it on the table next to the container of cantaloupe I'd cut up yesterday. No, I didn't make him eat that health food—he said Froot Loops and the chocolate cereals tasted artificial, and far be it from me to try and force the kid to eat junk. I figured I'd have enough of that during his teen years.

Ike stuck his tongue between his teeth as he struggled to open the container of melon. With a triumphant smile and a flourish, he pulled off the lid and offered Kate a fork and plate—*his* fork and plate. Cantaloupe was Ike's favorite food and he never shared. But here he was giving Kate his fork and plate and practically shoving the dish at her.

"Thanks, Ike. I appreciate the offer, but I've managed to stuff myself with donuts this morning and can't possibly eat another bite."

Ike set his chin in his palms and stared up at Kate, a look of wonder in his eyes. "You eat donuts?"

She sighed and shook her head. "Not often. But they're Jenna's—she's my boss—they're her favorite, so I got some. She isn't feeling too great today and passed on them, which meant I had to eat them."

"How many did you eat?" Ike asked. He shoved a bit of cereal in his mouth and crunched through the flakes.

"Three," Kate said on a groan.

"Wow. That's a lot of donuts," Ike said. "I can eat six donut holes."

"Yeah?" Kate asked. She settled further back into the seat. "Glazed?"

Ike nodded, serious as he always was about his food. "The white kind. Chocolate is weird."

"True," Kate said. "Do you like fruit with your donuts?"

"Yep. Melon. Or berries."

Kate smiled. "Me, too."

I wished I'd bought a dozen donuts so that we could eat them together.

Ike studied Kate, his eyes taking some time to focus on her features. "I like your hair. It's kind of like cantaloupe, but prettier. I like when the curls bounce around your head."

Kate opened her mouth, and I caught her look. I hoped my expression didn't show how freaked out I was because I'd never seen Ike take to a person so quickly.

"Th-thanks," Kate stuttered. "I like your buzz cut. It's chic."

"What's chic?"

She grinned. "Stylish."

She reached forward and tapped the frame of his glasses. His too-large eyes blinked back, magnified through the lenses.

"Like these," she said.

"You like my glasses?" he asked, sitting up straighter. The start of one of Ike's beaming grins formed, transforming his face into sheer delight.

Each time I saw one of *those* smiles, my heart tried to burst with happiness.

"You know it," Kate said.

"He's a bit self-conscious about his glasses," I said.

Kate started when I spoke but kept her eyes on Ike.

"The kids at my preschool call them Coke bottles," Ike said as he scooped up another bite of cereal. "I like Coke bottles. Especially the old green ones my grandfather has. But those kids don't mean it to be nice."

Kate flashed a look at me. I stepped forward, hoping I managed something more than a banal or inane comment that would ease Ike's frustration.

"Hmm, well, those kids don't know what awesomeness they're missing. I never had glasses, but I had braces on my teeth for four years. And headgear," Kate added.

"What's headgear?" Ike asked.

"It's like a horse halter for your head that helps your teeth straighten out." She tapped her front, top pearly whites. "These stuck way out, like a rabbit. The kids called me horse teeth."

Ike frowned as he reached across the table and took her hand. "That's not nice of them. I'm sorry they hurt your feelings," Ike said.

My stomach tumbled as Kate smiled at Ike, a little lost in her past even as she clearly appreciated the sweetness of my son's heart.

"I am, too. But I'm even sadder kids made you feel bad about your *tres chic* glasses." She leaned forward and met his large eyes. Then, she whispered, "I think they're just really jealous."

Ike settled back in his chair with a giggle. Kate glanced over at me, and whatever face I was making must have worried her. She cleared her throat, then stood up, smoothing her skirt.

She liked skirts, and I liked looking at her in them. This one was a soft yellow, like diffused sunshine, and she had a wide white belt with it. It was longer than the one yesterday, hitting her mid-calf and reminding me of something out of the fifties. Kate rocked the style.

"I have to get back to work, but I'd love to chat again soon, okay?" Kate said as she shot me another nervous glance.

"Promise?" Ike asked.

Again, Kate looked startled, but she lifted her hand and hooked her pinky finger. Ike sat there, clearly unsure of what to do. Before I could move forward, Kate lifted his small hand and helped him hook his small pinky around her delicate one.

"Pinky promise. Which is unbreakable," she said, her voice solemn.

"So, you'll come by again tonight? We have dinner at six, and then I get to play cars before bed."

Kate's throat convulsed as she swallowed. "Um…"

"You pinky promised," Ike said.

"I'd love you to come to dinner," I said. "Ike, finish your cereal. I'm just going to walk Kate out, okay?"

"Yeppers," Ike said. He stared at Kate. "No take-backsies with a pinky promise." Then, as if the matter was settled, he shoved his spoon into his bowl.

I gestured for Kate to walk out first, mainly because I wanted to watch her skirt swish around her legs. I had it bad if I was this enamored with a woman's calves. They were fantastic. So was her ass. Shapely and round. Yeah. Kate's back was a masterpiece of femininity. As long as I only looked, I'd be fine.

Except I didn't want to just look. I wanted Kate. Yes, because of the chemistry we shared, but because I liked her. I liked her mixture of vulnerability and strength. I liked how much she enjoyed my son.

She stopped at the door and I managed to drag my eyes up her small waist to her face.

This close, I could see the dark circles under her eyes, which reminded me why I'd asked her to come in in the first place.

"You okay? I mean, are you worried about that roadie bothering you again?"

"I'm *fine*," she said.

She sounded like she was reassuring herself. That didn't reassure me. Much as I wanted to fix the problem for her, I didn't know how.

"So…dinner," I said.

She raised an eyebrow.

"It'd be great if you showed up about five-thirty."

"Is that an invitation?" Kate asked, her eyes widening.

"You were already invited," I clarified. "I'm just giving you the details."

Kate glanced over my shoulder. "I don't want to cause problems with your son—"

"Which is why you'll be here at five-thirty. Bring that camera of yours, so you can take some of those photos you mentioned."

"But I thought—"

"Ike's off-limits to the press and social media," I said.

She folded her lips over her teeth as she studied me. "Fair enough. And, for the record, I'd never take photos of your son without your permission. I always talk to the performers about what they're comfortable sharing when we come up with the campaigns. I want you to get more out of the week or two we spotlight you than we do. That's how we work."

Before I could think of anything to say to Kate's revelation, she stepped out the door. She made it nearly to the corner before

I pulled out of my stupor.

"We're having spaghetti and meatballs," I called.

"I'll bring some garlic bread," Kate said over her shoulder.

"It's a date," I said.

Kate's gait hitched for a moment before she continued walking. Only after she disappeared toward the parking garage did I head back inside.

Ike looked up from his bowl. He pulled his spoon from his mouth and munched. Milk dribbled off his chin. I handed him a napkin.

"I like her," he said, wiping his face.

"I noticed," I said.

I picked up my cup of coffee and took a sip. Ike ate some more, seeming deep in contemplation.

His spoon clattered into his bowl, signaling he'd finished his breakfast. "Can we get flowers?"

I frowned. "Flowers?" I asked.

"Yep. I need to have a bouquet for Kate."

A strange sensation built in my stomach and spread into my chest. "For Kate?"

"Yes, Daddy. Kate needs to have flowers. C'mon. All princesses get flowers."

And just like that, I realized my five-year-old had way more game than I'd ever hope to achieve.

CHAPTER THIRTEEN | Kate

It's a date.

Those words ran through my head on a constant loop all afternoon. *It's a date.*

Just words. A figure of speech. He hadn't meant it was an *actual* date—a get-to-know-your-son opportunity. In fact, Rye would never have invited me if Ike hadn't done so first, and he would have negated the invitation if Ike hadn't been insistent about it.

But the sweet little boy had.

Those glasses made his eyes huge, almost cartoonish in his pointed face. I'd been able to study his irises, which were a honey brown with darker brown flecks—like bits of melted chocolate. Such pretty eyes and thick lashes. I worried that I'd stared at his eyes too long, but not because I was troubled by his obvious issues. Nope, I'd been intrigued by his earnest expression and the smattering of freckles brushed across his cheeks and nose.

Ike was adorable. And, if his bone structure played out, he might give his daddy a solid run for a who-was-more-handsome contest in a few years.

Rye's initial reaction told me he was sensitive to Ike's issues, and Ike was small for his age, which, based on his speech, I guessed was around five or six. But his cheerful face and disposition created a wonderful aura I wanted to soak in.

I'd always loved kids. Unlike my brothers, who'd focused on sports and ranching and *way* too many girls, I'd enjoyed babysitting the neighborhood children. In fact, by the middle of my sophomore year of high school, my first boyfriend broke up with me, complaining I never had time to see him thanks to all my babysitting jobs. My brothers were ecstatic over my ongoing singlehood.

That'd been fine because I'd enjoyed spending time with the kids more than the boyfriend. I sighed. If only I'd made that same decision in college when I dated Brett. He'd shredded my heart when he broke up with me, citing his need for a more "attentive relationship." He'd meant he wanted me to be more fixated on him, and I'd wondered if I should have been, until I saw him all handsy with a freshman two days later.

I'd managed to sew the pieces of my heart together and move on, concentrating on the internship I'd landed with a large aerospace company in Chicago. But the exhilaration quickly turned to jadedness, and more heartache, thanks to my coworkers.

Troy and his friends had at first enjoyed giving me the worst of the assignments, sabotaging them so I struggled to complete them at all. They lied to me about what was required and what was expected.

Once they realized I was managing to do the work they needed completed, they'd started taking credit for what I did. I didn't realize that at first either, because Troy made sure I didn't attend the meetings with upper management. And, through all those months, I thought we were friends with the possibility of *more*.

Troy strung me along, promising dates that never materialized. He brought flowers or chocolates to my desk when he needed something else. And for months, I continued to work ninety-hour weeks, always anticipating *this* project would be the one I received a well-done for from my boss. Or maybe a kiss from Troy. I'd wanted both equally.

One night, I decided to catch an early dinner so I could see Cam's concert. But when I happened to overhear the four of them laughing about me in the bar across from our offices, I'd walked out of the pub without my coat. Too hurt to go to the concert, I called Cam's bodyguard, Chuck, and told him I was sick. Then, I went home and cried because I hadn't realized Troy was using me. Seeing him laughing at my pathetic crush when I'd worked my ass off—doing both *his* job and *mine*—turned my sadness to white-hot rage.

I'd been naïve because I believed we were supposed to be on the same team, but I was no longer willing to be duped. That Monday, I'd settled into the conference room for the weekly meeting, smiling sweetly at Troy when he walked in.

"What are you doing here?" he'd asked.

"I wanted to see you in action," I said, batting my eyelashes in what I hoped was the same lovesick look I'd been giving him for weeks. Troy bought my continued adoration even as I swallowed down the nausea building in my stomach. I'd smirked as Troy gave the false presentation I'd sent him. When it became obvious that his numbers were incorrect and he didn't know any of the projections, let alone the actual business plans, he pointed at me, sputtering out some nonsense about working with me.

I'd stood, straightened my skirt and gave a hell of a presentation with the correct numbers and excellent suggestions to top the previous quarter's ROI. After the meeting, the department boss called me into his office and told me we were supposed to be team players, not embarrass our colleagues. He wouldn't let me explain my reasons. Which was how I'd walked out of that office with a cardboard box of my personal items an hour later, desperately trying to ignore Troy's smirk as he leaned over his cubicle wall to watch my walk of shame.

Between Troy and my father, I understood I had issues with lies and coverups. I detested manipulation, too, which was why I was having second thoughts about dinner with Rye. He hadn't told me about his son, not even when I'd opened up—unwisely—about my issues with my family.

If I hadn't promised to have dinner with one of the cutest little boys in the world, I'd ditch Ike's sexy-as-sin Viking father.

——— ★ ———

I left work at five on the dot, causing Jenna to take notice, I'm sure. Though I wasn't overly concerned, because Jenna still looked a little peaked from her earlier bout of illness.

Lyle told me he'd get Jenna home, and I'd texted Cam to let him know Jenna might need a little prodding to take it easy. And TLC. His prompt reply let me know he'd ensure Jenna's evening was just what Dr. Kate ordered.

I smirked at Cam's playful banter but didn't reply.

Thanks to traffic and my stop at a local bakery for garlic bread, I arrived at Rye's house ten minutes later than I'd planned.

Ike opened the door, a huge grin beaming from his face.

"I saw you walking down the hall," he said. "I'm so glad

you're here."

"Thanks. Me, too," I said. "But I'm guessing you're not supposed to open the front door."

"You're not," Rye said. He threw a dishtowel over his shoulder and crouched down in front of Ike. "We talked about this."

Ike nodded, his lip quivering. "I gots excited. I wanted the fun to start."

Rye closed his eyes, and I didn't know if he was seeking patience or if Ike's words affected him as much as they did me. I tried not to notice how long Rye's lashes were—in that same brown that lightened to sun-kissed blond, tangling together as he squeezed his lids together.

"The rules are there to keep you safe, buddy," Rye said.

"Yes, Daddy."

Shifting a little, I said, "I brought you this." I offered Rye the loaf of garlic bread.

His thighs tensed, pulling the faded, soft denim tight as he rose from his crouched position. I swallowed and lifted my eyes but my cheeks still burned with awareness. My body wasn't going with my mind on this one—Body-Kate liked everything she saw and smelled about Rye, completely disregarding Mind-Kate yelling that continued attraction was both pointless and stupid.

"Thanks," he said.

"Smells good," I said, trying to behave like a normal person and not a lust-crazed maniac who wanted nothing more than to plaster myself to Rye's chest and pull his mouth down to mine.

"Daddy's a good cook," Ike piped in.

Perfect. Ike grabbed my attention. He was adorable and kept

my mind from picturing all the ways Rye and I could use the kitchen other than for its intended use.

This inability to control my own thoughts agitated me, and I squirmed. I took an unobtrusive deep breath and loosened the belt of the light-weight cardigan I'd worn over my thin, silk blouse.

"I'll take your jacket," Ike said. "That's what hosts do, right, Daddy?"

Rye's lips disappeared into his beard as his eyes sparked with humor. "You got it, son."

I folded my cardigan and handed it to Ike, who tossed it over the back of the couch. I caught Rye's eye and we both stifled a smirk at Ike's disinterest in the rest of the social niceties.

"What did you do today?" I asked.

"We went to the doctor," Ike said. "I got my eyes checked again."

I bit the tip of my tongue to not ask "why". Ike would tell me if he wanted me to know.

"Then, we went to the hospital and Daddy played music for the kids chemico."

I frowned. "Music? Chemico?"

Rye shrugged. "He means chemo. I help out sometimes with the kids who're struggling with pain or their therapy. Bring some instruments so the kids can make music. A buddy of mine started the program. He's an ER doctor but spends his free time jamming with the kids up in the children's ward."

"All the kids like it," Ike piped in. "I do, too, because I can just be in my body and not worry about my eyes not focusing. Jamal said he likes music because it takes the pain away."

"Jamal?" I asked.

"He's super tall and wants to be a basketball star. He told me before he and Daddy played drums."

Rye shifted, clearly uncomfortable.

"Not away," Rye said. He ran his hand down his hair. "It's more like puts the kids in the moment—pulls them out of their bodies' distress."

"Have you mentioned the program to Cam?" I asked.

Rye's shoulders tightened under his tee. "No. Why?"

"He likes to volunteer his time, especially to kids and veterans. Those are the causes closest to his heart. I was just thinking he might know people in the business who'd want to help."

"The kids aren't there to be exploited," Rye snapped.

"Is that what you think I'd do?" I asked, a frown forming between my brows. "What Cam would do?"

Rye sighed as he ran his hand over his bearded chin. "The kids don't need cameras in their faces and a media circus. They need to have some fun and, hopefully, heal."

"And Cam would bring press," I said, crossing my arms.

"Doesn't he? Everywhere he goes?"

I pursed my lips, but before I could ask a follow-up question, Ike grabbed my fingers.

"Come on, Kate. I need to give you the flowers."

I let him because hanging out with Ike was much, much safer than standing near flinty-eyed Rye. I didn't have a child so maybe I couldn't understand the defensiveness that bubbled up and over when I made the suggestion to include my brother. Cam enjoyed helping others, and I'd already created a mental list of musicians I knew who would jump at the chance to perform small, intimate sessions for kids.

Ike grabbed a mason jar filled with an interesting array of flowers and shoved it into my hand.

"I picked them out myself." He beamed.

"Thank you," I said, still trying to wrap my head around the cluster of blooms.

"I told Daddy you needed the prettiest flowers. But I wasn't sure if I could see them all cuz my eyes don't work great. I hope they're pretty," he said, fidgeting.

I heard Rye's footsteps, but I avoided glancing at him and how good he looked in those jeans. He went to the stove and turned off a pot.

I rearranged the vase, almost stabbing myself in the eye with some of the greenery, and wrapped Ike in a hug. "Calla lilies are my favorite."

"Which one's that?" Ike asked.

I showed him that particular flower and thanked him for the bright colors. Sure, the oranges and maroons clashed horribly, but it was, without a doubt, the most thoughtful bouquet I'd ever received.

"I'll treasure it," I said, and I was serious. "I'm going to put these on my desk at work so I have lots of reasons to smile."

Ike grinned, but he'd clearly lost interest in the flowers.

"I want to show you my backyard. I think it's big enough for a dog but Daddy said no, not yet."

Ike tugged me outside into their small patch of fenced yard.

I glanced back one more time and gulped at the sight of Rye in that gray, V-neck T-shirt. While not tight, it showed off his thick pectoral muscles and the flat slabs of his abdominal muscles.

Yes, searching for puppy escape routes was much, much safer than staying inside with the prickly, single dad.

CHAPTER FOURTEEN | Rye

For the second night in a row, I lay in bed, reliving my evening with Kate. A faint smile pulled at the corner of my lips as I pictured her in the tiny backyard, peering behind some scraggly bush. Thoughts of her took my mind off the message from my father-in-law, stating I was on my own for the surgery costs.

I'd expected as much, but I'd hoped…well, I'd hoped he'd be decent. The cost with insurance was staggering—nearly sixteen thousand dollars. But without insurance…Dr. Tenaka's office manager had shaken her head.

"I can't give you an exact cost, but…you're sure there's no insurance option?"

I shook my head. She shifted uncomfortably in her seat. "Um…we give a discount," she began, clearly uncomfortable. "But, you have to understand, it's not just Dr. Tenaka's fees. There's the anesthesiologist, the operating room, the recovery room, follow up visits…"

"Ballpark it for me," I said.

She blinked, her mouth twitching. "The last one of these I billed insurance over two hundred fifty thousand dollars."

I'd asked Ike if he minded going to the hospital after, needing the music and time with the kids, an escape from the cold reality that I couldn't afford my son's best chance to see.

So, now, I focused on our evening with Kate.

Ike adored her. More so with each passing moment they spent together. She shook her head at Ike's attempts to spin the spaghetti onto his fork and ended up showing him how to use a spoon to help him wrap it. He'd crowed with delight and asked her to help him with his next bite before he'd managed to do it on his own.

I'd loved the concentration on his face, the tip of his tongue poking through his teeth, as he dragged the noodles around and around. Kate watched, a proud smile gracing her lips.

That, in and of itself, was so different from Deirdre's interactions with Ike. When he'd failed at some task like spaghetti twirling, she'd let out a frustrated sigh and then cut his food into tiny bits, never heeding his attempts to do it himself.

Ike even sat next to Kate when she took a few photos of me with my new guitar. When I began to strum out one of my favorite tunes, Kate's eyes turned smoky with desire.

"Did you get enough photos?" Ike asked.

"What?" Kate asked. "Um. Yes. Of course." She stood, a blush staining her cheeks.

"For now. We have to discuss those…parameters," I said, following it with a wink that caused Kate to inhale on a tiny squeak.

"Cool. Come play cars with me."

"Absolutely," Kate said, hurrying off down the hall toward Ike's room. I followed after I settled the guitar in the case, needing a moment to overcome my own raging need to hear more of Kate's squeaks and sighs.

Kate made cute little motor sounds as she sat on the floor of his room, puttering a red race car across the carpet—again, not something Deirdre ever showed any interest in doing. When Kate saw the racetrack pieces in the box in the corner, her eyes lit up.

"Ooh! Can we build one? My brothers never let me play."

"You want to build a racetrack?" I asked, shocked.

"Yeah, so I can beat you both." She practically bounced up and down and her gray eyes sparked with eagerness.

She and Ike built the track, and she did win—the first time. The second, she pushed her own car off the track with a casual foot bump. Ike never noticed, too excited at the flashes of color speeding around the track.

She congratulated him with a high five, and he'd thrown his arms around her, hugging her in one of those tight embraces I hadn't seen Ike give anyone but me, leaving me awed at Kate's connection to my son.

Awed. But also concerned.

When I realized Kate had let herself out of the condo while I was getting Ike ready for bed, disappointment slammed against my belly, stifling me. She'd left me a note on the kitchen table:

Thanks for the fun evening! Cars are my new favorite activity. I'm planning to do a short intro video campaign to let our fans know you'll be spotlighted with Cam as our South by Southwest performers.

I'll touch base with my preliminary plan tonight before I post any photos and videos online.

Kate

Right now, I reviewed the posts she wanted to post. They were fantastic. She'd caught me looking pensive, no doubt attempting to keep those money worries at bay. I wasn't sure which filters she'd applied or how she'd edited the video clips so seamlessly, but I sounded great. The theme for the series was relaxed and simple—the perfect series to showcase Camden Grace's opener.

Kate was talented. I told her so when I responded. She told me they'd be online within the hour.

I tried to ignore the unsettling reaction rocketing through me. Quentin, Deirdre's father, had agreed for me to have this month with Ike while he sought a new nanny.

Music might be my passion, but I had to face the reality it wasn't creating the lifestyle I needed to give Ike the future he deserved. There was only one way I could do that—I'd have to agree to my father's demands that I take over his car dealerships. At least I'd have a steady income and health insurance. There was no other way. Ike and I were running out of time.

I stared at the images of me, singing. I'd give South by Southwest my best performance. Because, now, I understood it would have to be my last.

CHAPTER FIFTEEN | Kate

When Rye called me the next morning, I hoped it would be to ask me out again. I couldn't have been more wrong.

"Kate! I'm so glad I caught you. Listen…is there any way you'd be willing or able to hang out with Ike today?"

I glanced around my desk and the overflowing pile of paperwork. I hated a messy desk, and after the last couple of days, I was more behind than ever. A muscle under my eye twitched as I considered the hours I'd need to put in to get caught up. I'd worked for two hours last night and barely put a dent in it. "Um…"

"I wouldn't ask, but I really need to go see my father. It's urgent." Rye's swallow was audible. "He's got MS, and my sister called, asking me to drive up to Dallas."

That slammed into my chest like a meat mallet. "I'm so sorry," I whispered.

My father might have been a liar, cheat, and all-around terrible husband, but he'd been my daddy, and I'd loved him. I loved him still, even knowing he was lower than a snake in the grass. Losing him had blown up my world. Or maybe my world was in the process of blowing up and Daddy's death was the rock bottom of those few months.

Paperwork be damned. Family was more important. And,

yeah, I got how rich that was since I could barely stand to be in the same room as some of my family members.

"Of course. When do you need me?" I asked.

"Oh, thank you so much. I owe you *big* for this."

"What time?" I asked again, trying to focus on the practical.

"That's why I called you. Beatrice, she's the lady I hired to stay with Ike—her son's been in a car accident and she left about an hour ago, right before I got the call from Aubrey. I didn't think it was a big deal…"

"But it's become one," I said.

"Yeah," Rye said. "I'd take Ike with me, but my dad…he's not easy to be around. Last time he asked me all about Ike's issues as if Ike wasn't even in the room."

I closed my eyes and tipped my head back. Hadn't Cam said the same words about my father? *Not easy to be around.* Such a pleasant euphemism for the pain that had settled behind Cam's eyes. And if the man was saying things about Ike, no way could I allow that to go on. No wonder Rye was concerned. Desperate, even.

"I'll be there," I said. "When do you leave?"

"As soon as I can. I need to get back to meet Cam at the venue at eight-thirty."

"That's cutting it awfully close."

"I don't have a choice," Rye said. "Your brother's the main draw, and I'm just the opening act."

"Why don't you just ask Cam to postpone?"

"I can't. He's already… Look, if it's too much, I'll…I'll figure something else out. *Shit.* This *is* too much to ask of anyone. You don't have to hang out with my son. He might freak out. There've been a lot of changes in his life these past couple of weeks."

"You know he's going to be fine with me," I said. "We get along great."

I waited. Rye did, too. Finally, he said, "Ike really connected with you."

"I'll meet you there in an hour. And, Rye?"

"Yeah?" he asked, distracted.

"Focus on your relationship with your father." I bit the inside of my cheek to keep from saying more. He didn't need a lecture or my feelings about how lucky he was to still have the chance to yell at his father like I wanted to yell at mine. Who asked a seven-year-old to lie for them? Why had I put faith in my father for so long after his obvious betrayals of my mother?

"Thanks, Kate," Rye said.

I refocused my attention on him, glad to exit the memories and self-flagellation they brought up.

"Seriously, I can't even begin to tell you—" Rye began.

"You don't have to. Just let Ike know I want a car race rematch, okay?"

———— ★ ————

When I told Jenna I needed to leave to watch my friend's son because of a family emergency, she shooed me out of the shop. I made it to my car before I realized I hadn't grabbed my day planner. I still preferred the pen-and-paper method of scheduling. I ran in to get it, pausing when I heard the sound of retching. I considered knocking on the door, but Lyle shook his head.

"You'll get her home?" I asked in a quiet voice.

"I already called Cam to let him know she's sick. He's on his way."

I nodded, glancing back at the bathroom once more before I hustled out of the building.

Cam would take care of Jenna. No reason for me to insert myself into her illness—or contract it myself. Especially if I was going to spend the day with Ike, who might struggle with some auto-immune issues. Or maybe not. I only knew one preemie, and that was my friend Sana's son. Josh was an absolute fire-cracker of a kid, but those first few years were rough as his little body struggled to make up for the time he hadn't stayed in his mama's womb.

I frowned. No way I wanted to get Ike sick. Sana used to freak about every sneeze and runny nose. I'd already realized Rye was a worry-wort. He needed to settle down a bit, enjoy his son more—at least, that's what it looked like to me. But I hadn't been around Ike for more than a few hours and wasn't aware of the situation surrounding Ike's birth or time in the NICU.

If he spent time in the NICU.

See? So much I didn't know.

I ran upstairs to my place long enough to change out of my work clothes and grab a couple of board games I kept in my closet. I wasn't sure either would hold Ike's attention long, but I'd learned during my years as a babysitter that newness always trumped older toys.

After a moment's debate, I tossed a small bag on my bed and packed some essentials—a toothbrush, and a change of clothes for work tomorrow. Not that I expected to need them, but better to be safe than sorry. Plus, the nanny Rye had hired, Beatrice, might be back before Rye anyway. I ignored the pang in my chest at the thought of cutting my time with Ike short.

I pounded down the building's stairs and headed toward Rye's door. I smiled at the sight of Ike standing in front of the large picture window as if he'd been waiting for me again.

I heard Rye call out to Ike that it was okay for him to open the door. He did, and I opened my arms.

"You ready for some fun?" I asked, trying to be peppy.

"I'm so glad you're here," Ike said on a deep, heartfelt sigh.

When he hugged my legs, my heart burned with happiness. I brushed my hand over the top of Ike's head and admitted what my heart had known since our very first meeting: I was head over heels in love with this child.

CHAPTER SIXTEEN | Rye

Much as I loved seeing my sister, Aubrey, I didn't relish going back to the large, cold house I grew up in. I straightened my back and squared my shoulders, using one of my dad's favorite lines to give myself the pep talk I needed. *Man up*.

If there was one phrase that epitomized my father, that was it: Man up. He'd been a colonel in the army, and warmth wasn't in his vocabulary.

When my mom divorced him while he was still on tour in Kuwait—back when Aubrey and I were in preschool and kindergarten—he'd seemed to go along, unscathed by our absence from his life.

He'd "done right" by us with generous child support that allowed my mother to work part-time and be at every one of my baseball games, then my concerts.

My father never attended either; he even missed my high school graduation and my sister's college one. He seemed uninterested in Ike and never invited me home. Which was why my father's decision to reach out to me now was such a shock—especially since it came right on the heels of me making the decision last night to accept the role he'd offered me last year.

I hugged my sister at the door, trying to gauge her mood and, possibly more importantly, our father's.

"How are you, Aub?"

She hugged me back. "When did Dallas get so far away?"

I patted her cheek, smirking because I knew she hated when I did that. "When I started traveling more for my music again."

When Quentin refused to let me see Ike every week like I wanted.

Her eyes softened. "You do good work, big brother," she said. "And you still sing like an angel." She grimaced.

It wasn't that Aubrey couldn't sing—it was that my voice was clearer, and, as she put it, had soul. She wouldn't listen to me when I told her she also sang like an angel.

"C'mon. He's this way."

"This about the family business?" I asked. I was fairly certain that's why I'd been summoned. I hoped it was why Dad wanted to see me. The weight of that huge number for the eye surgery had kept me up most of the night. There wasn't another solution for me. At least not one that included me pursuing anything other than the newest models of high-end vehicles.

Aubrey dipped her head in a curt nod.

"You still interested in running all the car dealerships?" I asked her. My father owned eight luxury-brand showrooms across Dallas and Denton counties.

Again she nodded, but this time, her eyes lit up brighter than the Christmas tree in Rockefeller Center.

"But you know Dad won't pass the business along to me," she said on a sigh. She deepened her voice and said, "It needs a strong, firm hand."

"That's BS, and we both know it," I said, offended for my

baby sister. She had the brains for business—a truly brilliant mind when it came to numbers, not unlike Kate.

Numbers and car models were definitely outside my area of expertise.

We walked down the long, dark hallway that led toward the back of the house—the farthest space from potential visitors, quiet and interruption-free. Just how our father liked it.

"It doesn't matter what I think or want," Aubrey said, her lips twisting in a grimace. "And, Rye," she said quietly.

I waited.

"No matter what he says to you, the doctors are telling me he's running out of time. He postponed this call as long as he could. Yesterday, he had a seizure at the office."

I walked into my father's study with trepidation. He sat behind his desk, expression a mix of exasperation and…maybe?…pleasure.

"What did I tell you about your hair?" he barked.

Which was part of the reason I'd grown it out—to annoy the old man after those years of forced buzz cuts. The man couldn't bother to actually visit, but he called my mother, yelled at her, then at me, if my hair was more than a quarter of an inch longer than he deemed acceptable. Yeah, the irony of Ike's hairstyle of choice wasn't lost on me.

"You wanted to see me?" I shoved my hands into my pockets. For this trip, I'd pulled out one of my two pairs of dress pants and a nice button-down shirt. My father did not approve of jeans, and he sure didn't approve of comfortable clothing.

Sharp dressing, that's what he called it. *Look successful, be successful.* How many times had I heard that refrain?

"Damn straight, I did. We need to discuss you taking over my company."

While I respected the men and women who worked for him, I'd never been interested in cars, and I sure as hell never considered myself a salesperson. My singer-songwriter's salary wasn't stable enough, the judge told me at the last hearing Quentin forced me to attend, though we both had known it was an excuse. I made more than the average family—this was a way to keep me from my child, the continued penance Quentin felt I needed to pay. But Deirdre had been making noise about supporting my decisions—mainly because she didn't want to be responsible for Ike. Taking the job my father insisted on would solidify my ability to provide for Ike, and get Ike into my home full-time. I'd already asked for a different judge in our next hearing. One not in Quentin's pockets. If I took this position, I'd win at least split custody. We all knew the outcome.

All I had to do was agree to work for the man—my father. In a job I would never like.

I unclenched my jaw. I needed to think about how to benefit Ike, to get him the best future possible.

"Aubrey—"

"Is twenty-four years old and still working on her master's degree," my father said with a dismissive wave of his hand. "She's not ready to take over this large of an operation, and, as I've told her, she doesn't have a strong enough personality to run a company comprised mostly of men."

How my baby sister continued to live with this man boggled my mind.

"Aubrey's young, but she understands the business better than I do," I said. I needed to try to win him over to Aubrey's side. She deserved the chance to be in charge. Even though I needed some position in the company, that didn't mean I wanted to run it—or that I wanted to take something from my sister. And my father had known that for years. It was the main reason I'd refused to work for him up until now.

"That may be so, but it doesn't change the fact she's too young. And pretty," he added. Like that was a detriment.

Aubrey had sat in on more meetings with the executives than I had and understood way more about car sales and customer service than I ever wanted to learn.

"What's your plan of succession?" I said, not waiting for him to invite me to sit in the chair across from the desk. "What if we developed a plan for Aubrey to step into the CEO role over a time frame?"

My father settled back in his wheelchair, eyeing me as if I'd sprouted two extra heads.

"What would you plan on doing?" he asked. "More of the music?"

"No. I'd be here, helping Aubrey with the day-to-day operations until she took over."

My father narrowed his eyes. "And you'd take the title of CEO, have the executives report to you? You'd be in charge? No more running off to perform?"

"I'd be here." Because my father's company was my only shot to get more time with my son. I detested my dad's methods; Quentin and he both tried to bend others to their will. I didn't like being controlled.

I kept hoping my music would take off and I'd be in a position like Cam—on top of the industry and making more money than I could spend in my lifetime. Instead, I was a steady mid-charter. I needed more than that to be the father Ike deserved. That realization slammed into me while I looked at the numbers Dr. Tenaka's office manager wrote down for me yesterday.

"But I want Aubrey compensated for her time. If you don't set that up now, I will as soon as I take over," I warned.

"I didn't expect you to be so reasonable," he muttered. "I need you here full-time. I'm not able to handle the day-to-day details of the business anymore."

I resisted the urge to massage the back of my neck.

Performing at South by Southwest had long been a dream of mine. Perhaps it would also be the pretty bow wrapping up my youthful dreams. I knew the statistics of who made it in the music business, just as I'd watched families fall apart, thanks to the pressure of touring and constant studio sessions.

Kate's face swam through my mind. If I moved back to Dallas, I'd have no reason to see her again. Having her in my building was an added bonus—one I really wanted to take advantage of.

If I didn't move, Ike would lose out on his last chance to be with me at least half the time, as well as his vision.

I'd considered asking my father for the money to pay for Ike's surgery, but knew he'd tell me to man up. Or just ignore me until he got his way and I worked for his company—probably for a worse salary and benefits than if he thought he had to woo me, as he did now. Letting him think he was manipulating me was the best way to get what Ike needed.

I sucked in a painful breath and met my father's sharp eyes in that haggard face. "Let's discuss the conditions and my role. Specifically, health benefits for Ike and me."

When my father opened his mouth, I held up a hand.

"I'm not saying yes. Not until I see the healthcare package."

And made sure this deal with the devil included well-respected scleral buckle surgeons.

CHAPTER SEVENTEEN | Kate

The second time Ike tripped, this time over the hose in the tiny back yard, I realized just how much his eyesight must be a hindrance. Not that Ike seemed to care—he was in a state of perpetual motion, which was what caused the second header. I managed to catch him before he splatted on hard Texas dirt, but my heart hammered as I stood him back up.

I wrapped up the hose he'd tugged out to water the shrubs that he swore were rose bushes without making mention of Ike's near-miss. He pretended everything was fine, and I let him.

I'd been self-conscious about my teeth as a kid before I got braces. Granted, Ike's vision was completely different, but I'd also learned from my experiences that focusing on the positives of his personality and his capabilities would help him build confidence and try new adventures.

"How about a trike ride to the park?" I suggested.

"Really?" He smiled up at me, his glasses glinting in the sunlight. "I get to pedal all the way there?"

I patted the handlebar attachment that allowed me to hold and steer the trike if necessary. "We'll take this just in case you get tired, but yeah. You can pedal. Just let me change into my exercise gear."

"I'll put on sunscreen," Ike squealed as he ran into the condo.

I winced when he banged his shin on the door.

Rye must have been hard up to trust me with his son. I hoped I could keep Ike in one piece until Rye arrived home.

CHAPTER EIGHTEEN | Rye

Thanks to my trip to Dallas, I was running late to meet up with Cam at the venue. I lived in a perpetual state of too much to do and too little time. On my way back, I called to check on Ike.

"He's doing great," Kate chirped. "We made some cookies and he rode his trike to the park."

"By himself?" I asked, concern sizzling over my veins. I exited my car and jogged toward Cam's trailer, my other hand wrapped tightly around the guitar handle. No way I was going to let anything happen to my new baby.

"I was with him the whole time," Kate said. She managed to soothe me by sounding matter-of-fact. "I had that bar thing that goes on the back, but he stopped at the corner without me asking." I could hear the smile in her voice when she said, "It was great exercise for us both. Way better than the treadmill."

The image of Kate in tight Spandex, running and laughing next to Ike swirled through my mind, making me dizzy with longing. I wanted to see that. Be part of that.

I stopped moving for a moment as the idea of not seeing Kate again sliced deeper than a twelve-gauge nail. I needed to respond to Kate, but my chest ached as if the nail were buried deep in my heart.

I cleared my throat and started forward again.

"Thanks for being there with him today. I don't know what I would have done otherwise. Beatrice called me earlier. She's not going to be back until Saturday morning." And the show was Saturday night. My pulse escalated but I took a deep breath. I'd figure something out, even if it meant getting Aubrey to drive down. This gig was officially my last one, and I was performing with an incredible talent. No way I'd mess this up…more than I already had, anyway.

"It's been great. Seriously, don't worry. We've eaten sandwiches and apple slices and watermelon, and we just finished pigging out on cookies. He'll be in bed in ten minutes."

I opened my mouth to tell her no more than two, but then snapped it shut. Cam strolled around the corner of his trailer, his eyes narrowing in irritation as they zoomed in on me.

"He around? Can I say hi?"

I spoke to Ike for a moment, making sure he was comfortable and okay with me coming home after he was in bed.

"Kate's going to stay with me. She promised to read me four books."

"That's great, son. Sleep tight."

Kate took the phone back and told me goodbye.

Pocketing my phone, I straightened my posture as I faced Cam and readied myself for the slew of accusations and questions about where I'd been.

Cam shoved his hands into his pockets and rocked back on his motorcycle boots. Had to admit, the dude oozed confidence; the kind of appeal women lapped up and other men wanted to emulate.

I'd *never* been him—or anyone like him. For a while, I'd thought that was okay, that I was going to make my own mark in that area between country and folk and alternative—my own sound. But some dreams remained ephemeral no matter how much we wanted them or how hard we worked to achieve them.

"I'm just going to ask, and I hope you'll tell me the truth. What's up with your kid?"

I pulled the elastic from my hair so I could run my fingers against my scalp, hoping to ease the throbbing there.

"He just turned five."

"And?" Cam prodded.

"Ike was a preemie and he's got…"

Cam's face softened further. "Special needs?"

I snorted. "Not like you might be thinking. His immune system is fragile, meaning he's more susceptible to the flu and viruses, and he's…" This was the hardest part to talk about because my anger at Deirdre and her family made hot emotion lash up my throat. "He's got ROP."

At Cam's questioning look, I began the spiel I could recite in my sleep.

"ROP stands for retinopathy of prematurity, and it affects infants born before thirty-two weeks. Ike only weighed in at one pound fifteen ounces, which made him more susceptible to ROP. It often leads to vision impairment and blindness."

"Sorry, man." Cam shook his head. "That's rough. For him, but also for you."

I shrugged and looked at the ground.

"Jen's pregnant," Cam blurted, and my gaze snapped up. He

dropped his head a little, almost sheepish now. "We...ah...we haven't told anyone because we're both kind of freaked out about the baby being healthy."

That wasn't something I'd worried about before Ike came so early. I was more apprehensive about being a father within months of being legally old enough to drink alcohol. Partying was shunted to the bottom of my to-do list as soon as we found out Ike was coming.

Yeah, at twenty-one, I'd been a self-absorbed asshole who thought my music was the most important aspect of my life.

I nearly rolled my eyes at my whacked-out set of priorities. I'd been working since to correct them—to live up to the faith my son had in me.

"She's had a difficult time," Cam said, his voice rough.

I nodded because the entire world knew Jenna's story—the overdose of GBH meant for her friend and the subsequent trial. Since she started dating Cam, more of her history and struggles came to light, but those weren't any of my business. Just like my son's health wasn't something the rest of the world needed to know or speculate about.

"She seems good now," I said. "Solid. Happy from what I saw the other night."

Cam narrowed his eyes. "Damn straight she's good. Like I'd let her be any other way."

I smirked at his caveman statement until I saw the fear shifting in his eyes. Maybe if I'd been more like Cam, Deirdre would have conquered her fears and let Ike get the surgery earlier—maybe then my son would still have a mom in the picture *and* functional sight. But I hadn't been that man; I still wasn't capable of setting aside all *my* worries and perfecting the stoic, alpha protector that Cam found so natural.

Cam ran his hand down the back of his neck. "She…ah…she worries she'll mess it up. Carrying a child, I mean."

Holy hell. Who knew I'd have so much in common with one of the biggest rock stars in the world? But then, when it came to our kids, our hearts were no longer our own.

"I don't have any good advice if that's even what you're asking me for. Follow the doctor's instructions: rest, vitamins, water. Carrying a baby…it's work. One of the most profound and miraculous things I've ever seen in my life. Me—you—we need to remember we can't do that. Which is why our job is worse. You just get to stand by, watching, waiting, and being there for her."

Cam smirked as he stepped closer. "Hell, now I see why the label wanted me to give you a shot. You're deep. Sensitive. And all gooey at your center."

At my scowl, he threw his head back and laughed. "Don't worry, I won't say anything. But maybe cut the crap with the chip on your shoulder. We all got shit we're dealing with."

It was my turn to shove my fists into my pockets and rock back on my boots—which were an exact replica of Cam's. Crap. We had the same taste in guitars and footwear. We were probably destined to be buddies.

Just what I needed—to bond with a freaking global phenom. That wouldn't keep Ike out of the public eye long, nor would Cam's success make me giving up my dreams easier to swallow.

"No one gets a piece of my son, Camden."

He frowned. "I don't see—"

"Definitely not the press. I refuse to let people pry into his medical records or take photos of him so trolls can make fun of glasses or his small size or—"

Cam held out his hands, palms up. "I get it. And I don't want that for your boy, either. I'd never throw out that kind of bone to the reporters." He sucked in a long slow breath. "I'm going to pretend you said that out of concern for your son only and not because you think so lowly of me."

I dropped my head so that I once again looked at the pavement. "I don't. I'm worried about what you and the world think of me."

Cam clapped me on the back. "You should come to dinner at the ranch tomorrow."

"What? No, I couldn't—"

"My mama wants to meet you. And I don't like to disappoint my mama."

I shook my head at his down-home talk. We both knew Cam did what he wanted, when he wanted. I was flattered he wanted me to meet more of his family. And I loved the idea of spending more time with Kate.

"All right. I'd like that," I said.

"Excellent," he said.

He strode onto the stage as if he owned it, talking about what he'd like to do with my set and how to transition it directly into his opening song.

We finished the exchange within an hour, and I had to hand it to Cam—the idea for the seamless transition was brilliant. My last tune flowed well into his, almost as if we'd planned it.

Cam slung his guitar on his back as he fist-bumped his band. "That was awesome! Kate sure knows what she's doing."

"That was Kate's suggestion?" I asked.

Cam nodded. He strolled off the stage and toward his trailer. "She's been humming the tune. I asked her why she was singing my song when I saw her at the shop last evening, and she got this funny look on her face and blurted out the idea."

I couldn't help the smile that slid over my face. "Your sister's smart."

"She's pretty, too. She's also dealing with some things." The last was said in warning.

I raised my hands. "I wouldn't hurt her. Have you heard anything about the roadie?"

Cam scowled. "Yeah. He's gonna do time. Kate's not the first woman he's assaulted. I've got Chuck making sure these charges stick—and he gets the longest sentence possible."

"Good."

Cam studied me for a long moment. "We'll see you tomorrow. Six sharp. My mama's going to want to hug your boy and maybe Kate'll show him her horses."

The man knew exactly how to lay the trap.

"She rides?" I asked.

Cam grinned. "Like the wind."

CHAPTER NINETEEN | Kate

I set my e-reader to the side as Rye walked through the door. He lowered his guitar case to the wood floor in the living room before pocketing his keys.

"Hey," he said, hands still in his pockets.

I smiled at him, resisting the urge to press my hand to my chest. Each time I saw him, my heart flipped and somersaulted like a trapeze artist.

He inched closer until he was at the edge of the couch, his eyes heated with a sizzling electricity I appreciated all the more because I returned it.

"Thanks for the suggestion to Cam. About the song."

I grinned. "It worked out?"

"Yes. It's a fresh way to get the crowd excited about the music." His expression turned speculative. "You're really good at marketing."

I shrugged.

He came closer, settling next to me.

"You look good on my couch," he said, his tone a little rough. His attention slipped back to my legs. "In those pants."

I had on a pair of capri yoga pants and an overlarge top that hung off my shoulder, showing off the thin bra strap underneath. Rye's warm look of approval swept over me again. Goosebumps cropped up along my skin.

"Thanks." Real snappy, Kate.

Rye tucked some loose curls behind my ear. "I've been thinking about kissing you, Kate. I'd really like to do that again."

I tipped my face upward so that our lips nearly touched. "Yes, please," I whispered.

I caught the start of his smile before his lips settled over mine. He moaned. His arm slid around my waist and pulled me closer.

When his tongue slid across the seam of my lips, I opened for him, and the kiss heated up. Rye's tongue danced over mine, tasting me. He tasted of coffee and something else, something delicious. I sucked his tongue and he did something with his arms so that I ended up in his lap.

His hands slid up from my waist and over my chest, which I pressed against his palms. Rye tilted his head and nibbled at my lower lip before placing soft kisses along my jaw to my ear. He nipped the lobe and I gasped, grinding into his lap. He lifted his hips. I bit my lip as I felt his growing desire there behind his zipper.

Oh, how I wanted him. I was desperate for this man. For everything he could give me.

That thought finally broke the sensual haze that had soaked over my brain.

"Wait," I gasped. "Wait. I'm not...this is... Too fast."

Rye dropped his hands to my waist before he leaned his head back on the couch. I watched his Adam's apple bob. "Right. Yeah. Of course."

Rye set me on the couch beside him and then stood. He walked toward the kitchen.

I picked up my e-reader and powered it down. "Um…are you mad?"

He filled a glass of water. "No. You were right to stop me. We… My life's complicated, Kate."

I bit my lip, wanting his comment to reassure me. It didn't.

"How'd it go with your father?" I asked, desperate to change the subject to something less awkward.

I peeked at Rye from the corner of my eye and saw the disappointment flash across his face before he schooled his features. "Fine."

Hmmm, that conversation path didn't work. If anything, the air around us now vibrated with discomfort.

"That's good," I said.

Rye tugged the elastic from his hair and ran his fingers through the mass. I wanted to be the one weighing the silky strands across my fingers.

Time for me to go before I further messed up what had been the hottest make-out session of my life. I grabbed my purse from the kitchen table and tucked my e-reader inside. I dug out my keys and glasses from their case and settled the cute purple frames on my nose.

Rye leaned his hip against the edge of the table. "What's with the glasses?"

"They help me see better at night. I'm a little near-sighted."

His gaze ran over the frames almost like a physical touch. "Just at night? Not for reading?"

"Near-sighted people get more near-sighted in the dark, apparently."

"You didn't wear them the other night."

I shrugged. "I wasn't as tired." And because I hadn't wanted him to see me in them. Now, though, there was no reason to keep pining. His life was *complicated*. And I felt very much like one of those complications.

"You okay? To get home?"

"Of course," I said. "It's just up the stairs, really."

"Well, I want to make sure you get home safe. That you get a good night's rest."

"I will," I said.

"Okay." He looked at me and I fidgeted, unable to meet his eyes. He cleared his throat but made no move toward me. In fact, he gripped the edge of the counter, anchoring himself.

"Then, good night," Rye said. "And thanks again for your help today. I'm sure I'll hear all about it from Ike."

"Bye," I said, heading toward the door.

"Wait," he said. Urgency filled his voice.

I turned back toward him.

"Do Cam and Jenna plan to tour much this year?" he asked.

That seemed like an odd question, but I shook my head.

"Not really," I said.

"That's good," he mumbled. "Really good. Do you know if they have a rocking chair?"

"Nope." I frowned. "Why?"

Rye cocked his head before his lips slid into a flat line. "No reason."

There was a reason. That was an odd question. I blew out a breath. "Did you need something else?"

He sucked on his lower lip, which caused his beard to shimmer in the low lights. "So, your brother heard me talking to Ike earlier tonight. He asked some questions…"

"About your son's eye issues?" Then I blushed. "Sorry, I already know that's a touchy subject, but since I hung out with Ike today, I noticed…" I hesitated. "My friend had a son three months premature. He has ROP. Is that what Ike has?"

Rye's expression tensed and a few seconds of silence filtered by. He seemed to weigh his options before he nodded. "Yeah. Glaucoma from it. He's stage IV."

"He's a great kid, Rye."

"Yeah, he is," he said, voice thick.

"I hope you get what you want for him," I said, my voice soft.

Pain and tension radiated from him, so I moved close enough to place my hand on his wrist, an unwitting attempt to offer comfort. Warmth spread through my veins. He turned toward me, caging me against the counter. His mouth landed on my neck before either of us did more than breathe.

I moaned as he placed small kisses along my jawline before settling his lips against mine.

My second moan turned to a strangled gasp as I cradled his growing erection against my stomach.

"Rye."

"I thought about you today, Kate. I shouldn't. I know that. But you…your gorgeous hair and this soft magnolia scent. I'm addicted to it."

I loved his words. I wanted to believe them. I teetered there, my heart aching, my core warm and soft with need.

"Let me introduce you to Dr. Tenaka," I blurted out, wanting to do something for him, wanting to help Ike.

"He was Sana's son's doctor. Caleb was stage IV, but almost stage V—bad, right? And now Caleb's got most of his vision. I'm sure Dr. Tenaka could help you come up with a payment plan like he did for Sana—"

Rye stepped back, putting the table between us. "I've met with Dr. Tenaka. And I've already talked to his staff about payment options."

"Oh. Well, good."

Rye stiffened, his mouth set in a rigid line. "The surgery is astronomically expensive. It's all state-of-the-art, cutting edge equipment. Plus, the hospital won't do it without proof of insurance or a hefty down payment. I have insurance—a crappy policy for *me*. But that doesn't help out Ike." He narrowed his eyes. "And there's nothing wrong with Ike the way he is now."

He wrapped both his hands around the back of his neck. "Shit. Now I sound like Deirdre," he mumbled.

I tucked the name away. I'd already looked Rye up and knew he had been married before. To Deirdre Keen Lawson. They divorced last year. I also knew Rye was six months younger than me.

But I wanted to know more. So much more.

Rye dropped his hands. He looked tired, wrung out as if he'd worried himself sick.

"I want Ike to have this surgery—I want him to have every chance at a normal childhood," Rye said.

"I'm sure he will. You're a good dad, Rye."

He barked out a laugh. "Tell that to my ex's father, okay?" He shook his head, but his eyes were flat with anger and hurt. "Look, I don't want to fight with you about this. Ike may get the surgery. He might not. There are a lot of moving pieces."

"All right," I said, mainly because I didn't know what else to say.

"Thanks for today. Seriously. I know Ike had a blast, and I should have focused on that when I walked in. I'm sorry. Your brother got to me earlier, too." He leaned his palms on the table and dropped his head forward. "Defensiveness seems to be my default when it comes to Ike. Defensiveness and overprotective-ness."

I rested my hand on his shoulder. I hoped he took it as the gesture of comfort I meant it to be. My fingers curled into his muscle, seeking to get closer.

Rye shifted, his muscles loosening as if he liked my touch. That spark rekindled in my belly.

"I'm not trying to pry. I just know Dr. Tenaka is the premier doctor for this surgery. Ike's such a great kid, and since you're here, it made sense to me that—"

"*My* son is none of your business," he snapped.

My eyes flashed up to his blue ones, which were filled with so many turbulent emotions. My chin quivered once before I managed to slam my lips together and nod. Message received.

CHAPTER TWENTY | Kate

I vacillated between tears and anger during the short walk back to my place. Why couldn't Rye see that I wanted to help him and Ike? A deep hollowness grew behind my breastbone. I tucked myself into bed and slept fitfully.

The next morning, I sipped the last of my cup of coffee as I finished applying my makeup. It was heavier today, due in large part to the ravages of lack of sleep.

Jenna hadn't arrived when I opened up the shop. Hopefully, Cam kept her home until she was back in top shape. Mainly because I didn't want the stomach bug. I shuddered. I hated vomiting. A fever—that was annoying. Body aches hurt, but medication caused them to fade. But the inability to control one's stomach had always upset me more than my mama said it should. She'd tell me just get it out and be done with it. But I struggled to remain in control for as long as possible. So, yeah, I feared the idea of puking my guts up.

I squirted enough hand sanitizer to coat my hands. Maybe that'd keep the bugs at bay.

I threw myself into the paperwork I needed to complete. Jenna walked in a couple of hours later, pale and wrung-out, and strode straight into her workshop with hardly more than a raised hand in greeting. I knew she was behind schedule on crafting a superb specimen for a friend of our sister-in-law, Regan. While not as big a name in America, the young singer-songwriter was tearing up the European charts.

In defiance to my brother's country roots and Rye's soulful, folksy music, I set my playlist to some of Regan's newest songs, all of which left me feeling more empowered. I finished the last of the accounting for the month and turned my attention to the Instagram campaign I was building using photos of both Cam and Rye. This one was painstaking work, where I needed to build off the previous image and caption. The account had over three million followers, something I took pride in even if Jenna was married to Cam, who had millions of fans.

As I designed the campaign, using different images I'd taken at Rye's the other night, I felt another pang of concern. I finished my plan and then clicked through some previous posts, making sure this was in line with the branding and message we wanted to convey. The promotional arm of the business had led to more exposure for Jenna, the shop, and the process of custom-made instruments.

Not that Jenna had been hurting for customers or cash flow before. But now, thanks to my efforts, she had a dedicated following of people who admired her work, whether she was married to Cam or not.

As I worked on the next campaign, using some of the photos of the partially-made guitars Jenna was currently building, I smiled a little, shocked as I always was that I worked for such a prestigious name in the music business.

Definitely not the future I mapped out for myself as I'd

finished up my undergraduate degree or even as I worked in
Chicago, but, in many ways, a better one.

A hand touched my shoulder. I jerked and screamed.

I turned, tangled in my headphone cord, and nearly tumbled
from my seat. Cam caught me before my butt hit the ground.

"Not quite the reaction I was expecting," he said.

"You scared the bejesus out of me," I said, trying to catch my
breath.

"I called your name first, but I guess you didn't hear me."

The music pounded through my headphones. "I had the
music turned up."

"No kidding," Cam said with a frown. "That's going to mess
up your eardrums."

I settled back in my chair, switching off the music. "Well,
thanks for giving me a heart attack. Now I don't have to worry
about destroyed hearing."

Cam clucked as he set the headphones on my desk. He picked
up my hand, turning it over to examine the fading bruises around
my wrist. His scowl grew.

"These from the roadie?" Cam asked.

"It's fine," I said.

Cam touched the worst of the bruises and I flinched. Cam's
scowl deepened. "It wasn't this bad on Tuesday."

"I had time to grow into it. How'd you know?"

He flashed a glance up at me. "Rye told me last night. Wanted
me to make sure you were feeling okay this morning."

My heart squeezed. He'd told me his son was none of my
business, but there he was, butting into my life as if he actually

cared about my physical wellbeing.

I wish Rye wouldn't act sweet. I wanted to be mad at him. Except I didn't. I wanted to kiss him again. I wanted to go back to our time on the couch and have him stretch me out there and love every inch of me.

My cheeks heated at my thoughts—thoughts I was having in front of my brother. I took a measured breath and blinked back the fantasy.

"Seriously, Cam, I'm fine. The pain is less than it was, and I keep getting reassured the guy will serve jail time."

"Oh, he will," Cam said. "Chuck's coordinating with the local police to make sure they stay on top of the case."

"Thank you," I said.

"I'm so sorry it happened in the first place," Cam said. "You sure you won't let me hire you a full-time guard?"

"I don't want to live with a shadow, always worried someone's watching me."

Cam's gaze settled on something far away as if he were trying to work out a complex issue. "There's a price to fame I never really considered until I was already in too deep to step out of the limelight. If I'd known…" Cam shook his head.

"What? You love the fans. The concerts. You feed off it."

"Yeah. But Jenna shies from it. So does Mama. And you were hurt because of someone's beef with me. That…"

"Could have happened whether you were famous or not."

Cam dipped his head in acknowledgment. "Maybe. You coming to dinner tonight?"

I glanced at the clock and cursed under my breath. Nearly

five—I'd been lost in work all day. Now that I knew the time, I needed to pee, and my throat was drier than one of the local creeks in August.

I grabbed my glass of untouched water and downed it, buying myself a moment to put my thoughts in order. Forgiving my brother and building on our former relationship was one thing. My mother—her lies and what she let me believe… That pain rocketed back through me. Pain and shame. Because, for years, I'd blamed my mother for my father's cheating. I'd kept his secret, the mortification of knowing it was wrong growing with each passing year. And my mother, with her silence on my father's many affairs, reinforced the falsehood he was a decent human.

That's what made the entire situation so difficult for me. I'd idolized a selfish, weak man, always believing I had the best daddy in the world. And, the whole time, he'd been hurting the rest of the people who I loved.

"At the ranch?" I asked.

"Yeah. Carter and Regan are stopping by."

"I'll think about it," I said. I started to swivel back in my chair to face my computer, but Cam placed his hand on my armrest.

"It'd mean something to all of us if you'd come," he said, his voice softer, coaxing.

Damn his magic voice. I wasn't mad at him, not really. Just wounded by his lack of trust, and I wasn't sure how to get around it or over it.

"Mama wants you there."

I crossed my arms over my chest and scowled. "Then, maybe she should have told me the truth about our family. *That* would have made me feel included a lot more than a guilt trip about a missed dinner."

Cam dropped his head down toward his chest. "I get you're upset with her, and, if it's any consolation, you're in the right here."

He pulled out a Werther's candy and popped it in his mouth. I hadn't seen him do that in a while. Cam sucked on it for a moment before he continued.

"But life takes unexpected turns, Katie Ro…*Kate*. I never got a chance to make the situation right with Laurence."

"Do you wish you had?" I asked. I'd wanted to know but hadn't known how to ask him.

Cam hesitated before he nodded. "What he did to me was unconscionable, but yeah, I do. Even if that 'right' was to slug him for being such a…" He trailed off, side-eying me. "I have to carry the heartache of not trying my best around in here." He pressed his hand to his chest, over his heart. "And that's a heavy weight."

I must not have looked convinced because he said, "Look, my experience with your father was different than yours. But we can agree on the fact Laurence loved you to pieces. He hurt our mama but he will always be the only father figure any of us will ever know."

Cam's eyes turned stormy with regret. "I let him die without trying to understand his side of the situation."

I nodded as I picked up a paper clip. I fiddled with the edges, hoping I looked busy instead of nervous. "I caught him cheating on Mama."

Cam cursed.

"Do I even want to know how old you were?"

I glanced up at him from under my lashes. "Seven. He told me it was a one-time thing. That mama wasn't giving him enough sugar.

"So, I don't think you need to carry around any weight about Laurence. He made his bed long before he died in it."

When Cam opened his mouth, I held up my hand. "I'll come to dinner. But no promises about forgiving Mama. She made choices and I have to live with those."

"Yeah, I understand."

And I knew he did, which warmed me more than just about anything else could have. Cam stood, eyes on Jenna as she walked through the door, rubbing sawdust off her hands with one of those flannel rags she liked so much.

"Oh, and Rye's bringing his boy out," he said.

Good thing Cam's attention was so utterly taken because blood rushed to my cheeks once again.

What had I gotten myself into now?

CHAPTER TWENTY-ONE | Rye

Why had I agreed to spend the evening with the Grace family?

Because Camden Grace asked me, that's why. I might be giving up my music career, but I wanted to stay in Cam's good graces. A part of me thought, maybe, just knowing someone of Cam's stardom would make it possible for me to complete another album, to make a comeback. Eventually.

And, yeah, I wanted Kate's brother to like me, to approve of me as her partner. I craved more time with Kate. I craved that beautiful smile, craved her joy when she played with Ike. And that sexy ass in those tight Spandex pants.

I needed to apologize for snapping at her. She didn't know how Deirdre's family controlled my relationship with Ike. She didn't know of my father's years of manipulation and efforts to force me to work for his company, mocking and disparaging my music career.

Thinking about Kate was nearly as dangerous as thinking about my upcoming takeover of my father's dealerships. I'd signed the paperwork earlier today, sending the documents back by courier. My father called a couple of hours ago to let me know it had been delivered—and to get details about when I would arrive in Dallas.

My throat cinched closed at the thought of giving up music,

of sitting in an office all day. Panic built but I forced it down, tucked it away. Just as I had my desire for Kate. I couldn't have her—not if I was moving to Dallas in less than a week.

I still couldn't believe I was leaving Austin, a place I'd always wanted to live, to move into my father's oppressive house. Nothing about this situation smacked of *me*. Nope, I'd sold out for health benefits and would turn into a corporate drone, even if technically I'd be the boss man. Still, this career change was the only way Deirdre and her family would no longer dictate Ike's care.

Dr. Tenaka had affirmed in that appointment a few days ago that the window for Ike's surgery had narrowed to a critical point. We had mere months left before the pressure to the optic nerve grew too high and the damage was irreversible.

Months. All because I'd allowed my ex-father-in-law to dictate terms to me.

I gritted my teeth as the war inside my head waged on. Not that my feelings mattered—Ike's future hung in the balance, and if that meant giving up my dreams...

Unfortunately, I couldn't see another way to achieve the outcome Ike needed. The one he deserved, and the one I was going to give him. No matter the personal cost to me. It was my penance for failing him years ago when Quentin bribed that cursed judge.

While those thoughts circled through my mind, I dressed in a nice pair of jeans and a new gray Henley. I picked up a bottle of sparkling water for Jenna and a six-pack of the local brew for Cam. Ike ran to the car and managed his own buckles, something he'd been practicing since he came to stay with me. I double-checked to make sure his safety harness was straight as surreptitiously as possible. He'd been complaining about how Deirdre's family treated him like a baby. No way I was making the same mistake.

We drove to the Grace's family ranch with the radio blaring Ike's favorite songs—some of Camden's tunes intermixed with my own.

"I get to meet him?" Ike said as one of Cam's songs faded.

I turned down the volume. "Sure do. You'll like him. He's nice."

"Is he big like you?"

One of the coolest things about having a kid—they think their daddy is the biggest, baddest, most amazing specimen of manhood on the planet. Not that I liked to discourage such things, and my chest puffed out with pride when I said, "Almost."

Cam and I were both tall and athletic, though his muscles were from scaling walls and sprinting through the hot sands of the desert. Or had been. Mine were from hours in the weight room as part of the varsity football team and, later, lugging around heavy equipment to shows before I built up enough of a following to have staff to do it for me.

I pulled into the white gravel driveway of a surprisingly modest brick ranch-style home with a white wraparound porch. A riot of flowers in a variety of colors and feathery petals grew in large, well-tended beds interspersed by huge oak trees. Soft hills undulated behind the house, rolling down into a wide meadow surrounded by pipe-fencing. Four large barns painted crimson sat to the left and a few horses were in a large corral off to the side of one of the barns. The place was neat and well-maintained but not ostentatious.

I released a long breath. "Ready?" I asked Ike as I collected the bag of drinks from the passenger seat.

Ike remained quiet so I turned around to look at him. His face was twisted. "What if there are kids and they tease me about my glasses or move too fast so I can't see what's going on?"

Aw, hell. Ike knew how to bring me to my knees. I got out of the car and opened the door next to Ike. I squatted in front of him and rested my palm on his knee.

"No one will tease you. There aren't any kids." I gulped, hoping that didn't freak him out more. "And if anyone moves too fast, we'll just ask them to slow down."

"The kids at preschool don't. They speed up, and they say I'm stupid for not being able to see like they can."

I hated that I hadn't been there with him to at least talk to their parents about being kinder. Deirdre's father wouldn't do either; Deirdre had all but abandoned Ike. That's why I couldn't fail him now.

I wouldn't.

"I'm sorry to hear that," I said, trying to keep my tone even. "I'll be sure to talk to your mom and grandpa—"

Ike shook his head so hard his glasses slid off his nose. I tucked them back on and waited. His mouth screwed up in a scowl.

"Don't talk to Mommy. She just cries."

Before I could answer, another car pulled into the drive. I swiveled around in time to see Kate's cherry-red Mustang convertible slip to a stop on the far side of the drive. A nude stiletto attached to Kate's trim leg crunched in the white gravel. She shut the door and, over the roof of the vehicle, saw me crouched in front of Ike's seat.

A frown settled on her beautiful face as she walked toward me, hiking her purse up on her shoulder so that her top showed a small sliver of skin on her stomach. That pale flash of flesh caused my heart rate to ramp up.

"Kate," Ike cried.

He scrambled over me, knocking me flat on my butt there in the gravel as he dove to clutch Kate around her legs. She patted his back as she raised an eyebrow at me. I rose and dusted myself off.

"Glad you could make it to my mom's place, Ike. She makes the best fried chicken."

"Is that what we're eating? I've never had it before."

Kate took his hand in hers. "Then you're in for a treat. Crispy and juicy and dee—licious." She laughed as she laid on the accent as thick as Cam.

"I get to meet your mom?" Ike asked as he skipped up to the porch, his earlier fears clearly forgotten.

"Yep."

"Do you live here, too?"

A flash of pain flashed across her face, but she masked it with a smile.

"No, sir. I live in my own place. It's in the same building as you. Because I'm all grown up and that's what grown-ups do."

Ike scratched the side of his head near his ear. "I thought grown-ups got married."

"Some do," Kate said.

"You live in my building? So you can come play cars with me tonight? And again tomorrow?"

Kate hesitated. I smiled at her, but she glanced back at Ike, still seeming nervous. Right, because of my harsh words to her. I needed the clear the air and soon.

"We'll see," she murmured as she opened the white front door. A blast of raucous laughter spilled down the hallway, wrapping us in the happy sound. I took a deep breath and wondered when I'd last heard so much cheer.

Not in a long time.

The front entry was a bit dark, highlighted by a large chandelier that wasn't on. The hardwood floors glowed with a patina caused by years of foot traffic and waxing. A bench sat to the left of the stairs with a pile of shoes in front—everything from cowboy boots to small, feminine flip flops ringed the seat.

Before I could ask Kate if we should remove our shoes, more laughter spilled down the yellow-painted halls.

Ike hung back a little. Kate noticed and dropped his hand. When he refused to move forward, she knelt in front of him.

"What's got you so worried?" she asked.

"I wear glasses," Ike said.

Kate smiled as she straightened them. "I see that. They make you look very distinguished."

"What's disting…ish?"

"Handsome and smart at the same time," Kate said.

That sweet look coupled with her willingness to reassure my son ignited a longing in my heart.

I swayed a little, shocked by how much I wanted more of Kate's affection. For Ike, sure, but for me, too. I'd *never* felt anything like that. Ike had the power to bring me to my knees with his questions and tears. But, no, not even Ike's contagious belly laugh made me want to wrap him in my arms and hold onto the moment with both hands, drawing it out forever.

"Really?" Ike asked, hope brightening his face and pulling me out of my terrifying realization that I didn't just lust after Kate. I already cherished her. Deeply.

Kate leaned in closer. "For sure."

Damn if my heart didn't pound harder as Ike sucked in a breath and nodded with solemn intensity. "That's good."

"It is. Did your dad tell you," she said, "that I wear glasses at night? And even sometimes when I work on my computer."

"I loved your glasses," I murmured.

She shot me a look that I found difficult to interpret, but the heat building in her eyes caused my body temperature to spike.

"So does Carter," Kate continued. "He's one of my brothers. His wife says his glasses make him look very distinguished, too."

She stood in a lithe movement that had my mouth drying out. This woman kept me spellbound.

"You want to meet Carter? I heard him laughing, so I bet he's telling one of his silly jokes. Be sure to ask him the one about the turtle."

Ike perked up even more. "I love turtles," he said.

"Me, too."

Kate held out her hand again, and Ike took it. Part of me smiled while another part mourned the loss of Ike wanting and needing *me* to lead him into that room of new people. Kate glanced back before she moved, as if to make sure she had my permission.

I smiled at her, and she smiled back but it remained tentative.

Right. I still needed to correct my defensiveness from last night.

The kitchen was as dated as the front hall. The appliances were white, a bit dented, and scrupulously clean. The countertops appeared to be that uniform engineered stone, but the cabinets were yellowing oak with a wide grain reminiscent of the eighties, and an inexpensive laminate supposed to simulate brick covered the floors.

Copper pots lined the walls, covering much of the faded wallpaper, giving the space a warm charm. People maneuvered around the long island in the middle. I waved to Cam and Jenna as I tipped my chin up at Chuck, Cam's buddy and head of security.

Another man who looked identical to Cam—except he wore glasses—turned as Kate entered.

"Katie Ro… Kate!" he cried, moving forward to hug her. Ike wrapped his arms around her leg at the guy's exuberance.

The man must have seen Ike's movement because he looked down. "Hey, little man. I'm Carter."

Just as Kate had, Carter dropped down to meet Ike at his level. I couldn't help but like this family. They had a natural, easy way with kids that put Ike and me at ease.

Carter stuck out his hand and Ike clung tighter to Kate's leg, his cheek pressed into the soft gray fabric of her skirt. Smart kid that he was, he'd figured out the best place in the room was plastered to Kate's side.

"This is Ike, and he's my date tonight," Kate announced. "He's never had fried chicken and he likes turtles. So, as you can tell, we have lots in common."

Cam chuckled as he pressed a kiss to Jenna's temple while

Carter's wife, Regan, a pop diva turned bluegrass singer, leaned back against the counter and whispered into an older woman's ear. By her good looks and graying reddish hair, I decided she must be Mrs. Grace, Kate's mom.

"You picked a good man there, Katie," Mrs. Grace said, wiping her hands on her apron.

I noticed the stiffening in Kate's shoulders as well as the pointed look from Cam. Why? Because I noticed everything about Kate, and I didn't like the idea of her being uncomfortable.

Mrs. Grace gave Kate a quick squeeze and then turned to Ike. She said hello in a friendly manner that had Ike relaxing his hold a little on Kate's leg. Then, Mrs. Grace turned her attention to me.

She had Kate's eyes—large and expressive—but with more years of living and regret buried in their depths.

"Hi, there. You must be this cutie's daddy. I'm Jasmine."

I fumbled with my bag so that I could shake her hand. It was work-roughened but warm.

"Ryland Lawson. But most people call me Rye. Thank you for having me to dinner, Mrs. Grace."

"It's Jasmine, honey, and I'm glad you're here. Same with you, Ike. I hope you like fried chicken and pie. That's what my boys like to eat."

"What kind of pie?" Cam asked.

"I made you apple and Carter cherry."

Cam smirked. "Good. Cherry's for suckers."

"Will you stop?" Jenna said with a little laugh. She stepped forward and took the bag from my hands. "What do you have here?"

"Just some drinks. I wasn't sure what else you needed." I felt nervous. I wanted Kate's mom to like me. Not because I wanted her approval. Fine, I did. I'd never gotten Deirdre's dad's consent to marry his daughter, and that always bothered me.

My eyes drifted back to Kate, who was hugging Carter's wife, talking to the other woman even as she kept a hand on Ike's back.

Seeing them together made me smile. Deirdre had never been so comfortable with Ike. But he and Kate, they'd bonded instantly.

If I could fall into lust with her with one look, I guess my son could fall in love. That should worry me more. I knew it should. But right now, I couldn't think of a good reason why.

"That's so sweet," Jasmine said with a smile. "Ike, how do you feel about lemonade?"

"He and I will both have some," Kate said. "We'll go out on the back porch, and I'll show him my turtle's nest."

"You have a turtle?" Ike squealed.

The adults chuckled.

Kate accepted the two glasses from her mother, one with a striped paper straw, which Kate offered to Ike.

"Thanks," she said, but the strain was there in her voice and in her facial expression. I resisted the urge to wrap my arm around her.

"Kate's been in love with turtles since she was littler than you," Mrs. Grace said. "She managed to lure one up into the yard to lay eggs about twenty years ago, and that girl or one of her babies has been coming back ever since."

So Kate hadn't been playing up her interest in the reptiles to Ike. Interesting.

"Did she tell you what she named her?" Carter asked, laughter shimmering through his words.

"Don't tease her," Jenna said.

Kate shrugged. "I was six. And I loved The Beatles."

Cam grabbed her shoulder and pulled her into a side hug. "You listened to those albums nonstop." He faced me, a proud smile playing across his face. "Kate has the *best* ear for talent. She'd slow down the songs on the turntable, play them over and over."

Kate shook her head. "I wanted to be a Beatle."

"What did you name your turtle?" Ike asked.

"Sergeant Pepper. After my favorite album. And because that turtle brought up a squad of friends." She shrugged but her cheeks were pink. "Made sense when I was little."

"I want to see Sergeant Pepper," Ike said, eyes wide. "Does he still have friends?"

"She's a new turtle, and I haven't seen any others in the yard in years."

"Laurence didn't like 'em much," Cam said, eyes narrowed.

"It was all we could do to keep him from shooting Sergeant Pepper," Jasmine said. "Remember, Cam?"

Cam's shoulders tensed and Jenna wrapped her arm around him. His eyes softened and the hard, sharp look dropped from his face. "I remember. C'mon, Jen, let's go find one of those albums. I'm in the mood for The Beatles."

Lots of emotions swirled through the Grace family. Jasmine followed Cam and Jenna's retreat with troubled eyes. Carter stood stiff while Regan murmured at him. Ike bounced up and down, excitement shining from his face.

"I'll take you out to meet Mrs. Sergeant Pepper," Kate said with some false cheer, shooting her mother a look.

Before Jasmine could respond, Kate sashayed out of the house, Ike following a half-step behind, chattering at her about the turtle facts he'd learned. Which was a lot. We read a book about turtles pretty much every night.

"So, where's your wife?" Mrs. Grace asked just as Kate reached the kitchen door.

I froze for a moment. "We're divorced."

CHAPTER TWENTY-TWO | Kate

Unfortunately, Rye's quiet response sucked the air out of the kitchen. My mother was typically good at social situations, so I had no doubt she'd recover from her faux pas with her normal aplomb. Though, the fact she'd brought up my father—the terrorizer of Cam's youth—rocked me, but not as much as it shook Cam and Carter. My brothers hadn't blamed me for my mother's comments, but I hated how my mother's obvious nervousness at my arrival reminded them of just how hard Cam's childhood here on the ranch had been.

I led Ike outside, thankful for a moment away from the tension in the house. Setting my drink on a small table, I said, "Put your drink here, and we'll go check the nest."

Ike did as I asked, holding his glass with both hands and taking care to make sure it was stable before he removed his hands. His little tongue darted out between his teeth as he concentrated. Such a cute, endearing habit.

I took a deep breath and released it slowly. I'd felt a rush of desire when I took in Rye's outfit of well-fitting jeans that showed off the thick slab of muscle in his thighs. He wore a charcoal Henley, a thin black sports coat, and…yes! A new pair of Chuck Taylors. The man's sense of style was dreamy.

I adored shoes—all shoes—but there was something especially

sexy about a guy in faded jeans and Converse.

When he caught my eye, his expression appeared somewhere between apprehensive and begging for help. I'd been surprised then flattered to help him with whatever was going on with his too-cute son.

"I don't have on the best shoes for traipsing through the meadow," I said. "You mind holding my hand so I don't fall in any gopher tunnels?"

Ike took my hand as we walked down the steps into the grass. Sure, my stilettos were a poor choice for the tough, native grasses, but I wasn't sure how poor or blurred Ike's vision was. I held his hand to ensure I was extra careful with his balance and safety without making the sweet boy self-conscious.

"You have gophers, too?" Ike asked.

"Sure." Mainly because we couldn't get rid of the suckers. They loved to munch on the roots of mother's peonies. That caused annual battles between mom and rodents. *No one* messed with her peonies.

I led Ike over to the spot between two large asparagus plants. I pointed. "Can you see the bits of eggshell?"

Ike peered closer, leaning closer until his nose almost brushed the piled grasses.

"I do," he breathed. "That's from Sergeant Pepper?"

He was too precious, and his willingness to use the name I'd given years before without question warmed my heart.

"Yes. But we can name this turtle something else if you want."

Ike shook his head. "I like it. Daddy plays The Beatles, and I like that song. But I like the hold-hands song better. Holding your hand is nice."

How could I not tumble harder in love with Ike? He was so genuine, so in-the-moment. He bent back toward the nest before he peered around the grass.

"There were babies here?" he asked.

"Yep. We get a few eggs every year."

The door banged and I turned, unsurprised to see Rye striding toward us.

"Here comes your dad," I said.

Ike nodded. "He worries about me. He thinks I'll get hurt."

I filed that piece of information away to process later. I kept my wave friendly. "No turtle, just some bits of eggshell."

Rye stopped about a foot from me and shoved his hands into the pockets of his jeans. Seriously, did he have to look that good? His shirt had two buttons undone that showed off his strong, tanned throat and a hint of firm chest.

Get a grip, Kate. We were at my mama's house. His son was holding my hand.

"Y'all ready for some dinner?" I asked.

Rye nodded. I led Ike to his father. Instead of dropping my hand to take Rye's as I'd expected, Ike positioned himself between us, each of us holding one of his hands.

"Swing me," Ike said.

"I'm not sure—" Rye started.

But I was already counting. Ike took a running start and lifted about a foot off the ground. He squealed in excitement. "Again, again."

Rye's lips twitched in what I hoped was pleasure as we swung

Ike again. The third swing had Ike landing on the porch step. I felt a pang of disappointment I couldn't keep playing with him. He really was a precious child.

My mother came to the door and smiled, even as lines of tension formed around her eyes. The moment of joy I'd created with Ike popped, and as much as I wanted to live in this bubble of childhood perfection, I couldn't. I cast a quick glance at Rye and saw the same flash of disappointment in his eye.

He held the door open for my mother. Ike followed her inside. When I moved by him, Rye leaned down and whispered, "I'm sorry about last night."

His eyes were clear and full of regret.

"Thanks. I shouldn't have assumed you'd want help. Or that I knew your situation well enough to offer it."

Rye ushered me inside the house, his hand on my lower back. His fingers lingered there in a caress. "I wanted you to know I felt terrible about how we left things." His voice dropped lower. "Especially after how well we were getting along on the couch."

My breath hitched at his words.

"I'd love to be that friendly with you again soon, Kate," he murmured against the shell of my ear.

He pressed a soft kiss there and my breath hitched again, my pulse spiking.

"Soon," I breathed.

I was pretty sure I heard him say, "Not soon enough."

CHAPTER TWENTY-THREE | Rye

We sat around a large, oval oak table with matching ladder-back chairs. The cushions appeared home-made with the same French-inspired rooster design Mrs. Grace—Jasmine—seemed to prefer.

Ike devoured his dinner. The Grace family's easy-going nature and flowing conversation, especially between the twins, had Ike more relaxed than I could remember, and he ate with relish.

He gravitated toward Kate and the two of them shared multiple quiet moments together over the course of the evening. I wanted to be involved, as well, but forced myself to focus on Cam. A bite of chicken stuck in my throat when I realized Cam's ability to smooth over my problems with the label executives wouldn't matter next week. I wouldn't be in the music industry anymore.

I cleared my throat and gulped down my sweet tea, wishing I hadn't agreed to this dinner—to reinforcing everything I was giving up.

"I have to ask," I said, though butterflies jittered through my stomach. "Why didn't you and Regan team up for South by Southwest?"

"Cuz Regan's too popular to help me out." Cam snagged his beer bottle off the table and took a drink.

"Shove it, Grace," Regan replied without any heat. She

turned to face me. "I'd already booked tour dates in the Bay Area. Carter needs to meet with his team there, and I wanted to go with him."

She said this with a casualness that belied the difficulties of the logistics. When he raised her hand and kissed her knuckles, all while staring into her eyes, I knew she meant what she said.

I'd never had that level of connection with Deirdre. She hated my touring, hated the bus, the hotel rooms, and the fans. She'd liked my rising fame and the money that came with it, at least until she decided she couldn't mother a kid with health problems and poor eyesight and cleared out our apartment while I was on the road. Next stop, I'd been served divorce papers.

"Which leads to our reason for asking Mama to host us tonight," Carter said, pulling me from my past. His voice lacked some of the twang Cam seemed to play up, but was similar in rich baritone.

He turned to face his mother. "Regan and I are expecting."

Jasmine clapped, her face lit with joy. She rose and hugged both her son and daughter-in-law, pausing a moment to cup Regan's face and place a soft kiss on her forehead. Kate, who held Ike snuggled in her lap, his head drooped against her shoulder as he snored softly, offered her quiet but heartfelt congratulations, smile filled with warmth. Just before I turned away, I saw the sadness flash through her eyes as she stared at Carter and Regan's soft touches.

Cam and Carter hugged with lots of back slapping. Jenna and Regan conferred in excited tones.

The longer they talked amongst themselves, the more Kate and I seemed set apart. Without realizing it, I'd taken her free hand, unsurprised to find it trembling a little. She breathed out on a soft hiccup.

No one else noticed her burgeoning distress, which caused my frustration level to increase.

When Cam announced that Jenna was also pregnant, Kate leaned toward me. "Ike's down for the count. Want some help to get him to the car?" she asked.

"Sure," I said. "But I'll carry him."

Kate glanced down at my son, her face softening with affection and something that looked too much like longing. "I got him."

Even as I wanted to protest, she rose.

"I'm going to help Rye get Ike in the car. Then, I need to head out. No, no, don't get up. You have lots to talk about."

I witnessed the collective realization they'd completely left her out of their joy.

No wonder Kate had issues. While unintentional, there was definitely a fine, filmy curtain between Kate and the rest of her family.

Jenna seemed the most distressed, but Cam whispered something in her ear. She relaxed into him and nodded.

"I'll see you tomorrow," Jenna said.

"Course," Kate said, mustering a smile.

Since she insisted on carrying Ike, I grabbed her handbag—a pretty one with an expensive label. Kate liked luxury brands. I might not be up-to-date with women's fashions, but everyone knew the iconic red bottoms of those heels she'd worn into a field tonight—just to show my son bits of turtle eggshell.

"Guess I know why you asked about the rocking chair," she

said as she settled Ike into his car seat. "Cam must have told you about Jenna."

I hated to hurt her more, but she already knew that I knew. "Yeah, he told me. He mentioned she's pretty freaked out about messing up the baby."

"Did you buy it?"

"I was thinking about it—as a thank you for the guitar. And being so decent about working around my schedule. It's a good one—the kind the NICU nurse suggested I get for Ike."

She nodded. "You should. They'd appreciate the gesture." Her hand lingered on Ike's car seat for a moment longer before she stepped away.

Kate dipped her head but not before I saw the sheen of tears. Maybe it was that feeling she'd been dealt a shitty hand that had me blurt out, "Want to come back to my place?"

She'd just finished buckling Ike into his seat and turned to look at me over her shoulder.

"Yeah," she said. She cleared her throat, drawing my eyes to the long, elegant line. "I'd like that."

CHAPTER TWENTY-FOUR | Kate

"Kate?" Rye hesitated for a moment. "For what it's worth, I think your family's missing out on what you have to offer."

I sucked my lower lip into my mouth for a moment as I absorbed the pain of being left on the outside of their shared excitement—and the embarrassment that Rye saw it happen. I yelped when Rye laid a hand on my hip. He turned me slowly, carefully.

"You're kind and funny and obviously a brilliant marketer. Jenna admitted tonight she'd be lost without you running her place."

I snorted. Because that praise was faint and ridiculous. Jen's reputation and beautiful instruments would more than keep her afloat. I just added a bit of icing to her cake.

Rye wrapped his arms around my waist, snuggling our chests together as he rocked back and forth in that gentle way parents seemed to develop.

"It's their loss," he murmured against my curls. "They don't deserve someone so selfless."

I rested against him because he smelled good, he felt good, and the words he said made me feel good.

"You don't even like me," I mumbled.

He chuckled wryly. "That's where you're wrong. I like you." He cupped my cheek and tipped my head back. "And I'm so damned attracted to you, it's driving me insane."

His lips settled over mine in a soft, sensuous brush of sweetness. The kiss remained light, almost a dream. His rich, clean scent wrapped me in a cocoon as warm as his arms. I reveled in the feel of his interest.

His touch ignited the same soul-deep desire I'd tried to ignore since hearing him sing. Whatever was between us was strong, a compulsion, and now that we'd kissed, I didn't know how I would go back to my life now knowing what his lips felt like. How his beard was soft and tickly against my cheek and chin.

I opened my mouth in a gasp as he aligned his stomach and thighs to my curves. He was hard everywhere, and I marveled at his strength.

Then his tongue slipped past the seam of my lips and stroked along mine. Rye held me even more tightly to his body as our mouths fused together and his tongue seduced me.

I wanted more.

"Daddy?"

Ike's plaintive cry had Rye stumbling back with a curse. He shoved his fingers into his hair, tugging those long, burnished locks loose from the band. Damn, that hair was sexy. I *really* needed to run my hands through it.

After a heated backward glance, he strode toward Ike, leaving me leaning against the side of my car, breathing labored, thighs quivering, and heart in tatters.

I wanted to call Rye back, to beg him to focus on me. But that was wrong. Ike needed his father. Maybe I would *never* hold anyone's focus or deserve the undying love Cam shared with

Jenna and Carter felt for Regan. Wasn't that what I'd learned from my few boyfriends? Hell, my own father, the man I'd idolized, couldn't stay involved with just his own family. He kept looking for someone better than the people who loved him at home.

I was throwing a pity party for myself, but I still couldn't believe Jenna hadn't told me she was expecting. She knew how much I liked kids; she understood how much I ached for a family of my own. Yet, she'd said nothing.

Because I might be her friend, but I wasn't her confidant. That was Cam's position. And with Regan also pregnant, I wouldn't even be able to share pregnancy milestones—not when Jenna and Regan had each other.

Once again, I'd proven to be good but not good enough. As a sibling, as a friend—hell, as a would-be lover to the man already striding to his son's side.

He spoke to Ike in a soft voice before bolting back to me. He scooped me into his arms and kissed my mouth like a starving man at his first meal in days. He pulled back slowly, hands cupping my face, thumbs against my cheekbones, staring at me as if I was precious. "If you don't come to my place, I'll head up to yours."

With that, he climbed into his car and shut the door, leaving me annoyed, pleasantly shocked by the demand, and very turned on.

CHAPTER TWENTY-FIVE | Rye

I glanced back to see Kate's soft, lustrous skin glowing in the porch light. I wanted her riotous curls tangled around my hand again. I'd loved how, with each shift of my fingers in her hair, I seemed closer to her sweet lips. Even now, the light scent of magnolias trickled across my senses.

I shifted in my car's seat, cursing the uncomfortable cloth seats in my five-year-old sedan. This must be the twentieth time, but I simply couldn't get my raging hard-on to calm down. Kate was everything, and I meant *everything,* I'd ever wanted in a woman. A little shy but full of passionate hunger—all centered on me.

I bit the pad of my thumb as I turned off the ranch's road. I struggled with how to proceed—with Kate, sure, but also in Cam. I liked the guy. My phone beeped, but I ignored it. No way I'd check a text message while I was driving—especially with Ike in the car. No way in hell I'd jeopardize his safety.

Once he was tucked into his bed, I checked my phone.

The message was from Cam. Two words. My heart pounded at my own stupidity. *Call me.*

Sucking in a breath, I did.

"Y'all get home all right?" Cam asked.

"Yes. Ike's in bed."

"My sister there?" Cam asked, his bluntness taking me by surprise. So, he had seen me kiss her.

"No."

"You got a thing for her?"

"I…" I'd started dating Deirdre when I was eighteen. She was the sum total of my romantic experience outside of a few—very few—random hookups, but I manned up and said, "Yes. I think I do."

The mere thought of Kate's bright, happy smile again caused my lips to curve upward.

"I'm not sure how I feel about that. About you kissing her like that. But Jenna pointed out that's between you and Kate. So…all I'm going to ask is for you to be careful with her, man. She's had a rough time. And I don't think we made things better tonight."

I rubbed my hand through my hair.

"She doesn't connect to you, or your brother, or your mom, especially when you close ranks and exclude her, intentionally or not."

"You noticed?" Cam said on a sigh.

"Hard to miss."

"Right. Well, there's tension. Just don't use that to seduce her and then leave her. Cuz if you do, I'll bury your chance at a second shot with the label."

I couldn't tell Cam I was actually more worried about *my* response. Damn me for being a selfish bastard. That kiss…I wanted Kate too much to leave her alone. Maybe she'd be okay with a long-distance relationship. It was only about three hours between Dallas and Austin.

We could make that work—spend time together on weekends.

I licked my dry lips. If that was my best shot with Kate, I'd take it. She held my focus, and I craved more time with her.

"I…" I blew out a breath. Much as I wanted Cam to know how much Kate meant to me when the bottom fell out, I wasn't prepared to tell him I might well already be halfway in love with his sister—and definitely in such deep lust I'd never clear my head of her. I stared at my trembling hand before I clenched it into a fist.

"Congratulations to both you and Jenna, and to your brother and Regan," I said. "That's so cool you'll have kids so close together."

"Yeah, I'm shocked we're having babies before Katie Rose. She was always so into little ones. Obviously, Ike picked up on her love."

Cam's words caused another ominous shudder to pass over me. "Kate wants kids?" I asked. My voice sounded choppy and my heart pounded.

"Yep. Always has. Plans on a brood of 'em. I guess if y'all get together, she gets a jump start."

He chuckled.

My responding chuckle was faint and pitiful. "I'm not… I don't…"

"I pushed too hard," Cam said, contrition dripping from his tone. "Just know I love my sister. And you've grown on me, Lawson. Treat my sister right and we'll be fine."

Cam rang off. I stared at my phone, which shook in my hands.

"What have I got myself into?"

There was a knock on the door. Kate.

The thought of her on the other side of the slab of wood and metal made my blood sing and melodies explode in my head. When I opened the door and saw her standing there, eyes wide and nervous, I pulled her into my embrace.

I leaned her against the wall, arm cinched tight around her waist, and kissed her. I kept kissing her until we had to break apart, panting, desperate for air.

I dove back in, my tongue rubbing against hers in the intimate way I wanted my body plunging into hers.

"Rye…"

"Kate, I need you. Let me have you."

"Please," she gasped as I sucked on her neck. "Please, please," she chanted.

I picked her up and carried her to my bedroom, making sure to lock the door. Ike had a habit of wandering in my room at strange hours.

I held her so she slid down my front. Her breasts cushioned against my chest, her hips cuddling against my hardness.

"Let me touch you," I said, running my hands up and down her body. "Let me love you."

And she continued her litany of pleases. Best music I'd ever heard. I could listen to Kate's breathy pleas forever. Except I needed her naked, all that pale, lush skin mine to learn, touch, taste.

We moved together, in perfect synchronicity, removing clothes, all while kissing or touching. When my fingers skimmed her naked breasts, I held my breath, shocked by my body's response to the mere proximity of those lush curves.

CHAPTER TWENTY-SIX | Kate

Rye, so attuned to each response, slid his arms around my waist and hoisted me up so that I was aligned with his naked hips. As I wrapped my legs around his waist, creating a delicious friction, his legs seemed to give. He stumbled to the bed, his lips on mine as we tumbled downward, his arms cushioning my head and back.

"Kate."

His tone was ragged, a seeming prayer. I arched into him, needing more contact, needing *him*. He kissed me again, the hunger between us exploding into raw ardor. I couldn't get enough of his mouth, I needed more of his skin against mine. His hands once again covered my breasts and I bowed my back, exposing my neck. He kissed my throat. My fingers tunneled into his long hair, tugging before settling against his scalp, cradling his head as he licked and sucked the sensitive skin of my neck, collarbone, and finally, my breasts.

He pressed his hips tighter against my sensitive center as he sucked a nipple deep into the warm cavity of his mouth. My hips bucked against his and, as he released me with a hiss, he softly scraped his beard against my pebbled bud. He moved lower, his lips a hot trail down the center of my chest, across my belly. He nipped at my navel before he licked away the sting. I trembled as he continued downward, the kiss deeply intimate as he licked and nibbled and suckled my heated flesh.

I bit my lip, trying and failing to stay quiet. As soon as he slid a finger into my opening, I stiffened. When he licked my clit, I bowed my back, fingers buried in his luscious hair. He nipped my delicate flesh as he curled his finger up, into that spot. I unwound around him, the back of my free hand over my mouth to quiet my cries of pleasure.

He continued his ministrations, slowing them as my body relaxed. He pressed kisses to my inner thigh, which caused my hips to twitch in response.

"Sensitive?" he asked as he turned to my other thigh.

"Yes."

"Want me to stop?"

"*No.*"

His chuckle was as dark and rich as ganache and twice as decadent. I burned for more.

"Please," I whispered. "I need you inside me."

But Rye had his own agenda. "I told you I was going to love every inch of you. Roll over."

He eased away from me so that I could. I buried my face in his pillow, moaning loudly this time as his hands covered the globes of my bottom. He molded them before sliding up to my waist, then further up to the sides of my breasts. His lips followed all the way up to my ear lobe, leaving a trail of fire that sparked deep in my belly.

"I need…I need…" The rest of the sentence failed me.

Rye seemed to understand. He flipped me back over and kissed me, long and deeply, as if we had forever. I'd never had a man focus on me so intently, and I reveled in it, wanting to give him the same pleasure. My hands glided over his firm back, cupping his taut buttocks before I roamed back up to his shoulders and over his pecs, down his ridged abdomen. His breath stuttered as I clasped his erection in my hand. My fingers didn't quite meet as I tugged my hand forward to the wide purple crown. I rubbed my thumb over the drop of precum. Rye threw his head back, jaw clenched, before he dropped his forehead against my collar bone, his hips jerking against my continued pumping.

"Stop," he said.

I didn't.

"Kate, *stop*. I want to be in you when I come."

"Hurry."

He reached over to the nightstand and pulled out a handful of condoms. My eyes widened. "Four?" I said.

He stared down at my body and licked his lips. Then he pulled two more from the box. A burst of giggles escaped my lips and Rye's eyes crinkled.

"I've never had a woman laugh in bed," he murmured. "With you, I like it."

I wrapped my arms around his shoulders and brought him down to kiss me again, effectively cutting off thoughts of anyone but the two of us.

When we finally broke apart, both of us breathing heavy, a fine sheen of sweat covered my skin. Rye ripped open a condom and rolled it down his impressive length. I ran my fingertips down his chest to his quivering belly.

"I need you, Kate."

I spread my legs wider and he slid that thick length inside my body in one heavy, smooth glide.

"You're perfect," he said on a gasp as his hips bumped mine.

I was wet and throbbing. I needed more so I shifted, causing more friction against my clit. I closed my eyes and shifted again.

"Fuck, yes," Rye said.

And he pulled out to the very tip before slamming back into me. Again, and again, hard enough for the headboard to hit the wall. He lifted my legs by my thighs, dropping my knees over his shoulders as he continued to pound into me, each of his pelvic thrusts hitting my clit. I'd never been that vulnerable or that turned on.

He gripped my waist for more leverage, the slick in-and-out making my heart pound. I went over first, this orgasm stronger than the last one. I convulsed, clutching at his shoulders even as my body squeezed his hard cock. He froze for a moment, eyes wide, lips parted, breath held, before he slammed into me hard, his movements less controlled, his pupils dilating.

He came with my name on his lips.

CHAPTER TWENTY-SEVEN | Kate

The next morning arrived much too soon. I smirked at the number of empty condom wrappers before I sat up. I winced as muscles twinged in protest—both at the lack of sleep and overuse. But the smile remained fixed on my face.

I glanced at the clock. Before six. Good. I'd leave before Ike rose. That way, Rye wouldn't need to feel anxious about what to tell his son. As I started to slip from the bed, his hand cupped my hip.

"Where are you going?" he asked.

"To my place. I need to shower."

Rye sat up, the sheet falling to reveal his chiseled chest. He yawned, turning sleep-heavy eyes toward me.

"You can do that here."

I paused in pulling on my shirt. "I…um…I thought, you know, with Ike…you wouldn't want to…um."

Heat flamed over my neck and raced across my cheeks.

Rye's smile was soft, gentle. "Thanks for thinking of Ike. That means a lot to me."

I shrugged. "I just didn't want to make things awkward."

Rye stood and came around the bed, wrapping me in his arms. I luxuriated in his warmth—even though I wished he was naked and we had more time to love each other again.

"It's probably best—for now. But I know Ike will love that we're dating."

I nodded, even as a pang of disappointment rippled through my chest. Waiting to tell Ike about the progression in our relationship was the appropriate course of action. I knew that, even as I wanted Rye to ask me to stay.

"Come back for dinner tonight," Rye urged. "Stay with me again."

"Are you sure?" I asked, warmth swirling through my chest. I peered up at his face, wanting to be sure.

His eyes gleamed brightly. "Yes."

"Okay."

He leaned down and pressed a soft kiss to my temple. I clasped him tighter. After a long moment, he stepped back.

"I'll miss you today," he said.

I finished dressing and he walked me to the front door. This time, he kissed my lips in a long, lingering moment that left us both overheated.

"Hurry back."

I nodded. He waited until I was around the corner of the building at the elevators before he shut his door. I hugged myself all the way up to my place, feeling both dreamy and exhausted.

I turned my shower to the hottest setting I could stand and stripped out of my clothes. I leaned forward over the blue granite counter and stared at myself in the soft vanity light, looking for signs that my life was different.

My eyes glowed and my cheeks remained flushed. My lips

were swollen and my skin was lightly abraded from Rye's beard.

"You've been well-loved," I whispered in the mirror.

I skipped into my large, glass-fronted shower, my heart light as I pondered the rest of my day. It would drag because all I could think of was getting back to Rye.

—————— ★ ——————

I wasn't surprised when Cam strode into the shop with Jenna later that morning. He lingered over a shared kiss. I finished typing out an email. When Cam pulled away, I stood, smoothing my skirt.

"Hey. Can we talk a minute?" I asked him.

Surprise flared in his eyes but he smiled. "Sure."

"What do you know about Rye's deal with the record label?" I asked.

Cam settled his hip against the desk. He tried not to grimace because he didn't like it when anyone commented on the pain in his leg.

"I know the label has an option on a new full-length EP, meaning they have the right of first refusal."

"So, this is outside of his contracted albums?"

"Yeah, it's the extra one. They only put that in the contracts of people they'd like to sign longer."

I sucked on my lower lip. "So, the label people want him to keep performing—to keep making music."

Cam raised his eyebrows. "The man has immense talent, but his deadline's past. By almost six months. If this show for South by Southwest hadn't been booked all those months ago, he wouldn't have this opportunity," Cam stated.

"I wondered why he was here," I murmured.

"Me, too. I mean, our work meshes well. He's got that down home vibe he probably wouldn't like me to mention."

I shrugged. "All the genres are stretching. There's more overlap across many more of the styles than there used to be. Look at what Regan's doing and how it dovetailed into your last album."

Cam nodded, thoughtful. "I swear you'd make a better producer than half the people in the industry."

I shrugged. Creating music was Cam's trajectory. After my last—only—stint into the male-dominated world of aeronautics, I wasn't interested in diving into another misogynistic group. I stared at my computer screen, unseeing. "Why would he let it linger for so long?" I asked.

Cam crossed his arms over his chest and scowled. "I don't like the idea of him losing out because of his home situation."

"Could you do something? Like help him finish his album?"

Cam remained silent. I understood he was ticking through possibilities in his head, weighing the benefits and the dangers. That's what Cam did—everything was an army mission, still, and he never made a move until he was certain he could deliver on his promises.

"Let me ask around," he said. He refocused on me. "Are you sure that's something he'd want me to do? Because this'll be me calling in a favor. Maybe many."

"Which isn't something you'd do for just anyone," I said. My tummy tumbled.

He tugged at one of my curls, just like he used to. "I'd do it for you, Katie Rose."

I didn't bother to correct him. I stood and wrapped my arms around him. He gathered me closer and hugged me tight, like he used to when I ran to his room during thunderstorms.

"Thank you, big brother."

He pulled back and tousled my hair. "Is he worth the fuss?"

I smiled, cheeks heated. "I think so."

"Well, all right, then. I'll make some calls."

CHAPTER TWENTY-EIGHT | Kate

Regan and Carter stopped by and treated us to lunch before they flew out to San Francisco. I tried to enjoy myself, but my siblings and their wives watched me like they were worried I'd shatter. But I wouldn't break.

If Troy's hurtful words and easy dismissal hadn't broken me, nothing would. I made a point to smile and tease throughout the meal. I finished the day and left before five, unusual for me, but Jenna looked done in and wouldn't leave until I did.

Because it was still early, I changed into my yoga gear and then headed to a nearby studio that offered Bikram. I wondered if asking Cam to help Rye was the correct solution or if I'd over-stepped. And I worried that Ike wouldn't like me anywhere near as much when he found out I was his dad's girlfriend.

The thoughts caused me to struggle through the class in the steamy room, and I didn't feel any more relaxed or centered afterward. Just sweaty and with fizzed-out hair.

Getting home, I was surprised to find Rye leaning against the wall outside my door. My feet stuttered to a stop. My hand shot to my hair and I bit back a groan.

"There you are," he said, as if I should have been expecting him.

My heart thumped way too fast, but I refused to admit it was due to excitement.

"Hi," I said, digging out my keys. I tried to ignore the sweat still trickling between my cleavage and pooling at the waistband of my skin-tight yoga pants. "What are you doing here?"

"Ike and Beatrice were making a cake, so I wanted to see if you'd like to catch some dinner."

"She's back?"

"Yep. Got in a couple of hours ago. Ike was sad she wasn't you."

"Um." I fumbled with my keys, finally unlocking my door. I held my breath, trying to remember if I'd tidied the place.

No such luck. Two pairs of heels flopped on their sides near the couch. A suit jacket was tossed across one of the barstools at the raised kitchen counter. Dishes sat in the sink. Not horrible, but not as nice as I'd want my place to look for company.

At least my geometric rug was clean and the bright-patterned throw pillows were on the couch. The chenille blanket was tossed over the back and my vibrant purple leather club chair always added a nice punch of happy color.

"Dinner?" I asked. "I…um… I need to, you know, get cleaned up."

Rye nodded. "I can wait."

I set my things down. "I thought I was supposed to visit you later."

Rye's mustache twitched a little. "I want to take you out."

He stepped forward so the heat from his chest mingled with mine. He smelled woodsy and fresh, making me feel even grungier. Before I could move back, he ran his fingertips down my cheek.

"Your skin flushes when you exert yourself," he said.

"The curse of the redhead," I replied.

"Where would you like to go?"

I smiled. "Kind of hard to get a table at Stubb's."

"The barbecue joint?" he asked, eyebrows raised.

I nodded.

His eyes glinted with humor. "You're a Texas girl through and through."

I wanted to shake my head but Rye stepped into my personal space, his large hand cupping my cheek as his fingers speared into my hair.

I wet my lips and Rye's eyes flared with heat as they dropped to my mouth. His breathing hitched and he leaned in. But he didn't kiss me, just stood over me like some kind of sentinel.

I tugged at my top, not liking how it clung to me. "I need to shower."

Rye's smile appeared pained but he thrust out his chin. "Take that shower. Then, we're going to Stubb's."

I headed into my room.

"Kate?" he called.

"Yeah?" I pulled clean lingerie from my drawer, some white cotton panties that cut up high on my butt cheeks and a white bra. Nothing too fancy because I didn't want Rye to think I was trying too hard to seduce him.

"I saw those posts you put together today. Thank you for those."

"You're welcome," I replied. This current round of images and videos had been some of my best work. Already, those images had over five hundred thousand likes and lots of people seemed to be clicking through to Rye's official page. I was pleased with the interest and excited about what the boost in popularity might do for his career.

Hopefully, Cam would be able to come through and get Rye a good producer. Even better would be a collaborator like my sister-in-law. I loved the idea of Rye and Regan teaming up on some kind of steamy love song. I was pretty sure their voices would harmonize beautifully—even better than that Lady Gaga-Bradley Cooper duet that was so popular a while back.

"You're a brilliant professional and I'm really looking forward to sharing a meal with you."

His words snapped me out of my fantasy of Rye and Regan singing on the Grammy stage. I wanted that for him—just as I'd wanted the accolades for Regan and for Cam.

I smiled, pleased that Rye thought highly of my skills. I put back the conservative panty set and picked out the pale pink silk and lace set that pushed my breasts up to their full advantage while playing peekaboo with my most sensitive skin.

The smile was still on my face as I stepped into the shower.

CHAPTER TWENTY-NINE | Rye

I gripped my hands behind my neck and tipped my head up to stare at the ceiling. What the hell was she doing to make me want more with her? *How* was she making me question all my hard-and-fast rules since my relationship with Deirdre deteriorated?

Kate had blown past my barriers, and I was…yeah. I was okay with that. We could make the long-distance thing work. I'd bring it up, soon. After the performance tomorrow night. That would give me time to show her how good we were together. Show her why we were worth the extra effort of a few hours' drive.

Sure, I wanted Kate. Sexual tension tugged at my gut, the situation was worse now that I'd tasted her mouth and had my lips all over her gorgeous curves.

She brought out my most primal masculine instincts, but also the need to shelter and cuddle. No, I wanted to *cherish* this woman. After I pounded into her body until I couldn't think or feel anything but her wrapped around me.

Those thoughts were not helping to calm myself down.

I focused on the photos she had placed on her mantel, and a few on the wall. There was an artsy shot of the Sears Tower as the sun rose or set, I wasn't sure which. I'd bet Kate took that one. I'd seen how she used light and objects in her Instagram posts to really magnify the emotion she wanted to evoke. The woman was talented, whether she believed me or not.

Next was a picture of a much younger Kate and her brothers standing near a corral fence. From the soft undulating hills and oaks dotting the background, I surmised they were on their ranch. Kate had a lasso looped over her shoulder and a gap where her front teeth should have been. Cam and Carter looked to be in that state of constant growth, stretching into the bodies they now lived in with such ease.

Kate's hair had been tamed into a long braid, but some of those curls refused to stay restrained and danced about her head, glinting with sunlight. Freckles dotted her nose and cheeks. Her eyes shone bright with love and joy.

I viewed a few more—Kate wearing a pair of chunky black frames in one that got my imagination shifting into sexy buns and pencil skirts. Yeah, Kate could totally pull off the buttoned-up librarian look, and I wanted to be the one to muss her.

And…back to how hot our sex would be later tonight.

The shower shut off. I spun away from the hall, which tempted me toward her bedroom door. I wanted to push through it and straight into her bathroom, to see the droplets of water clinging to her pale flesh.

I clenched my hands and turned, nearly knocking another, smaller photo off the bookshelf. This one was an adult Kate, taken more recently, and an older gentleman. I guessed he was her father. He looked down at her, a slight smile gracing his lips. I recognized that expression because it was the same one I wore when I looked at Ike.

Why was it tucked back, behind others?

"Mind if I blow dry my hair?" she asked.

When she saw me holding the photo, her face shuttered. She seemed poised to march across the room and snatch it from my hand. Instead, she spun on her heel and headed back down the hall.

Something told me this photo—her relationship with her father—was integral to understanding Kate.

This time, I followed.

"So, what's the deal with your dad?" I asked.

"He's dead," Kate replied. "Heart attack about a year ago."

More to that story. Much more, if I had to guess by the set of her shoulders and the pain building in her eyes. "You were close?"

"Yes," she said. Her shoulders bunched tight under the thin straps of her loose, filmy tank top.

"And?" I asked.

She whirled around, face tight with controlled emotion. "And he wasn't the man I thought he was, and thanks to that—to his lying and cheating—I...my family smashed to bits."

I smashed to bits. That's what she planned to say, until she realized she'd be revealing too much. So, yes, her brothers' lies and omissions hurt her. But her relationship with her father, a man she adored and respected...that's what nearly broke her.

Cam warned me about Kate's fragility. Perhaps he understood the depths of her confusion and hurt. Or maybe he didn't. I'd been to their house now, seen the relationships they'd fostered between Cam and his brother, their mother, and their wives.

Far as I could tell, Kate didn't feel connected to that.

Maybe *that's* what sent her reeling, adrift. And that was something I could understand because I'd always craved my father's approval, even if I knew it was not worth the price of my goals and dreams. At least, it hadn't been until Ike's future hung in the balance.

Pain seeped into her eyes and she wrapped her hands around her elbows, as if already absorbing the blow she expected me to deliver.

Like all the men from her past, starting with the most important one: Her dad.

And with that look, I folded in my desire to share my plans to leave for Dallas. Right now, Kate needed reassurances. She needed to understand she was the most important woman in my life.

CHAPTER THIRTY | Kate

"Stop looking at me like that," Rye growled.

"Like what?" I asked, choking the words out of my dry throat.

Rye set the picture down and crossed over to me in two long strides. His fingers dove into my wet hair as he tipped my face up to his. His lips rested millimeters from mine.

"Like you expect me to hurt you."

My breath hitched as he seemed to stare into my soul. His eyes burned with ferocious truth.

"I won't. I want this, what we're building, Kate. I want you in my life. No, I *need* you in my bed and part of my day."

"Until—"

But Rye's lips crashed over mine, his tongue at the seam of my lips just as they parted with a gasp. He slid his tongue inside my mouth as I sagged against him.

Kissing Rye was unlike kissing any other man. The way his hands clasped me to him, the pressure of his lips and the soft, velvety touch of his tongue spoke of intense focus. He made me feel treasured, even as my heart rate spiked and my belly quivered with desire.

He rubbed his lips across mine, his beard rasping across my chin. My breath stuttered as he pulled back.

Then, before I could catch my breath, he tilted his head

so that he could deepen the kiss, taking my mouth with such seductive intent that my core clenched. My hands swept up from where they rested on his shoulders so that my fingers could worm into his hair, which was just as silky and warm as I remembered.

My palms sensitized as I ran them over his skull. I pressed my chest tightly to his and he cinched his arm around my waist in a steely band. He bent me over slightly, his beard another sensual caress against my lips and cheeks.

The kiss went on and on, and I never wanted this moment to end. Desire poured through me, lighting up my nerves.

Eventually, Rye brought me back to upright, his large hands spanning my waist. His pupils were dilated and his breathing ragged.

"Dinner," he said.

"What?"

Yeah, that was my smart reply. In my defense, the man had kissed me senseless.

My lips tingled, legs were jelly, and the space between my thighs craved more stimulation. I wasn't just turned on, I was afire. And I wondered, not idly, if I could have orgasmed from Rye's kisses.

I was thinking yes. I wanted to try.

His lips twitched under his beard. "Dinner. I want to take you out."

I tried to come up with an argument as to why he should simply take me to bed *right now*.

"Kate," he said, as he brushed my damp curls from my face.

He mapped my face almost as if he were memorizing each line, the freckles I could never bleach away.

He groaned and stepped away. "I want to lose myself in your scent and your tight, perfect body. But I want to talk to you, to see you throw your head back when you laugh. I love the line of your throat and how your eyes dance. I want to see other men looking over at me in envy as I sit with you, take your hand. I want to wrap my arm around your shoulder as I lead you out of the restaurant, knowing I get to bring you home."

His voice dropped to a sultrier tone that seemed to have a direct line to my core.

"When I get you home, I'll spread you out on your bed and feast on that luscious skin and perfect tits before I finally love you. Hard."

His breath sped up as he talked, as did mine. I shifted, my panties damp from his sexy talk. He pressed his thumb to my lips.

"Grab your purse so I can do all that."

I stared at him for a moment. He waited, his breath fraying. Oh, he wanted me. The need swirled around us, heady and insistent.

I darted my tongue out and ran it over the pad of his thumb. He cursed, lunging toward me as I spun away with a gasped laugh.

"You promised me a meal before this hot night of sex," I said, glancing over my shoulder.

He tilted his head to the side. "I did. Let's feed you. Because I need to fuck you soon."

CHAPTER THIRTY-ONE | Rye

Dinner was fun, easy, one of the most enjoyable meals I'd ever had. The barbecue was delicious and tender—perfect, really. The ice-cold beer proved a great counterbalance. But I ate without much thought because our table was beset with a driving sexual tension I'd never experienced. The heady sensations made me want to draw out the moment.

Our first official date.

We finished our beers. Kate dabbed her paper napkin on her lips, her eyes warm pools I wanted to fall into.

"You ready?" I asked.

"Yes," she breathed.

I rose from my chair and reached for her. As I'd expected, many male heads turned toward us, their eyes appreciating each of Kate's gorgeous features. My chest puffed as I held her hand and led her from the crowded establishment.

I smirked back at one of the guys, who hung his head when he realized I'd caught him staring at Kate's perky ass.

I slipped my hand from hers and settled it on her hip. She glanced up at me in askance. My smirk turned to a smolder as the words I'd said to her earlier drifted around us.

"You do collect quite the fan club," I said as I held open the door for her.

She chuckled. "I'm pretty sure those ladies were all lusting over you." She patted my cheek. "You do rock the Viking look."

"Viking?" I asked.

"Big, buff, just a little too wild."

I narrowed my eyes. "I'll show you wild."

She licked her lower lip. My eyes followed the slick trail of moisture.

"I'm planning on it," she whispered, breathless.

The ride back to Kate's condo was filled with music and conversation. I'd never experienced this easy back-and-forth with anyone. I liked it. I was addicted to our banter.

I turned off the ignition and leaned over the console. I covered her mouth with mine. She tasted of tangy barbecue sauce and beer but also that unique flavor that was all Kate.

This kiss started slow, with soft licks and gentle pressure, a glide of lips over each other. Then, Kate moaned and pressed closer, and my composure began to crumble.

Pull me close, I wanted to say. *Take the chance on me. I'll give you everything I have.*

She did, in her bed. And I gave her all of me.

For the first time in months, maybe years, I was content. No, I was happy. Now, all I needed to do was talk to her about our future. I hugged her closer.

Soon.

Very soon, we'd talk. And plan.

CHAPTER THIRTY-TWO | Kate

I visited Cam's trailer, planning to snap some more photos of him before his show. I wanted to post some of Cam interspersed with Rye, showing the two men collaborating.

"I asked about South by Southwest and his album," Cam said, setting down his guitar and grabbing a glass of iced tea. I knew it was my mother's recipe and that she sent Cam a couple of gallons each day he was at the venue. Chuck was an even bigger fan of my mother's cooking, and Mama had adopted the big, quiet man into the family—same as she seemed to be doing with Rye and Ike, if the container of cookies and the jar of lemonade were any indication.

My mother showed her love through food.

Cam shoved a box of sweet treats with my name labeled in my mother's neat cursive into my hands. I wouldn't eat them, but I was finally at a point where I appreciated the gesture.

And I wouldn't eat them because if I started, I wouldn't stop. I'd found that was the only way to combat my mother's delicious cooking—ignore it if possible.

"Big wigs said yes, if I wanted to go to bat for him they'd give him the studio time and some promotional support."

I sat, setting the tin in my lap. My leg jiggled, making the tin bounce. "Would you?"

Cam dipped his head. "Jen and I talked it over. Rye's got the talent, the looks for success. He's just had some bad breaks—first with Ike arriving days before the start of his national tour and Rye's inability to reschedule the large-scale multi-month campaign soon enough."

Cam sucked down his glass of tea. "Fans can be fickle. Rye managed to overcome a lot of that with his next album, which goes to show how good he is, but this last one he's worked on has been postponed—my guess, now that I know him, is that it's related to Ike's health."

I nodded. "He's really put Ike first." I sucked on my lower lip, both wishing Rye felt that much devotion for me and terrified of what I'd have to sacrifice if I loved him that much.

"To the detriment of his career," Cam said. He shook his head. "I get that. It's noble, but this fourth album needs to be completed, not just the couple of songs he's released—great as they are. The trickle isn't building him the rabid fan base he needs." Cam leaned forward, eyes bright. "Your campaigns might, though. The numbers are stellar. You're a damn good publicist."

Cam's praise caused warmth to bloom in my chest. "Thanks. I hope it's enough to get him the recognition he deserves."

"Me, too. By the way, Jen said she's willing to call up some of her buddies in Seattle to see if they can work up a few songs together. Like Asher Smith or Hayden Crewe."

My eyes widened at those names. Cam was a superstar, but Asher and Hayden…they were *royalty*.

If they were willing to help Rye with his album, it would at least get the promotional support it needed and listens from the legion of global fans both men enjoyed.

"But here's the question—would he want that?"

Cam looked into my eyes, and I realized Cam understood I had an intimate relationship with Rye. I bit my lip, my cheeks flaming.

"How could he not? Those are names anyone in the industry wants to work with."

Cam nodded once, eyes narrowing a bit in the corners. "True, but I just feel like I should talk to him…"

"I will. After the show." I became giddy at the thought. "It'll be such a cool surprise."

"If you say so," Cam said. "Jen hates surprises. She gets mad whenever I withhold information from her."

Cam's eyes darted toward the trailer's shut bedroom door. He'd carried Jen back there when she'd fallen asleep against his shoulder an hour ago and we hadn't heard a peep since. Apprehension on his face stamped deep as his hands clenched. This pregnancy was clearly hard on both of them.

I wrapped my hand around his wrist.

"Hey. It's going to be okay. Jenna's so strong."

Cam ripped his eyes from the door and met mine. "I'm really worried."

Cam's admission tugged at my heart. He was a former Army Ranger. He planned and executed missions—whether for the government or for his music career. But he couldn't direct the outcome he wanted here, not even with his formidable willpower.

"I'm here for you. Both of you. Whatever you need." As the words fell from my lips, the last of my distress faded. I knew from

Jenna that Cam had never wanted to go along with our mother's false narrative.

I rose and wrapped my arms around Cam's shoulders, pulling him in for the kind of hug I'd needed since life slid sideways in Chicago—and then fell off a cliff with my family.

I let out a slow, unsteady breath, and Cam did the same.

"Love you, Katie Rose."

"I love you, too, Camden. But stop calling me that."

And like a good big brother, he just laughed as he messed up my hair. That's when I knew we'd be okay—the whole family. And I agreed to another dinner at my mama's next week.

CHAPTER THIRTY-THREE | Kate

The crowds swelled in tandem with the noise. Jenna spoke with Chuck, my brother's large and taciturn head of security.

"Packed house, which is great for Rye."

I nodded, mainly because I couldn't speak. My nerves built and my heart seemed to expand, too large for my chest. He'd arrived late, wanting to eat dinner with Ike, who'd then asked him to play cars and read some books.

I hadn't had a chance to see him since that morning when he kissed me goodbye at my door. I'd missed him even as I took more shots and built out the next social media campaign that I hoped would help his career.

My breath caught and I gripped my hands tightly together as he strode toward us. He stopped in front of us, dipping his head and saying hello to Jenna, but his eyes stayed locked on mine. He pushed his guitar to his back as he stepped closer.

He snagged me around the waist and dropped a soft kiss on my lips. "Missed you today, Kate," he murmured against my cheek. His beard tickled my skin.

On cue, Jenna drifted off, stating she needed to talk to Chuck, but we both knew she left to give me privacy.

"I missed you, too."

He leaned in and brushed another kiss across my mouth, and

I melted into his large frame. I clutched his wrists, shocked by the emotion of *rightness* bursting in my chest.

When he straightened, his lips twitched beneath his beard. "I'm so glad you're here," he said.

His lashes swept down, covering his eyes for a moment. The ends near his lids were dark brown but the tips were so light, they were almost translucent.

Rye stepped back, pulling his guitar forward so that it provided a shield between us. "Will you wish me luck out there tonight?"

"You'll be amazing," I said. "Your voice blows me away. It settles over my skin, but more, it warms my soul."

I blinked up at him, shocked I'd said anything so revealing. My face flamed and I looked down at my shuffling feet.

He pushed the guitar back before he used his thumb and forefinger to tip my chin up. He leaned in and covered my mouth with his once more. This kiss was longer and it lingered. His muscles quivered under my touch as I slid my hands up his shoulders to the ends of his tied-back hair. I whispered, "Good luck," into his ear.

He pulled back, a huge grin on his face.

"I have you. I don't need luck," he said.

He eased me back as he placed kisses on my knuckles. With one last brush of his thumb across my cheek, he took his place on the stage to a large wave of screaming.

"Hey, there, Austin," Rye called. His voice was strong and sure. "Who's ready to party?"

The shouts and yells swelled to deafening levels.

Rye worked the crowd, telling a short anecdote about his first experience with the live music scene. Jenna ambled over, a slight frown forming between her brows.

"I really like him," she said, but her smile turned bittersweet. "He's an excellent performer."

Rye launched into his first song. I paused, my muscles quivering with longing. The power in his voice was raw and so full of emotion that I had to give him my full attention. Jenna cocked her head to the side, her long blond hair streaming over her arm.

When the song finished she blew out a small breath. "His voice is gorgeous. The guitar enhances it." She smiled, seeming pleased by her findings.

Rye segued into the next tune and then another. My feet tugged me closer to the edge of the stage. He stood in front of the mic, his forearms flexing as he played. He winked at a young woman in the front row who was fanning herself as Rye sang about yearning.

Jealousy swirled through me, but before it could settle in a hard knot in my stomach, Rye caught my gaze. His eyes blazed and I felt myself ignite in response. Up until this moment, I'd considered my brother and sister-in-law performers, the work they did out there on the stage just a part of their job. But with Rye, my reaction was visceral. My blood thrummed heavy in my veins as my body flushed. When he smiled at me, a small private one that held promise of something more, my back arched as if I'd just received a full body caress.

Rye held the note longer, his expression flaring in lust. Chuck came up next to me, hand on my arm. This time, my flush came from embarrassment. I'd been a step from entering the stage.

Rye tore his attention from me and once again focused on the crowd. I cleared my throat.

"Thanks," I muttered.

Chuck clucked. "All this unsatisfied sexual tension. Who knew so much of my job would be cockblocking?"

A tiny smile flittered across my lips. "I don't really want to hear about my brother's sex life," I said.

Rye once again talked with the crowd. They screamed in response to his question.

Chuck's gaze landed heavy on my head. "Who said I was talking about Cam?" he said.

I opened my mouth to respond but I couldn't think of anything to say. I snapped my mouth shut and turned my attention once again to the man on the stage.

He settled on the stool, his guitar in his lap.

"I need to let you all know this is my last performance."

What? My eyes widened and my jaw dropped. His last performance? How was that possible? No, no way he was giving up music.

Jenna's eyes were as wide as mine. "Oh my God. Did you know?"

I shook my head, shell-shocked and sick. I'd just asked my brother to call in favors… The crowd booed and cat-called and Rye shook his head.

"There are times you have to put aside dreams for the greater good," he said, simply.

What did that mean? The opening chords of the song swirled around me, wrapping me in another sensuous embrace.

"That's doubly hard when you want nothing more than to stay."

Rye's attention flitted back to me, and I stiffened further. Was he saying he wanted to remain in Austin? That he wanted to stay with me? The uncertainty swirled through me, making my chest ache. Jenna inched in closer, her hand reaching down to clasp my cold fingers.

"But dreams change, or they fade or, maybe, it's simply that they were never meant to be."

He picked up the pace of the melody, his guitar pick flicking over the strings.

"Your lips got me thinking…thinking of all the nights I wanted to hear…those three little heartfelt words…"

Jenna's soft gasp echoed in my ears and bounced through my chest.

Fuck no. I was *not* listening to him play a heartfelt ballad of longing when he'd so publicly dismissed me as not being enough.

I turned on my heel and left.

CHAPTER THIRTY-FOUR | Rye

Neither Cam nor Jenna told me anything about Kate. When I went upstairs to her place after the show, she refused to answer her door. She also refused to answer my calls or my increasingly pleading texts.

I still want to see you, I typed. *I just needed to make a public announcement about my retirement.*

I should have talked to you first. I'm sorry. I wanted to but we overslept this morning, and I didn't get the chance before you were out the door.

Still, no response.

I'd royally messed up. I hadn't needed to see Cam's face last night to tell me that. I just thought I'd be able to talk to her—explain that Ike had months for his surgery, and I didn't have the luxury of waiting for my big break anymore.

That didn't change the fact I wanted a future with Kate. I told Cam that last night—how I wanted to be the man Kate could count on to keep his promises.

"Unfortunately, I'd made choices before I met her or before I realized what I wanted with her—ones that could impact her happiness for years."

"Yeah, you did. And from what Jen said, she left mid-perfor-mance in tears. The last time she missed one of my shows, some scumbag in Chicago broke her heart."

So, Cam did know about Troy. I shook my head. "I don't plan to break her heart. I have to go to Dallas, help out my dad, get Ike his surgery."

Cam seemed to want to say something, but instead he turned and walked away.

But his earlier warning continued to cycle through my head; Kate deserved to be the top priority, and I hadn't been honest with her about my plans. Granted, we were new, but I hadn't shared the details of my life with her.

Her father's lies nearly shattered her, she'd said.

Hell. I'd fucked my chance with her.

Time to give her the unvarnished truth and hope she was willing to accept my messed-up life. The fear of her rejection gnawed at me, just as it had since I looked into those spectacular eyes and my mind clicked onto one word: *mine*.

In less than a week, I'd managed to mess it all up.

"Want to go see Kate?" I asked Ike.

"Yes, yes, yes! Where is she?" He looked around our empty condo. Beatrice and I had spent most of yesterday packing up the boxes, so all that was left to do was put our few items in my car. The movers picked up my minimal furniture, which I'd stashed in a nearby storage unit. I carried down our suitcases— the last items we needed to pack—then slammed the trunk closed.

Kate still wouldn't answer her door, so I led Ike to the car. If she wasn't at the shop I'd text her that Ike wanted to say goodbye. Yes, I was using my son for my personal gain, something I'd never done before. But Kate wouldn't turn him away, and I couldn't leave without talking to her.

Kate walked toward us, through the darkened shop's main display room, dressed in a pair of casual linen pants, a simple tank top, and ballet flats. She looked beautiful. And wary. How could I blame her?

She opened the door, accepting Ike's enthusiastic hug with relish. He darted into the shop with a low, deep hum of appreciation as Kate rose.

"What are you doing here?" she asked.

The words had a bit of an edge, and I winced. She had every right to be angry. In her position, I would be, too. Angry and hurt, much like I'd been when Deirdre kissed me goodbye as I headed toward my gig. She'd waved to me as I drove away, all the while knowing her lawyer would serve me divorce papers while I was on the road.

I breathed through that hurt, knowing the momentary pang would dissipate soon. Deirdre leaving had turned out to be a blessing. But that didn't mean I'd wanted it at the time— or even seen her departure as a possibility. I'd married her, planning on forever.

Even when we started having problems. Even when I made some choices that I now regretted, especially when I looked at Kate's smile as she watched Ike—especially when I'd seen that look of longing on her face when she stared at Jenna's tiny baby bump.

She'd make a great mother one day.

Yet another secret I'd kept from her that needed to be aired. But not yet. There was only so much a person could handle at a time. Still, the idea of keeping anything back left me antsy.

"We wanted to take you to lunch. Before we head up to Dallas."

Her mouth tightened, and I braced myself for a rejection when Ike came running back.

"They have a baby guitar, Daddy!" He practically danced in excitement. "Can I play it, Kate? Please."

Her whole face softened, and I could almost hear her objections melting as Ike bounced around her legs, his face beaming with pleasure.

"For you, honey, of course."

She didn't have to shoot me a look for me to get the message loud and clear: she was willing to put up with my presence for my son.

Kate seemed to enjoy showing him the workshop with some of Jenna's half-built creations. Ike was drawn to the ukulele Jenna had just completed for a friend of Regan's.

"This one doesn't sound like Daddy's," Ike said as he strummed out an F chord. Like most musicians' kids, Ike's proficiency with an instrument was high. He had an aptitude as well as knowledge and exposure.

I glanced up at Kate, expecting her to answer, but her preoccupation continued. Another flutter of concern beat through my stomach as I realized how much I'd hurt her.

"That's because it's not a small guitar, it's a ukulele. The distance of the strings is different and so is the width of the fretboard." I grabbed one of the guitars Kate had laid out on the gleaming metal table to show Ike the difference.

He nodded before he clutched his stomach. "I'm starving."

Kate snapped out of her daydream and smiled at my son. "We could hit up the food truck that's around the corner if you'd like. They serve gourmet burgers and all kinds of interesting fries."

Ike clapped his hands and jumped up and down, nearly slipping in a small clump of sawdust. She caught him before I managed to, and we all laughed. I snagged her gaze for a moment, and it was warm. Then, her eyes shuttered.

"Must be hitting a growth spurt. You were starving two hours ago…and two hours before that."

"Food it is," Kate said with a deepening grin. "But no more playing on this floor, please. I don't want you to get hurt."

"Okay, Kate. Let's go."

Ike trotted out of the workshop. I let Kate walk next, and as she passed, I wanted desperately to take her hand and squeeze her fingers in a gentle grip, but her expression warned me away.

Kate suggested that we walk because the weather wasn't much over eighty—that is to say, mild for a March afternoon. Ike wanted to be swung the entire way, which Kate seemed happy to oblige.

"Lucky for you," Kate said, "I have on great swinging shoes."

I gauged her interest in Ike's nonstop requests. She turned and smiled as we once again lifted Ike in the air. With another big jump, Kate squealed as loud as Ike, the two of them laughing together.

They looked happy, connected. As if they belonged to one another.

We arrived at the food truck before I had a chance to process that further. After Kate read the menu to Ike, we placed our orders. Ike settled in next to us on the wooden bench at the picnic table until a girl, maybe a year or two older, ran over and invited him to play with her and three other kids. Ike looked to me for confirmation before darting off into the small green area to the left. I shifted in my seat to keep an eye on Ike.

"I thought you were leaving this morning," Kate said when the silence between us grew heavy.

So she had read my texts. At least some of them.

I sighed. "After this. I wanted to head up to the hospital this morning. To tell the kids there goodbye."

Kate studied me. "Something happened?"

I nodded, wondering how she knew. "One of the boys I've been jamming with died last night."

She laid her hand over mine and squeezed. "That's so sad."

I swallowed hard, not just because of the pain of losing the child to such a beastly disease, but because I knew I didn't deserve Kate's sympathy. She'd told me about the men in her life, and I was continuing to follow the pattern. God, I was such an asshole.

"Yeah," I rasped out. "Good kid. His name was LeShaun. He played some mean Beatles and Hendrix." I tried to smile but it faltered immediately. "He had a thing for classic rock. I swear, he knew the lyrics to every song."

"He sounds like he was a great kid."

My eyes never wavered from Ike because I couldn't manage to look at the hurt in Kate's.

"I'm sorry," I said.

Kate sat back on her side of the bench. "For?"

"Not telling you about my plans to head back to Dallas."

Her lips compressed into a firm line. "That really should have come up before we slept together."

I ran my hand down the back of my neck. "Yeah. It's just... I didn't know how to tell you, so I—"

"Lied." The word held a wealth of emotion, none of it positive. She held my gaze. "You *lied* to me. About your intentions."

"I didn't mean—"

She made a slashing motion with her hand and I closed my mouth. "When I was seven years old, I caught my dad with another woman. My mother was inside the barn at the time, maybe fifty feet away." She looked away but I saw the bleakness in them. "He told me it was one time, just a little fun, that if I loved him and my mother, I'd keep the secret."

She had. I knew Kate well enough to understand she cared deeply about her family. She would have remained silent to ensure they remained one—at the cost to her own conscience.

I tried to imagine asking something so monumental of Ike. I couldn't. The selfishness of her father's act stole my breath.

"Years later, when I was in high school, I saw him with my brother's wife. They were both walking out of the barn. They had hay in their hair. I thought *no way*. I was mistaken. My father was a good man, and he'd *never* hurt our family like that—he'd made me stay quiet so I wouldn't hurt my mama. I found out recently, after his death, he was indeed having an affair with Cam's first wife. To hurt Cam, to hurt my mother. The man who I'd put on a pedestal *lied to me*."

She faced me and the sunlight hit her eyes, making them burn. "I look back now and see the pattern. His lies started small. Omissions."

She let that hang between us. I clenched my fists as her unsaid accusation settled over me like barbed wire digging into my flesh.

"Not telling you was a mistake," I said. "I was worried about how you'd react. And I wanted us to have a chance to see how good we were together. I planned to talk to you about me driving down here next weekend, maybe you coming up to Dallas the weekend after."

Her smile was sad. "I'm not sure I can believe that."

My heart fluttered harder. I was losing her. With each attempt I made to explain, I dug a deeper hole. One that made Kate relive the trauma of her broken family.

I watched Ike chase the little girl who'd invited him to play. They both laughed and squealed.

"I need to take the job in Dallas. The position gives me access to the insurance I need to afford Ike's surgery," I said. I swallowed the lump in my throat that seemed to expand with each breath. "I should have told you this when you were trying to help before. Dr. Tenaka said Ike only has a few months left before the pressure against his optic nerve is too high. Plus, his right retina will detach—there's no way they can stop it without surgery."

Kate continued to face forward. My stomach felt like it had been squeezed by a large, angry fist.

"You found out—the day I suggested you talk to him," Kate said.

"Yeah. I'm sorry, Kate. I was angry with myself—for not pushing harder to get my fair share of time with Ike, then. For not fighting hard enough to get a new judge. By the time I realized Quentin—my ex-father-in-law—bribed Judge Adler, Ike seemed to have adjusted. I thought...I thought I could go back to the studio, maybe finish up this album, get my shit together with the label. Get that elusive break and pay for Ike's surgery..."

I trailed off, my stomach aching at the image I'd wanted so desperately. The one I failed to achieve. And once I realized how unhappy Ike was, my album no longer mattered—getting him out of Quentin's house became my top priority.

Kate hesitated but still didn't look at me. Now, though, I noticed the tension shimmering off her body. "Would you consider another option? So you didn't have to quit making music?"

I snorted. "I've been trying to come up with one since before Ike was born." I hoped I didn't appear bitter. I wasn't. Though I was disappointed.

"Cam mentioned he had contacts to help you produce your album," Kate said.

Oh, God. No. My heart thudded with painful, rapid beats.

"I'm not going to be a charity case for Camden Grace," I said in a stilted tone.

Kate tilted her head, but her eyes remained sad. "Cam isn't planning to ask you to do a song or an album with him."

My gaze cut to Kate's before it settled back on Ike. She took that to mean she should continue speaking.

"Asher Smith may have something he's interested in working on."

I inhaled in a long steady stream before I released the breath just as slowly.

"Asher Smith?" I asked.

No way. She had to be playing me, trying to butter me up for whatever it was she wanted from me.

An ache built in my chest as I wondered just how far Kate would take this charade. She'd known which celebrity to dangle in front of me. She had to know how much any musician would want to work with Asher Smith.

That must be why she tossed out his name with such casualness. Like she knew him. She probably did. Not that he'd be interested in working with me. Asher Smith didn't know I existed. Why would he? Getting my hopes up…that was cruel.

"Yeah."

"And this is coming through your brother?" I said, my voice hitching. I hoped my beard obscured enough of my face so that Kate couldn't see my expression clearly.

"No," Kate said.

Again, my eyes cut to hers.

Our number was called. I rose, my legs unsteady as I thought about what Kate had said.

Asher Smith. Camden Grace. A fucking who's who of today's—this decade's—rock stars.

I went up to collect the baskets of food, willing my hands to quit shaking. Ike ran over, out of breath and flushed, his eyes gleaming bright behind his glasses.

"Did you see me, Kate? I caught Azalea twice!" He bounced on the seat until I set the red plastic container in front of him. Ike dove in, shoving about four fries into his mouth at once.

He must really be in the midst of a growth spurt.

"I did see you," Kate said. "You were faster than the Flash."

I continued to try to breathe like a normal person as I handed Ike napkins and then took a bite of my meal—one I couldn't even taste.

Ike spilled his milkshake, and I reordered a new one when Ike's eyes welled with unshed tears. Then, I cleaned up the spreading mess of ice cream on the table.

Ike ate more than I managed because I couldn't shake the worry mixed in with what was resentment that she'd talk to her brother about me. Trying to give me a leg up when I hadn't earned it.

Quentin had pressured me to work for his company once he realized Deirdre and I were serious about getting married. We were fine until Ike came early and our crap insurance paid practically nothing. The next two years, I spent every minute I had crafting a new album, touring, and spending time with my son. Quentin offered to make our debt disappear if I'd take a position at his company. When I told him no, Deirdre left me.

During that same time and up until I accepted his offer this week, my father pressured me to work for his company, dangling the much-needed health insurance as a carrot I could no longer ignore. He hadn't cared about my goals, my desires. He was willing to help me get the insurance that would allow Ike the new surgery only because he was no longer capable of railroading me to do his bidding. I'd made sure he knew that—even when the medical bills piled up so high, I wasn't sure I'd ever dig out of the hole.

But I had. Mostly. And I'd made peace with the fact that the only way to pay off that last fifteen thousand dollars and ensure I didn't go into debt yet again was by accepting a position I never wanted in an industry I didn't care about.

"Are you trying to get me to stick around in Austin because you don't want a long-distance relationship?" I asked as Ike ran to the trash bin to toss our trash.

Her narrowed eyes told me I'd struck a nerve. "How was I supposed to know you were planning to go to Dallas? I found out with the concert-goers last night."

And there was the crux of the matter. Kate felt that I'd lied to her. I'd never asked for her help—for a handout.

Sure, I knew now that Cam respected me. That made me happy. But Asher Smith. Asher freaking Smith…

I picked up Ike, who rested his head against my shoulder, breathing even and deep before we made it back to the shop.

"He's out," I murmured.

"He played hard.

I cleared my throat. "He's one of my idols."

"Asher?" she asked, but it wasn't really a question. Asher Smith was pretty much every musician's idol. The man's talent oozed out of him—and everything he did was stellar. Not great, no, that wasn't good enough for Asher Smith. He was top-shelf, as close as a musician could come to perfection. Working with him…I could barely wrap my head around how amazing that experience would be. Still, the idea of Kate manipulating the situation, going behind my back—not asking me if that was something I wanted…

I was hurt. And I was angry.

Our expressions probably matched as we walked back toward the shop.

"You didn't ask me if I wanted you to use your contacts." The words spilled out. "Like I said, I'm not a charity case."

"I never lied to you," she began, her tone furious. "*I* never led you on, never pretended I planned to be around, to build a relationship when all I wanted was someone to warm my bed for a week."

My breath hitched. I turned into the parking lot of the shop and strode forward to lean against the side of my small sedan. I opened the car and settled Ike in his seat. I stood back up to face her.

"The fact you think that about yourself upsets me. I never thought of you as a fling, Kate. Clearly, we don't know each other as well as I thought. Or hoped. Because I never would have lied to you. And if you knew me at all, you'd know how important it is for me to make my own way."

CHAPTER THIRTY-FIVE | Kate

"You're telling me *now* you want a relationship?" I sounded stupid, repeating him, but I was flabbergasted.

Who did that? He was correct—we obviously didn't know each other well enough. His omissions—telling his fans before me—*hurt*.

It flayed open a wound I'd thought had scabbed over years before.

From the tortured look on Rye's face, I could only imagine that I'd dangled the most precious of gifts in front of him. He wanted to grab this opportunity. I could see the desire on his face, but his need to prove himself was too great. This wasn't just about Rye's need to reach his goals; his ex-father-in-law and his own father as well must have done a number on his pride if he was willing to turn away from working with Asher Smith.

I didn't know that history, and, clearly, I'd stepped into a quagmire of old hurts that seemed to have healed about as well for Rye as they had for me.

I'd been giddy with hope yesterday morning. The world seemed so bright as Rye kissed me goodbye.

Apparently for the last time.

Because we were at an impasse, both of our worst fears raw and exposed. I hated this—hated how the ache in my belly and chest expanded with each passing breath.

We were too new to survive this level of emotional turmoil. Rye must have realized that, too.

He dug out his keys from his pocket. "You jumped to some pretty horrible conclusions about me. And now you want to control my life. That's a hard no."

"So you'll just throw the opportunity away? Like you're now throwing a chance at us away?"

I couldn't believe I'd succeeded in getting the words out. But I'd managed to keep it together through lunch. I'd wanted to extend the meal, extend my time with Rye, even if all he'd give me was half his attention.

Those were obviously the wrong words to say. Rye's jaw clenched.

"No. You did that when you believed the worst of me. And when you tried to control my life in a way that suited your goals and needs."

He opened his car door.

"For the record," I said, my tone bitter, "I asked Cam if he'd be willing to help you before I knew about your plans. It's the first time I've ever asked my brother for a favor."

Rye's muscles bunched and I thought he'd take a step toward me, thought he'd wrap me in his arms. Instead, he settled into his seat.

When would I learn? When would I stop yearning for a man who didn't care enough about me to stay—to fight for us?

CHAPTER THIRTY-SIX | Rye

Leaving Kate hurt like I'd just broken all of my ribs. I knew what that felt like because I had, indeed, broken one rib back playing high school football.

No matter how much I wanted to talk this fight through, no matter how much I wanted to believe her, I had to do right by Ike. I was his father, and he was my responsibility. My one-hundred-dred-something-thousand-dollar responsibility. And I was no one's charity case. *No one's* to control.

I would curse the current state of medicine in this country, but I'd already done that, many times, and without insurance, my dad's offer was the best deal I was going to get.

Kate stepped back, away from me. Just as I should have stayed away from her today. If only I'd been stronger, I could have saved her this newest cut, at least. She deserved all the happiness, especially after she went to this effort for me.

My dream…my greatest desire…Kate was offering me *everything*. But it was on her terms, done her way.

I'd promised myself to never, ever let another person manipulate or control me.

Some disagreements couldn't be fixed. I knew that, didn't I? That's how I'd ended up divorced before my twenty-fifth birthday.

"Goodbye, Kate," I said.

She straightened her spine, lifting her chin. I tried hard not to notice the pain swimming in her eyes. "I'll let Jenna know you turned down the offer," she said, her tone flat. "That way, you won't have to deal with Asher contacting you directly."

Asher Smith. My hero. The reason I'd gone into music. One of the best lyricists, as well as musicians, alive today. And he was interested in working with me. Producing my album. Or maybe Kate and Cam spun me as the feel-good story. Some dude with a bit of talent they wanted to help out so they'd be able to pat themselves on the back.

I glanced back at Ike, whose mouth had dropped open so that small snores emitted from his throat.

No, I couldn't think that way. Deirdre and her father had given up on Ike. I was the only one willing to give him the future he deserved.

Even if it meant depriving myself of my greatest wish.

I just wasn't sure, in that moment, if my deepest desire was Kate or the chance to work with Asher.

Didn't matter. I'd just closed the door on both possibilities.

CHAPTER THIRTY-SEVEN | Kate

Rye closed his car door and started the vehicle.

I stood there, the tears that had threatened all week shimmering in my eyes as he pulled out of the lot. But he never saw how close I was to losing it.

Because I didn't matter enough. Not even the opportunity to work with Asher—the best carrot I could offer any musician—mattered enough for him to reconsider his set course.

That pissed me off, and the anger got me moving.

I went back into the shop and pulled up the company's social media accounts. For the rest of the day I lost myself in making more posts from the images I'd taken at the show. I stuck to Cam because the idea of looking at Rye made my heart thud in a dull, painful rhythm. Once I finished the posts, I checked on the previous ones, cursing the popularity of Rye's campaign. Many of the comments were from women and oozed sexual innuendo.

Well, he was no longer mine. We'd had our first fight and I'd lost not just the war of words, but the man himself.

What had happened today?

I'd been justified in my anger—shocked and hurt by Rye's omissions about our future. Yet, he'd driven away from me today as if I'd committed some unspeakable crime.

That night, finally home after a double session of yoga that left me worn out but not relaxed, I received a text message from Rye.

We made it to Dallas.

I wasn't sure if his message was supposed to be an olive branch—if he wanted to try and work out our disagreement. I waited, barely breathing, for another message to come through.

It didn't. My surge of hope crashed into despair. I turned off my phone, not willing to respond to his inane text. There was nothing more to say. We'd spent less than a week together. He didn't try to contact me again. And…that was that.

I moped around for weeks.

"All right, girly," Jenna said one Friday afternoon a month after the concert. "I know I'm pregnant and a puking mess, but you've been walking around like a sleepless zombie."

"I hate you pregnant," I muttered. "You're perky and gorgeous."

She was, too. Her long blond hair glowed with vitality and her cheeks bloomed with color, her cheekbones sharp and her chin more angular due to the morning sickness, which had, thankfully, passed. From the back, she was still slender with a smaller waist than mine.

Jenna snorted even as she rubbed her palms over her belly, something she'd taken to doing often. I'd read it was a protective gesture, proving just how much Jenna already loved her and Cam's baby.

"You need help, girlfriend," Jenna said.

Actually, I needed to not be in love with a man who lied to me and dismissed me and my efforts, but we didn't always get what we wanted.

The fact I fell for Rye so quickly—and so deeply—shocked me. But the feelings were there. We'd had the start of something great—something with the potential of Jenna and Cam's grand romance. But Rye *left* me. And now I'd never know if we could have been more.

"Get up," Jenna said.

"Why?"

"We're going for a little ride."

"Jenna…"

"Look, if you make me pull the boss card, I will. But I'd rather do this as your sister."

"You're my brother's wife. We're not—"

"You're the closest thing I have to a sister in the world, Kate. That includes Abbi and Nes, both of whom I'd give a kidney to or shank a mob boss for. So, get up, get your stuff, and get in the car, kay?"

I did as I was told.

"He wanted to do what's right by his kid," Jenna said, as if she could read my stupid thoughts. More like blurted. We were at a stoplight in the afternoon bumper-to-bumper traffic.

"I've thought of that—that's why I didn't go push him when he left," I replied. No, I hadn't pushed more because I was ashamed of his anger. I was worried I really had done something wrong when I asked Cam to help Rye. That I overstepped and deserved to have it slap me in the face.

I lifted my feet onto the dash—sans stilettos—and slithered down in the seat. I used to sit like this when I had to travel alone with my dad. Then, I'd considered it comfortable. Now, I wondered if I sought this position as a way to make myself less conspicuous.

"I know you're thinking about this from a parent's perspective, and I appreciate the insight, but Rye dumped me." My chin quivered so I pressed my lips together.

Jenna repositioned her hands on the wheel but said nothing.

"Does Cam still talk to him?" I asked.

Jenna shook her head. "Your brother wouldn't do that to you."

"I don't own Cam's time," I said. "I know the two of them really hit it off."

"I read Rye's blog," Jenna said, cutting me off.

I frowned. "Oh. Since when?"

"Since he started one after your awesome campaigns went viral and people are so interested in him." She hesitated. "He decided to go public with his son's health issues."

I absorbed the information like a boxer took a blow. I scrunched tighter into my seat.

"We're here," Jenna said.

I sat up and cursed. "I wanted to go to *my* home," I said through clenched teeth.

"And Cam and Carter both asked me to bring you here."

I rolled my eyes because I did not want to be here to celebrate my mother's birthday. Yes, I was aware tonight my mom turned fifty-five, and I'd informed my brothers she could enjoy the milestone without me.

"Take me to my place," I said, crossing my arms over my chest.

"No can do."

I glared back.

"Before you say anything, I'll totally fire you if you don't walk in there."

My mouth fell open. "You'd fire me?" I stammered.

Jenna looked aggrieved. "I don't want to. The shop will collapse in a terrible implosion if you make me. And I'll forget to take my vitamins and be the worst mom in the whole world because you didn't help me in my time of need."

"Too thick," I muttered.

"And I'll probably inhale something bad for the baby. All because you don't want to wish your mother—the very woman who carried you in her body and loved you and sang to you and changed your nasty, nasty diapers—"

"I get it," I said through clenched teeth. I hesitated but the words tumbled from my lips, "You'd really fire me?"

My daddy, my mama, those early boyfriends, Rye, Ike, and now Jenna. No one…no one truly wanted me. Dammit. I was worth *something*. If people would toss me aside, would simply use me, then…I didn't know what that meant except I couldn't handle the pain of being tossed. Again.

I sniffed hard. "Give my best to my mother and Cam. Have a…" I struggled to keep the shrapnel in my throat, which caused my eyes to burn. "I hope you, Cam, and the baby have a great life."

"Don't do that, Kate," Jenna said, tearing up.

"Bye, Jenna."

I climbed out of the car and shut the door. My legs wobbled but I got them to carry me across the gravel drive and up the porch steps. I'd wait inside while I figured out how to get a cab or borrow my mother's car.

I opened the door to my childhood home—the one I'd thought was filled with loving memories. I caught a glimpse of my mother's face, a smile starting to bloom there before I caught the banister. And, just like I used to when I was in high school, I ran up the stairs, the sobs drifting back down behind me.

"Kate," Mom called.

Like the night in eleventh grade when Vince Worth dumped me at prom, deciding to spend the evening with Jodie Phipps instead, I flopped down on my bed and sobbed into my pillow.

Losing Rye cut deep. I missed Ike's sweet little face. And now I was going to miss Jenna so much, too.

"Dammit!" I screeched. "Love is a sad, sorry sack of shit, and I hate it."

"Hurts worse than anything in the world."

I gasped, choked and managed to lift my head to glare at my mother. "What do you want?" I asked.

"Well, seeing as how you're here, I guess I want to comfort you."

I flopped on my back, heedless of the tears and mascara streaming down my temples into my hair. "Why? I didn't matter enough to tell the truth to, so why comfort me now?"

Her face folded into lines of misery. "Oh, honey. You are hurting something fierce, and it breaks my heart."

My laugh was caustic and ended in a hiccuping sob. "You *broke* my heart when you lied to me about my family."

"I know."

I'd opened my mouth to continue my diatribe, but at her quiet words, my lips slammed shut and I pushed up on my elbows to meet her gaze.

She held out a beseeching hand. Tears spilled from her eyes, just as they did mine. "I…I fucked up."

My mom didn't cuss. She was of the generation of Texas ladies that believed "pretty women kept a pretty mouth." I'd heard that refrain so often I probably spoke it in my sleep.

So, to hear my mother drop an F-bomb shocked me to the tips of my toes. I gaped at her, unsure what else I could or should say.

She nodded. "I did, baby girl. This is all on me." She looked down at her hands. "I thought I was doing right to make us seem like a family. To keep the lie I'd created so long ago and…" She twisted her fingers into knots. "And I realized it wasn't a lie for you or your brothers, or even your father. *I* needed it."

I leaned back on my elbows as I processed my mother's words. "Why would you want to perpetuate that we were a perfect family? *You knew he was cheating.*"

She reached out as if to touch my cheek but pulled back. Then she leaned forward and rubbed what I bet was the mascara from under my eyes. Yep, her thumb was coated in black.

"Because I never loved your father," she said.

My jaw was going to hurt from this constant slew of revelations. "You…"

She dropped her chin to her chest. "I loved his older brother—your brothers' father." A dreamy look spread over her face. "Jensen was the best part of my life."

"Then why stay in a loveless marriage with my dad?"

She shrugged. "Laurence loved me. Until he didn't. He provided for you, your brothers. Until he didn't. And because

I just…I just didn't care enough about how he treated me, I let him hurt your brother."

I stiffened, hating this reminder of what a pile of garbage my father was—not just to my mama, but to Camden.

"I hate that he's part of me," I whispered.

Mom's eyes softened. "Oh, sweet pea. No. Laurence wasn't a terrible man. He loved you. So much."

I shook my head, adamant about this one truth. "Yes, he was. Look what he did to Cam."

"I've talked to your brother about that. We both think Laurence took out on Cam what he couldn't on Jensen."

My lips twisted. "He asked me to lie about his infidelity when I was seven."

My mama's gasp told me I'd managed to shock her. I averted my gaze, unable to meet her eyes. "And I did because I loved him."

"Fine. You're right. Laurence was a selfish ass."

I snorted. "And that hurts me—that I loved a man who was such an ass. Love shouldn't cause this kind of pain. It shouldn't have hurt Cam. Or you." My lip quivered as I held in the words I refused to say.

"Or you," my mother said, her hand running over my hair in that endless caress I remembered from childhood, easing my tension now just as it had then. "Especially not you, Katie Rose. You were always the best of Laurence and me. And he damn well took advantage of your sweetness. If he were here right now, I'd clock him one good."

The tears welled again and overflowed. Before I could think it through, I wrapped my arms around her and held on tight.

Nothing was as comforting as having my mama's arms around me, rocking me gently as I poured all my heartache into tears.

Finally, it subsided.

She brushed my hair back from my damp cheeks. She met my puffy eyes. "I know you're hurting, but I need to tell you that *nothing*, not one thing in this world, is worth more than selfless love."

I choked out a laugh. "Sure doesn't feel like it."

My mother shook her head. "My time with Jensen, having Cam and Carter, then you, made all the rest..." She waved her hand to encompass the years she was married to my father, the hell of his affairs, *my* treatment of her this past year. "I wouldn't change you, your brothers, or Jensen."

I stared down at my lap. "Does it stop hurting?"

Mama's sigh answered my plaintive question.

PART TWO

CHAPTER THIRTY-EIGHT | Rye

Today was Ike's surgery.

Over the past nine weeks, I'd taken Quentin Keen to court—with a new judge presiding—and won my share of custody of Ike once the bribery was exposed. Quentin was forced to pay a fine and no longer be involved in further legal decisions with Ike, which suited me quite well.

The solution wasn't complete or even perfect, but I'd managed to achieve my goal and get my insurance in order.

As soon as I had the piece of paper in hand to prove my benefits, I'd called the best ophthalmologist in Dallas. While we were at our first appointment, he mentioned a surgery slot had opened up, and I'd accepted the time.

Since I agreed to Ike's procedure, sleep evaded me, and last night, I never bothered going to bed. After a long, hard work out that was supposed to keep me from thinking about Kate, I showered. Once I stepped out, wrapping a towel around my waist, I looked in the mirror, shocked by the wild-eyed, hairy mess of a man I'd become. And not just because of my worry over Ike, either. I missed Kate. Every night, as I lay in bed, I tortured myself with the time we'd spent together—how her lips felt, the warm, heavy weight of her breasts against my chest.

But, mainly, I missed her smile, her soft voice, rich as honey and twice as sweet, as she spoke to Ike or looked up at me with those clear, gray eyes.

I'd tortured myself with the remembrance of my last glance back at her across the parking lot, her shoulders pulled down and in, arms wrapped around her waist. Over the past couple of months, I'd come to understand that I expected her to fall in line with my plan for a long-distance relationship, but when she'd made her own plan, instead of considering it, I left.

I'd been afraid—afraid Asher wouldn't think I was good enough. Afraid Ike wouldn't get his surgery. Afraid to fall back into such a huge, life-altering debt. And, yes, afraid that Kate would realize what a coward I was and look at me with disgust.

"Man up," I said to the hairy man in the mirror. "Man up and face those fears. It's time."

I pulled out the clippers I used to buzz-cut Ike's thick hair. I gave myself a similar treatment and then went to work on my beard. I stripped away the hair I'd hidden behind, first to annoy my father, then to shield me from unwanted scrutiny from Deirdre and her family, from the NICU staff about Ike, and even fans of my music.

Only after I left Kate did I begin to understand the scars Deirdre and her father had carved in me traced over the ones my father created when he abandoned us years before.

Because of those previous relationships, those previous betrayals, I assumed everyone worked in their best interest, not mine.

I assumed Kate was the same.

Because of that, I walked away from the best relationship

I'd ever been in—worse, I deprived Ike of Kate's love, too. He'd moped since I told him Kate was out of our lives.

Fear had been a strong motivator for too long. I glanced down at the sink full of hair, then back in the mirror. I studied the clean-shaven man who stared back.

This was me, Ryland Lawson. I was a single father, a musician who worked as an auto-dealership executive and hated it, and I was in love with a woman I was terrified to contact after she'd ignored my last message.

The first week of going into the offices I acknowledged that writing and singing songs weren't just my passion—it was the work I needed to do. Thanks to Kate's social media campaigns, the fans thought so, too. If Asher was willing to mentor me, that would be almost as good as having Kate in my bed and Kate loving us as much as Ike and I loved her.

Now, nearly two-and-a-half months later, I was no closer to a solution of winning Kate back.

By the time I needed to wake Ike up, I'd showered again, removing the hair from my body. The plus side to not sleeping was we were on time for our 5 a.m. arrival at the hospital. The downside was my brain fired on about a half a cylinder and my body ached from fatigue worse than any I'd ever felt before—and that was saying something.

I settled into a chair and propped my booted feet on the one across from me. That position became uncomfortable, so I took out my guitar and strummed a few chords. Soon, I found myself playing the haunting melody—the tune I'd come to think of privately as "Kissing Kate Goodbye".

I hummed as I played. Then, as the rest of the lyrics came to me, I paused to jot them on the back of a magazine I found.

"Here, use this."

I jolted, unaware of the audience now filling the waiting area. There had to be thirty people. Most wore scrubs, which told me they were staff, but a few were parents or kids, some of whom looked to be patients of the ward.

I raised my hand in a sheepish gesture. "I didn't mean to disturb you," I said.

The woman—a nurse or doctor based on her hot pink scrubs and stethoscope wrapped loosely around her neck—handed me a pad and paper and shook her head.

"Are you kidding? This was a great way to start the morning. I'm Dr. Ginger Halliday."

"Nice to meet you," I said.

She tipped her head. "Would you like to come into the kids' room? They're mostly finished with breakfast, and I bet they'd enjoy some music."

I put my guitar in its case, locked the buckles and stood. "Lead the way."

Her smile held both warmth and a hint of flirtation. "We do appreciate helpful-minded folks around here."

"I'm glad to brighten their day. But will Dr. Wainwright know where to find me?" I asked.

While he wasn't the doctor I'd hoped to do Ike's surgery, Dr. Wainwright was well-respected, and he was in-network. The thought of having to choose my son's doctor based on insurance made my jaw tick in frustration, but I breathed through it—as I did so many details these days. This was life.

Dr. Halliday shot me a questioning look.

"My son. Ike Lawson. He's in surgery."

I swallowed down my fear and gripped the guitar handle more tightly. It was the only thing holding me together at the moment, which was one of the reasons I was more than glad to perform for the kids.

Deirdre never called to ask about the surgery. Some part of me expected her to show up, but, just like every other time I needed her since Ike was born, she refused to get involved. I'd never felt so alone.

"Oh," Dr. Halliday's tone softened with understanding.

"He's having glaucoma surgery. Probably a scleral buckle, too." I swallowed down my fear and reminded myself that Dr. Wainwright had been optimistic in our pre-op appointments, calling Ike a good candidate.

Dr. Halliday nodded. "I'll be sure to let the staff know where you are so you can get updates."

"I know he's in surgery," I said. "They texted me that they were about to start on his left eye."

"Oh, that's good, then." She stopped at a door and gestured me into the space. The chattering slid to a halt as I entered. About twelve small heads, some even tinier than Ike's, turned toward me. I also captured the attention of the parents who were sitting with their children.

"Hiya," I said.

Dr. Halliday greeted most of the kids by name. She spent a moment catching up with them before she turned back toward me.

"This is…"

"Rye Lawson," I supplied.

"Right. And he plays the guitar."

"Nah uh," one of the older girls said. Her head was bald, but she wore a fuzzy purple robe over pink pajamas. "He's, like, a famous musician," she said. Her smile turned dazzling. "I saw you on Instagram. My older sister watched all your videos. She loves your South by Southwest concert that guitar maker posted," she said.

My chest ached once again as I realized all Kate had done for me—and how I'd walked away.

"My sister is going to be so jealous I met you."

Dr. Ginger's lips twitched but she said, "Then you'll have a story to tell her, Jaime. But for now, I thought you might want to hear Rye play. The song he was playing out in the waiting room was beautiful."

I opened my guitar case and grinned a little as pride surged from the intakes of breath. Yes, the instrument Jenna gave me was a sight to behold. I almost couldn't play it, though, because it reminded me of what I'd had with Kate…and let go out of sheer fear.

I should have held her with both hands and proclaimed she was *mine* to the rest of the world that first day we met. But should have, could have, would have got you nowhere in this world.

I settled into a chair and bent over the instrument, hoping to get lost in the music. I played my best-known hit first. When I glanced up and saw them all watching, pride whipped through me. I hadn't felt this good since I was on stage at South by Southwest.

Six songs later, I had to set my guitar down and ask for the closest vending machine.

"We'll get you some water," Dr. Halliday said.

I wondered if she needed to perform her rounds or whatever, but she seemed to linger.

"Come on," she said. "I'll take you to the doctor's lounge."

She led the way, and I stared at her springy dark ringlets, similar to Kate's hair. Though Dr. Halliday was a beautiful woman, I wasn't at all interested in her.

I wanted Kate.

I feared now I'd *always* want her.

While I'd loved Deirdre, that had been a young love that hadn't withstood our personality growth into our twenties and sure as hell didn't survive the stress of my constant touring and a premature newborn. Much as I hated to admit it, Deirdre and I would have been better off never getting married when we found out she was pregnant with Ike.

But we did, and I didn't regret Ike. Just the years I'd wasted feeling guilty for not loving Deirdre as she needed.

I squeezed the back of my neck, wishing those revelations had come sooner. So lost in my own thoughts, I didn't realize Dr. Halliday had offered me a bottle of water. Or that she was so close.

"You're very talented, Rye," she said, batting those long, dark eyelashes at me. "Talented and attractive."

"Um. Thanks, but…uh…I'm…I'm in love with someone."

"Lucky lady," she said with a hint of humor. "And for the record, so am I."

My cheeks flamed. Crap. I thought she'd been hitting on me. Ego, much? "Um, well, great."

Dr. Halliday grinned wider, her eyes sparkling at my growing discomfort. "I was wondering if you'd take a selfie, maybe sign an autograph for my wife. She will be bummed that you've cut off your hair. She said it's better than mine." She winked.

I couldn't help but smile in return, happy to take the photo and sign Dr. Halliday's prescription pad.

"Thanks," Dr. Halliday replied. "Ellie's going to love this. Seriously, your girlfriend is lucky to have such a caring man in her life."

"Not sure she agrees. But…she and Ike…they're all I could ever want."

Dr. Halliday pressed the cold bottle of water into my hand. "I hope she knows how you feel. It's not every day a man will admit that."

I shook my head. I wasn't going to discuss Kate with her. "Thanks for the water. I'll find my own way back to the kids' room."

I turned and trudged back down the hall.

And nearly ran over Kate.

CHAPTER THIRTY-NINE | Kate

I wasn't sure I should go to the hospital. But Rye had posted last night on his blog—which I read every single day—that he'd be at the hospital alone. I couldn't let him face Ike's hours-long operation and subsequent recovery without company. I'd made it to the waiting room where I heard Rye's voice floating down the hall. I followed the sound, but by the time I arrived, he'd disappeared further down the hall.

I stood, rooted as the beautiful woman in scrubs hit on him.

Hearing Rye say he was in love with someone broke my heart all over again. I struggled to catch my breath so I could scurry away before he noticed me. Unfortunately, I was too slow. He reached out and gripped my biceps, those gorgeous eyes meeting mine.

"Kate."

Just my name, but the word held so much emotion.

"Hey, Rye."

His tongue darted out and touched the corner of his upper lip. His bare upper lip. I lifted my hand, my fingertips skimming his clean-shaven cheek and up to his shorn head.

"For Ike?" I asked.

He hesitated, then blurted, "I needed to exorcise some demons."

Unsure what to say, I dropped my hand, wishing I hadn't

touched his warm skin in the first place, even as my fingertips curled protectively around the faint heat. "I-I wanted to see Ike."

He closed his eyes. Before I could move or even process the change, his forehead touched mine and his arms slid around my waist. I dropped the stuffed turtle I was holding and hugged him back.

"Kate…"

Whatever he was going to say disappeared when I pressed my lips to his. Maybe he was in love with Deirdre or someone else. But this…I needed this one last chance to remember. Once I'd calmed down from my crying jag on my childhood bed, I'd promised my mother I'd tell Rye how I felt.

Now, I stood wrapped in Rye's scent, willing him to love me like I loved him. He cupped my cheek, nudging my chin to the right as he tilted his head and opened his lips. He groaned when his tongue touched mine.

"The hallway isn't really the best place," said a sardonic voice.

I stumbled back a pace and blinked over at the pretty doctor. She wore a slight smirk. Rye gripped my arm, his palm slipping down to my hand to lace our fingers together.

"This is my girl, Kate," he said. He waved between us. "Dr. Halliday, Kate."

"Nice to meet you, Kate. I'm Ginger. I run this department. Your man is talented."

"Yes," I said, my cheeks flaming. "He is."

She smirked again as she took in my flaming cheeks and swollen lips. "I hope to talk to him about singing for the kids here again. They really enjoyed today's impromptu performance."

I nodded but I'd quit paying attention. Rye's shirt shifted
when he caught me or kissed me, and I caught the hint of dark
ink in what looked like a circle covering most of his left pec. I
licked my lip in anticipation. I wanted to see that tat.

Rye spoke with the doctor while I bent down to collect the
turtle and his empty water bottle, made more difficult because
Rye refused to let go of my hand.

Okay, then. Maybe he was happy to see me.

Before we were able to talk, another medical staff—a nurse—
came out to give Rye news about Ike's surgery.

"He's out of the operating room. Dr. Wainwright will talk
to you in a few minutes. Would you like to meet in the waiting
room or go back to recovery?"

"I want to see Ike, please," Rye said. His hand trembled
against mine, and my heart melted further at his show of vulnerability.

I started to release his hand, but he clasped my fingers more
tightly. "Will you…" His voice cracked. "Will you come with me?"

"Yes," I breathed.

Tenderness burned from his eyes as he brushed a stray curl
off my forehead. He leaned in, inhaling, as he pressed a kiss to
the spot.

"Missed you, Katie Rose," he whispered.

———— ★ ————

Rye grabbed the guitar he'd set down when he embraced
me, and we walked next to each other to the room. Much as I
wanted to offer words of comfort, we'd both known the risks of
this surgery.

Rye placed his guitar in the corner and went over to Ike, who took up basically no space in the long bed. I bit my quivering lip as I saw the bandages swaddling his face. Rye gently lifted Ike's small hand.

"Hey, big guy," Rye said, his voice gruff. "Daddy's here."

"He's still waking up," the nurse said. "And it will be a little scary when he can't see because of the bandages. So, Dr. Wainwright has him on a light sedative."

Rye dipped his head in understanding even as he lowered his hip to the edge of the bed.

I followed my instinct and went over, placing my hand on Rye's shoulder.

We stood like that until the doctor entered.

"Mr. Lawson," Dr. Wainwright said, shaking Rye's hand. "So, we have good news. But we also hit a bit of a snag."

The doctor might not have seen the tremor in Rye's jaw or the hollowness in his eyes as he spoke. I made sure Rye knew I was there. But then I realized we hadn't spoken about whether or not he wanted me to be a part of Ike's life again.

And…if he didn't, could I handle that?

I worried my lip, missing most of what the doctor said.

I came back to the conversation when Rye's breath hitched.

"As long as there isn't any swelling or infection, I feel confident he'll be able to see as well as you or I do. With corrective lenses, of course."

"Glasses are fun," I murmured. "And he looks so cute in them. Hey, we can pick out some cool goggle ones he was talking about."

Realizing what I said, I flushed. Damn my big mouth.

Before Rye could remind me Ike was *his* son once again, the doctor smiled.

"I like the way you think. Those are the best kind for an active kid."

"What's the snag?" Rye asked, his voice steady.

I pressed into his side, letting him know I was there for him. Rye wrapped an arm around my waist. His whole body trembled.

"His left eye didn't need the buckle. I didn't realize until I was already in there, so I did some retinal shaping. That eye should improve over time, but that hadn't been in our original plan."

When Rye remained silent, I asked, "Are you talking along the lines of LASIK?"

Dr. Wainwright pursed his lips. "Kind of. The pressure against the optic nerve was lower in the left eye, but the astigmatism was greater—like a football. So I used the laser to reshape the eye a bit. Over time, it should reduce the need for correction for the astigmatism, but I don't know how much it'll change his need for correction to his vision."

Rye nodded. His tensed muscles relaxed further.

Ike stirred.

Rye squeezed my hand as if I were his lifeline. Maybe in that moment I was.

"I'm here, son," Rye said, his tone gruff. "I'm here with you."

I tried to step back, to give him some space, but he tightened his hold. "And so is Kate. You don't need to worry. We're here with you."

"Daddy? K-Kate? I can't see."

CHAPTER FORTY | Rye

Ike struggled to stay calm. I appreciated the effort because I was able to try, too. But watching my boy freak out did bad things to my insides.

Kate held on to me, and her presence helped me hold my emotions in check. I worried I was cutting off the circulation to her fingers, but even so, I couldn't let up, let alone let go.

"Don't leave me," Ike said, his voice plaintive.

Kate settled onto the bed next to me and laid her free hand on Ike's knobby knee. "I'm right here, sweetie. I'll be right here. As long as you need."

She sniffled a little and then said, "I brought you something. It's Sergeant Pepper. Well, a stuffed version."

She wiggled her hand free of mine and placed the stuffed turtle on Ike's chest.

"It's so soft," he murmured.

"Much softer than the real deal."

As Kate continued to talk to him, Ike calmed.

"I see you're in good hands, Ike," Dr. Wainwright said. He patted Ike's foot. "I'll see you in a couple of days. Better yet, you'll see me, too."

"Okay," Ike said, his voice small but no longer on the verge of hysteria.

An orderly wheeled Ike, still clutching his new turtle pet, out of the recovery area and into his private room.

I blew out a breath as I searched for the best way to make things right with Kate. To let her know how much I missed her, how stupid I'd been to allow her to leave in the first place.

Words stated face-to-face weren't really my thing. I did much better when my feelings took the form of a melody. So, I got out my guitar and played her "Kissing Kate Goodbye." The song helped Ike relax, which was an added bonus.

She pressed her fingertips to her mouth, the tip of her nose turning bright red. "Play it again."

So I did. Then a third time because it said everything I wanted to say.

"That's beautiful," she whispered.

"I mean it. You're my home. My favorite place to be. And I'll kiss you goodbye every single day as long as I get to kiss you good morning and good night every day, too."

"I don't…" She sucked in a breath. Her skin was pale, her eyes luminescent with hope. "I've read your blog. Every post. Jenna told me about it."

My nostrils flared as I struggled to keep the longing and fear in check. I wrote those posts for her.

"What…" I cleared my throat. "What did you think about it?"

"About the blog? It's good. A window into your world—one your fans definitely appreciate."

She dropped her chin to her chest. I didn't want to talk about blogs either. I wanted to fix the distance between us.

She held up her hand when I moved in closer, intent on

pulling her into my arms.

She raised her head and the pain in her eyes stole my breath. "I just wanted you to have the best opportunities."

Finally, *finally* I realized I'd never be safe with Kate because whatever she was feeling, I felt, too.

"I'm sorry." I shook my head. "Those words aren't enough, and I know it, but I am so damn sorry I hurt you. I was scared. Of what I felt for you. Of what you were offering. It all seemed too good to be true."

She kept her gaze on mine, intent.

"Those posts…some were so personal. About…about how you felt like a failure for not being able to fix Ike's eyes with that first surgery when he was still an infant. How hard it was for you to realize that music was helping him—helped other kids—even though it couldn't save them. That help and fixing and saving were different and sometimes not enough. And when I read them…you broke my heart all over again."

"I am a failure, Kate."

When she opened her mouth, I pressed my finger to her lips. They were soft and plush. My very favorite lips to touch.

"My first marriage failed because I married the wrong woman. We got pregnant too young. I failed Ike by putting my music career before Deirdre's pregnancy. I failed Ike when I didn't fight Deirdre harder for the next—*this*—surgery, when I let her fear and mine overwhelm me. And I failed Ike again when I told him to stop seeing you, stop having fun and living his life."

I sucked in a breath and admitted the rest of the truth I'd wrestled with for weeks. "And I failed me when I pushed you away. That was easier than accepting you owned not just my heart, but Ike's. That each of your smiles brought us both such joy. That your frowns and tears caused us such pain."

She pulled back and said, "But don't you get it? I feel the same way. I want nothing but sunshine for you and Ike. I want his laughter to dance through the meadow, his shrieks of delight to whip through the wind. I want him to have that perfect, idyllic childhood that every child should have. But I don't want that because he's any child. He's yours…and…and I wanted so very desperately for him to be mine, too."

I could see that now. Deirdre carried Ike in her body and gave him life, but she'd never wanted to be a parent—even before Ike arrived and definitely not afterward. Kate had stepped so seamlessly into the role I'd almost missed the bond forming. Until I severed it.

"I think…I think you might be my world, Katherine Rose Grace. And when you're in it, it's bigger and brighter and just all-around better than anything I could have imagined."

Instead of responding with her own declaration, Kate leaned in and pressed her lips to mine. It wasn't a soft, sweet kiss. This one was all about longing and loneliness and possession rolled up into a perfect dance of lips, teeth, and tongues.

Ike grunted, causing us both to pull back. We looked over at him, but he seemed to settle back into sleep.

Kate caressed the back of my neck and I shivered at the feel of her touch. Her lips quirked upward. "I've missed you like crazy these past weeks."

"How crazy?" I asked, loving the sparkle lighting up Kate's eyes.

"Well…" she drawled. "Crazy enough for Jenna to fire me?"

I gawked. "What the hell?"

"That lasted all of about…an hour. She fell in my arms and cried all over me. She said I wasn't fired, that she was giving me a huge raise, and that she hoped I didn't hate her and then gave me extra time off so I could pack up and drive to Dallas."

"Huh. I knew Jenna was smart. Why'd she fire you?"

Kate's mouth twisted. "She wanted me to talk to my mother."

I raised an eyebrow, unsure how to respond to that. Kate had valid reasons for being upset with her mother.

"It was Mama's birthday and I was being stubborn," Kate said. "I didn't want to go. But Jenna saying she was ditching me…I cried all over Mama. Which, in retrospect was the best gift I've ever given her."

I didn't follow Kate's logic. "Why's that?"

"Because I gave her back my trust. She got to hold me together, which is what mothers do." Kate pursed her lips, a faraway look gathering in her eyes. "At least good ones."

"So, you're telling me you two patched up your relationship?"

Kate nodded, her expression filled with happiness. "We're working our way toward good."

Seemed like a great way to view all relationships: always a work in progress and always working to make them better.

A melody began to play in my head for a new tune. This is what Kate did to me; she gave me back my ability to create music as well as my joy for the process.

She smirked, no doubt aware of what was going on in my head. "Write it down."

"I'm holding you. No place I'd rather be."

With a long-suffering sigh, Kate bent down to the bag she'd placed at her feet and pulled out a notepad and a pen.

"I'm guessing you don't keep these on you."

"I do, actually. Dr. Halliday gave me one earlier that I put under my guitar. See—there in the case."

When Kate shook her head, I pressed a soft kiss to her mouth, but she pulled back much too quickly.

"Write it down first. So you don't forget the lyrics or the melody." She raised her eyebrows in question.

I grinned. "Both."

She thrust the pen and paper into my hands and rose to check on Ike.

And I could see it, this life we would have: Kate making sure Ike and I were organized and happy. Maybe a flame-haired little girl to tag along after her big brother. And maybe a third and fourth one just to prove our love to the world.

Because I meant to prove to Kate, Jenna, Cam, Carter, Regan, her mother, and the whole rest of the world what a beautiful soul I'd been lucky enough to find. One who knew her value to me, which was priceless.

Except the nagging realization that I couldn't give her that future she so richly deserved hung over my head.

CHAPTER FORTY-ONE | Kate

Much to my surprise, the nurses brought in release papers not long after they unhooked Ike from the machines. Rye confirmed Ike's follow-up visit and checked his phone to make sure he had the time correct. Then, Rye lifted Ike's small body into the waiting wheelchair and the nurse pushed Ike from the room.

"Would you mind staying with them while I get the car?" Rye asked.

"No problem," I said.

The nurse waited until Rye sped down the stairwell while we walked at a more sedate pace to the elevator.

"He's a devoted father," she said.

I nodded, unsure what to say.

"You're a very lucky woman," she said with a smile. "I wish my own husband was half so in love with me."

"He's not…" I sealed my lips. No need to give this woman any fodder for the gossip mill. I smiled back, trying to make my lips less stiff. "I am."

We entered the elevator and tension built in my shoulders. Had I said the correct thing? I hadn't really understood the difficulties celebrities like my brother and sister-in-law, maybe even more Jenna and Carter, faced until this moment. I could say something that messed up Rye's image—the one he'd been so carefully crafting with each blog post over these past couple of months.

Yeah, no pressure.

"I'm sure your husband adores you," I blurted.

The nurse chuckled and shook her head. "Not like your man. But, hey, I don't have to worry about millions of women drooling over Ed, so there's my silver lining."

I gulped, once again unsure how to proceed.

"Kate?" Ike asked, his voice sounded frailer than usual.

I blessed him for the interruption. "What's wrong, sweet pea?"

"My head hurts. I don't like the dark."

I glanced up at the nurse, nervous ichor spilling into my stomach as I wondered what to do. Then I thought, screw it. This was *my* relationship with Ike and I hated the idea of him suffering.

"I'm going to pick you up and sit you in my lap, okay?" I murmured. "That way I can give you a big hug and maybe rub your shoulders a little to see if that helps with the pain."

"Okay."

I was careful, trying not to jar him, as I slid my hands under his shoulders and knees. The nurse held the chair steady as I sat, Ike resting against my shoulder, his small hand clutching my T-shirt.

"There," I said in a soft voice, rubbing my hand down his back. The doors opened and the nurse wheeled us out of the elevator. Ike snuggled in closer.

"I love you, Kate."

I pressed a kiss to the top of his head. I'd missed his thick hair and little boy smell. I'd missed his voice and his exuberance. "I love you, too, precious boy."

We made it to the front doors but Rye wasn't there yet, so the nurse waited, much more patiently than I would have in her position, as I rubbed Ike's back in soothing strokes.

His breathing evened out once more.

"He should be down for the night," the nurse said. "He's on a pretty good dose of sedative."

I hoped it meant Ike was going to sleep well and without pain. Before I could ask, Rye pulled up and hopped out of his sedan.

He scooted in through the doors, no doubt planning to scoop Ike out of the seat. I let him even as I felt a deep pang in my chest.

"Come on," he said. "I'll take you home."

I followed, trailing behind Rye until I realized I needed to open the car's back door, which I did. Rye settled Ike in his seat and double-checked the buckles.

"My car's in the lot—"

He leaned his hip against the side of the gleaming, new luxury vehicle. I missed his older, smaller version. Rye made a face. "My car didn't fit the image of an executive, let alone one who ran so many dealerships. The car was part of the package. I hate the lease payment." He fidgeted a little.

"It's a nice perk," I offered.

"Can we collect your car tomorrow?" Rye asked. "I'd really like you to come home with me—us—now."

"I need my suitcase."

"I'll grab it."

"Okay."

I assumed that meant Rye wanted me to spend the night. I worried over that until I decided I better get the details this go-round. I couldn't leave the situation open-ended as it had been before.

"You mean I should cancel my hotel reservation?"

"Yeah," he said.

I hadn't made one, so that wasn't a problem. But still, good to know.

We drove out of the trafficky mess of the downtown area and headed north on the Tollway. We both remained quiet.

"So, from what I gather, the doctor was able to keep Ike's retina on his right eye from detaching," I said.

"Yeah."

"So, he'll be able to see better than before."

"Yeah." Rye swallowed. "Just not as well from the periphery. If at all."

I reached over and clasped his hand. He held on tighter than I expected.

———————— ★ ————————

Rye maneuvered into the garage of a large home with a steeply-pitched, gray-shingled roof. The front was a Texas-original combination of red brick and native yellow stone. The porch was deep, with pristine white pillars and faux shutters on the windows. The interior was large and darker than I anticipated. The kitchen Rye led me through from the spacious four-car garage was top-notch, with high-end appliances and long, black granite countertops. Rye bypassed a narrower set of stairs right off the kitchen and, carrying Ike, headed to a broader wrought iron set that twisted around—the showstopper of the front entry.

Once Ike was settled in his bed in a room off the top of the stairs, Rye took my hand and led me down the hall toward his room.

"You own this place?" I asked. My stomach ached for a different reason. I'd thought we were more in-line wealth-wise, but after seeing this house—a far cry from the comfortable, even upscale condo that Rye had rented—made me realize Rye was much closer to my brothers' caliber of wealth. I didn't like the disparity between us.

Rye shook his head, shutting the door behind him and leaving his hand there, above my head. I re-situated my body into a more comfortable position.

"This is my father's house. He and Aubrey are in Houston to attend an exotic car show, and so my father can see a specialist."

"Oh, I wondered why they weren't there today. I'm sorry to hear he's struggling with a medical issue."

Rye clenched his jaw. "He wouldn't accept your pity."

"It's not pity." I frowned. "What's going on here? I just don't understand what I keep doing wrong—"

Rye kissed me. The first brush of lips was soft, tender even. Then his mouth settled over mine and he plundered my mouth, causing me to grip his biceps as I rose on my toes, inundated with pleasure and a bit of shock.

"I need you, Kate. I know I shouldn't push—we have things to talk about, but you being there today, meant the world to me. You were the only one who cared enough—"

"That's not true—"

"The only one who cared enough," Rye said again, rolling over my words, "to be there when I needed someone to hold my hand

and hold me up. Even my sister put work before my son." His face morphed into anguished lines. "If this surgery hadn't worked, I would have caused Ike to go permanently blind much sooner…"

Rye scowled. I was still getting used to seeing the soft, plump, pink skin of his lips. I'd wanted them on me before, but now, without the facial hair, I was able to see them in all their glory.

He had beautiful lips.

And a great jaw. Strong, sexy, determined. I shouldn't notice his appeal right now. He was right. We needed to talk.

"But Ike isn't. He won't go blind. Because you fought for him," I said, my voice soft.

Rye dropped his forehead against mine.

"There's so much I need to tell you." He hesitated. "I missed you, Kate. More than you'll ever know. I was so wrong about leaving the way I did, and—"

I pressed my fingers to those soft, plump lips.

"I know there's a lot to say. I know we need to get to know each other better. But, Rye…" I sucked in a deep breath. "I missed you, too. I hated how we left things between us." I blinked back tears. "You have no idea how hard it's been—"

"Yeah, I do. I've missed you every minute."

"And I just…I need to know you care about me. About us being an 'us'," I said.

I shocked us both when I picked up his big hand and placed it over my breast. My chest quivered as my lungs deflated.

I met his eyes. "Love me, please. I've missed you so much."

"Kate." My name was a moan. "There are things I need to tell you."

I rose up on my toes and drew his head down to meet my lips.

"If you care about me," I whispered against his mouth, "you can tell me everything tomorrow."

"Kate," he whispered. His lips slipped over mine, taking the kiss deeper. "I don't want to hurt you," he said, easing back.

"Don't you see? You hurt me terribly each time you draw back, pull away. When you stop accepting my love."

He stared down into my eyes for a moment that seemed to spin out into a lifetime of heartbeats.

I held my breath, more than half of me expecting him to push me away again.

CHAPTER FORTY-TWO | Rye

I wrapped my arms around her, tightening our embrace, the heat sizzling between us as my palms found their home on her waist. She pressed into me and my body adjusted, hardening even as my heart rate quickened with the need to kiss her again.

She raised her head, her expression wary but needy. Our lips melded as my heart crashed in a crescendo of longing.

My hands drifted down to their new, favorite place on her butt cheeks, which I gripped as I tugged her tight to my body. Passion exploded between us as Kate moaned into my mouth.

I loved her moans.

We fumbled our way to the bed, unwilling to stop touching. Her lips drifted over my neck, her palms rested above the too-hot skin on my stomach. Each place her fingers touched caused me to burn.

Finally, *finally* I was going to slake this need again. Our time together only made the deep-seated desire grow, because I knew what I was missing. And loving Kate wasn't just an emotion, though I felt her all the way into my soul. Loving Kate was a verb, one that left me more sated and happier than I'd ever been. Losing that connection nearly broke me.

"I'm so sorry," I murmured against the pliant flesh of her throat. "I should have realized you were trying to help me fulfill my dreams."

"Th-that's what I want," she stammered. Her palms splayed wide on my abdomen. "I want you to be happy."

"You make me happy," I said. And I ran my lips over hers, showing her how much she meant to me.

Exhilaration and lust built in my veins, popping in tiny bursts that kept me lightheaded.

I kept my hands on her hips, my lips on her neck as I walked her back until her knees hit the side of the bed.

Then, I raised my head. Even in the dim light, I could make out the bright hints of passion burning in her eyes.

"I want you."

"Yes," she murmured.

"Do you want me, too?"

"Yes," she said.

"You're sure?" I exhaled with a sharp, faint curse. I cupped her cheek, cradling her face. Tears pooled in her eyes.

She lifted her delicate hand to my wrist, holding me to her. I'd hurt her and, yet, here she was, trying to give more of herself. Her emotional strength blew me away. Where I'd been weak, where I'd run, she stood regal and steadfast in her beliefs.

She humbled me and I was damn glad she'd chosen me as her lover.

"Rye, I need you inside me. *Please.*"

CHAPTER FORTY-THREE | Kate

His response was to cover my lips with his while he slid his large, callused palms over my bare shoulders and down to the hem of my top. Instead of lifting it, as I'd expected, he placed his bare hands against the tender flesh of my stomach. I loved how warm his palms were.

I twined my arms around his neck and pressed closer.

He slid his palms up, to cup my breasts, which felt heavy and full with need.

"Perfect," he whispered into my neck.

I ran my fingers across his short, thick hair and warm skull, learning this new terrain, as I slanted my mouth over his, taking this kiss deeper, showing him exactly what I wanted him to do with me, to me.

Rye's groan was more of a vibration than a sound. The kiss turned hotter still. Then, my shirt flew across the room. And Rye was over me, his chest covering my bra-clad one. My nipples were hard little peaks and I writhed against him, seeking the pressure I needed. Rye unclasped my bra and tugged it gently down my arms. I wound my fingers back through his hair, arching my back as I held him close to my chest.

He worshipped one breast then the other, alternating back and forth. He settled on the left side and pinched my right one, causing a flicker of pleasure just this side of pain that shot directly to my core.

I panted and I struggled with the hem of his shirt. He rose long enough to do that male, one-handed tug from the back and his shirt flew across the room to join mine.

I ran my hands over his pecs and the new tattoo there. It was a beautiful combination of symbols and words that made the shape of... My eyes flew to his.

"Yes. I got the rose to remind me of you."

"It's beautiful," I said, my voice thick.

I slid my thumbs over the image before I continued down his hard, firm belly. His stomach quivered under my touch as one of my fingers eased below his belly button to the waistband of his jeans.

Rye blew out a harsh breath. He grasped my hand and brought it to his mouth, kissing the knuckles on each of my fingers before pulling the hand above my head.

"Don't tease me," he whispered in my ear.

"Why?" I asked.

He licked a hot path down my throat to the swell of my breast. He looked up at me, his eyes burning.

"Because I want this to last. I want to make tonight good for you. A memory you deserve."

My heart melted as every inch of my body softened further at both Rye's words and the look on his face.

"For the record, the fact that you just said that is amazing. And I want that for you, too."

His smile lit up his face and my breath caught in my throat.

Hovering over me, clean-shaven and broody, Rye looked masculine, in control. Like one of those warriors of old.

"You want to make this memorable for me?" he asked just before he dipped his head to take my nipple back in his mouth. He teased my sensitive skin, causing me to quiver.

"Y-yes," I gasped.

He let my nipple go with a pop and pushed off me in one lithe movement. He bent down and unlaced his boots, then toed them off. He settled against the headboard, rearranging the pillows behind his back. His eyes lit with that same wicked humor I'd seen before on that first night when he kissed my cheek before walking away.

"Strip for me, Rose."

I wrinkled my nose as I turned to look at him.

"There is a Rose called Katherine. I looked it up. It's pretty, but you are more like an Amalia Rose. A sweet, creamy, flaming-haired confection. I want you naked. *Now.*"

At my raised eyebrow, he added, "Please."

I lay there for another moment, soaking up his words before I rolled off the bed and kicked off my sandals. With slow, almost languid motions, I stripped off my pants so that I was clad only in my panties.

Rye's stare burned hotter than fire as it licked over my flesh.

"Come here," he said, his voice hoarse. The vein in his neck pulsed.

I lifted my hair off my neck as I turned to the side, giving him the view of my arched spine and raised, perky chest, my almost flat stomach and the profile of my rounded bottom cheek.

I faced him, loving how fast he was breathing. The tip of his tongue peeked out from behind his lips. Instead of coaxing me, he shot off the bed and pulled my body flush to his, his hands caressing me.

I became pliant in his arms, reveling in the feel of his big hands. My panties pooled around my ankles. His hand once more cupped my bottom and he tugged me tight to him until I was cradling his erection against the soft give of my belly.

I maneuvered so that I could slide my hands between us and I rested my hand over his turgid length, humming in the back of my throat in appreciation. I'd missed the slick, hard slide of him between my thighs.

He placed open-mouthed kisses up my neck, over my jaw and back to my lips.

I unzipped his pants and shoved my hands along the sides of his hips so that his jeans and tight cotton underwear fell to the floor.

I stepped back in until we were pressed skin-to-skin from lips to legs.

He slid one hand down my thigh to my knee and hitched my leg up, opening my body. His other hand cupped my warm center.

I pressed tighter into the kiss, my nails digging into his flanks. Slowly, he lowered me to the mattress and then settled between my thighs. I explored his length, squeezing him in my palm as he slid one finger into my body.

"Feel good?" he asked.

"Yes," I breathed. "So good."

"Don't stop," he said as he dropped back to take my lips in another steaming kiss.

The kisses turned frenzied as he pressed his thumb to my clit and worked two fingers inside me. My hips shot upward, only for Rye to press downward, keeping me tight to the bed.

He continued to work me with those incredibly dexterous fingers, and it wasn't long before I came in long, lush waves of pleasure.

Rye kissed and caressed me even as I sank back into the mattress, the tension fading from my limbs. My body remained warm and pliant and after a few moments of his ministrations, my skin flushed hotter.

He sat back on his heels as he surveyed my body. I'd let go of his thick erection to clutch at the bedspread when I orgasmed.

Rye slid from the bed and dug out his wallet, pulling out a few condoms; he kept one in his hand and set the rest on the bedside table. I smiled, loving his replay of our first time. He grinned back, eyes dancing.

"We have all night," he said.

"And you plan to use every minute of it."

"Damn straight. You are so gorgeous. I can't wait to be inside you."

Normally, I wasn't big on talking during sex, but Rye said such sweet, wonderful things to me, I never wanted him to stop.

He ripped open the condom before I could reach for it or for him. Instead, I raked my nails down his thighs and his hips jutted forward.

Covered in the thin latex, Rye held himself in one hand as he nudged at my swollen lips.

"So pretty and pink," he said.

The wide head slipped inside me and I brought my knees up, wanting to take more even as my body stretched to accommodate his girth. He pulled back and then pressed in, deeper this time.

I gripped the comforter again as he kept up his slow, gentle glide in and out, settling into me a bit more with each thrust until his balls slapped against the cheeks of my rump. His cock filled me, pulsing my welcoming warmth. I tried to raise my hips but Rye shook his head even as his hands moved to pin me to the bed.

"Let me love you nice and slow, Kate. Like you deserve."

My body remained taut and more than ready for another climax, but I tried to do what Rye asked. I wanted to move, I wanted to relieve the delicious pressure that grew with each of his thrusts.

He bent over me and nipped at my neck, rolling a tendon between his teeth. My breath hitched and my foot slammed against the bed. My head thrashed back and forth as that need coiled tighter and tighter in my belly.

Rye kept his pace deliberate and unhurried, nearly exiting so that just the fat crown sat inside me before pressing back in. I lifted my legs to wrap around his waist, but Rye grabbed each leg and bent my knees toward my chest, further opening me to his rhythm. His breath hitched, then sped up as he stared down at me, his mouth open slightly.

The change in position caused his pelvis to bump my clit. He swirled his hips, and I gasped. He did it again. I couldn't believe how deep he was inside me. I ached with the need to spasm around him, to release the pent-up tension quivering through me. He went back to his in-and-out pattern as his eyes began to glaze. The next time he swirled his hips, I exploded.

He held himself still above me, a sheen of perspiration outlining each of his features and the hard planes of muscle in his chest.

This orgasm was longer and more intense than the last. I couldn't look away from his desire-laden expression. As fainter ripples drifted through me, Rye bent and kissed me, harder and with less finesse than before. His hips bucked into mine, once, twice. On the fourth push, he groaned as he released deep, deep inside me.

CHAPTER FORTY-FOUR | Rye

I lay there on top of Kate, struggling to catch my breath. The force of that climax took me by surprise. She wiggled a little and I realized I needed to release my hold on her ankles.

"Give me a sec. I'll move."

She surprised me by wrapping her legs around my waist and her arms around my neck. "I don't want you to. Not yet."

Her voice was a little breathy and too sexy for me to handle, especially since I still had my hands on her sleek curves.

We stayed like that for a long time. Finally, I eased from her hold. "Be right back," I said, holding on to the condom with one hand.

I cleaned up and turned to look in the mirror. My lips were redder and swollen and wouldn't stop smiling. But it was my eyes that caught my attention. They were peaceful, happy even, and without the turbulent expression I'd become immured to since… well, since Ike's birth, really.

Kate sat up in my bed, her gorgeous hair spilling across the pillows and her creamy shoulders. I liked her there—very much.

She hadn't put on any clothes.

Good.

She nodded to the bedside table where a tall glass of water stood. "I ran downstairs. Thought you might be thirsty."

I settled my hip next to hers and picked up the glass. "Thanks."

I took a sip, then held it out to her, but she shook her head. "Already had some." Her gaze became serious, a bit worried. "Do you want to check on Ike?"

Much as I appreciated Kate's understanding, I wasn't ready yet to leave her.

Part of me had known I never would be, and now, the rest of me had caught up.

But that was too serious for this moment, so I set the glass aside and brushed her wild curls away from her face. "Sit tight, and I'll be right back."

Ike continued to sleep, his breathing deep and steady.

When I returned, she let the sheet fall from those beautiful round globes and I sat on the edge of the bed as I kissed her the way she deserved—languid and deep. She wrapped her arms around my neck and tugged me back down to her.

———— ★ ————

Later, much later, we were both so spent, I could barely pull up the sheet and comforter to cover our sweat-cooled nude bodies.

"How long can you stay?" I asked.

She laid her hand on my chest. "Jenna gave me a week. It's total guilt trip time off, but I'm taking it." Kate yawned. She snuggled closer to me.

"Thank you for letting me be here. I missed Ike so much."

I squeezed her tighter to me. "He missed you, too."

"I really love him, Rye. He's amazing. So strong, so positive." She lifted her head, eyes sleepy and sated. That was a look I'd never forget, the perfectness of languid Kate in my bed, even as I tensed under her.

Never had I thought I'd find a woman who could love my son as much as I did.

But, once I'd lost my attitude with Cam and paid attention to Kate, I'd seen a family who cared deeply about my son and me. I didn't know what I'd done to deserve their respect or interest and it worried me, still, that I couldn't reciprocate the way Kate deserved.

"He'll make an amazing big brother," she said with a smile.

And I could see what she wanted—her body rounding with our child as Ike rubbed her belly. The rowdiness of large family dinners and holidays. Ones her brothers, their wives, and mother could partake in, enlarging our family with even more love and laughter.

She snuggled against me. "You've given me a future, Rye. The one I always wanted."

Worry gripped my throat. I hadn't been honest with her. Not about the future I could offer her.

"Kate, I…"

Her deep even breaths stopped the words.

I pulled her tighter to me, knowing once she heard what I'd done, she'd leave. As she should.

CHAPTER FORTY-FIVE | Kate

Rye woke before me. I opened my eyes to find him looking at me.

"That's not creepy at all," I said.

He grinned but his facial features and shoulders seemed stiff, as if he expected bad news.

"I like watching you. It's easier to do when you don't know—that way you're not self-conscious while I'm ogling you."

The blush heated my cheeks. "Do you do that often?"

He nodded, his eyes solemn. "Every chance I get."

I grabbed his shirt off the floor, the closest item I could reach, and slid it over my head.

"I guess we should get up. Check on Ike, and, you know, make breakfast or something." I fidgeted with the hem of his shirt, uncomfortable now that I didn't know where I stood, even though I'd been the one to push for the hot sexy times all night long.

Rye rose and pulled on his boxer-briefs. I sighed with a hint of sadness as his muscled thighs and taut buttocks disappeared from view. He turned and gathered me into his arms. I rested my head against his chest, wishing I could stay there forever.

"I love you, Kate."

I wrapped my arms around his middle and squeezed. "I love you, too."

He held me long enough for me to feel the faint tremors in

his arms. "I need to tell you something," he said. "Something I really should have told you before. But I worried about what you'd say…"

I frowned, his nervousness making me nervous. "What is it? It's not like you're going to tell me you don't want kids, right?" I joked.

He paled further.

CHAPTER FORTY-SIX | Rye

Before I managed to explain, Ike stumbled into the room.

"I'm hungry," he groaned, holding his stomach.

"All right. I'll get you some breakfast," I said. "And I'll make Kate some of Grandpa's fancy coffee."

She stood rooted to the spot while I threw on a pair of jeans. I picked up Ike and carried him down the stairs, my stomach aching with the worry of where we'd left the conversation between us.

Kate took her time in the shower and getting dressed. Ike ate and was listening to some music, squishing some clay into awkward blobs when Kate entered the kitchen. Her eyes darted around cautiously.

I made her a coffee with lots of frothy milk and some chocolate syrup from my father's fancy Italian machine. She set it aside untouched.

"You need to tell me whatever it is that's bothering you," she said in a low voice. "Now. I'm freaking out."

Ike remained engrossed in his project. His small tongue poked out between his lips as he pounded the latest blob with both fists.

"Well, see…"

"Daddy can't have kids," Ike said.

"What?" Kate breathed.

"You mean what you were talking about upstairs? My mommy said that he can't have kids. That she made sure of it."

"You can't have children?" she whispered.

I rocked back on my heels. "No. I can't."

"May I ask why?" she asked, her voice modulated to a false neutrality.

I set my own mug of coffee on the counter.

"I had a vasectomy."

"When?" she asked, still using that carefully-controlled tone.

"After Ike was born."

Her mouth dropped open. "A doctor performed that procedure on you when you were…"

My cheeks reddened. I was young, stupid. I could see the thoughts because they now ran through my mind—more like screamed through it. I struggled to explain, knowing the words would be inadequate.

"I didn't want… We were having problems. Deirdre was freaked out she might get pregnant again, and we were still learning about Ike's eyes, trying therapies because of his preemie status…"

I didn't want to say the words, not there in front of my son. I didn't want him to know I hadn't been strong enough to even consider another child like him. That, for a brief time, I didn't see Ike as the blessing he was.

I crouched down. "Hey, buddy, it had nothing to do with you, okay?" I said, my voice soft. "I love you and always will."

Ike's face continued to remain twisted with anger and maybe frustration.

"You didn't want me to live with you for years and years."

My eyes slammed shut as pain lanced through me.

"I did want you, but the judge said that my job wasn't good enough. That's why I took over Grandpa's business." I turned a supplicating gaze toward Kate, needing her to understand. "Once I had *this* job, the judge said you could live with me and not Grandfather Keen."

"I like living here more. I love you, Daddy. I wish Kate was my mommy, because she's always wanted to spend time with me."

I stared down at my son, exposed, raw from his words—from all my failures.

Kate settled into the chair next to Ike and held his hand. She seemed to fall into a trance, a deep, painful place that, somehow, she and Ike shared together. I knelt on the wood flooring, knees aching, as I contemplated them both. And it hit me hard. Ike forgave me for my faults even when he shouldn't. To him, it was simple. I showed him love and was interested in him, unlike Deirdre and her family.

But Kate…maybe she was thinking about her relationship with her father, the man who treated everyone else around him as unwanted. The one who, she felt, pretended to love her out of spite for the rest of the family—to fracture it further.

She must also be thinking about her brothers who had kept the details of her parentage from her, not trusting her to handle the situation as they deemed most appropriate. Same with her mother. And now, me.

I'd done that to her. I'd not told her about my choice, before I knew her, to not have kids. I'd not given her all the information.

She must think that once she told me she loved me, I expected her to fall in line with what I'd already decided I wanted.

Like her father, her mother, and her brothers.

Worse, I hadn't treated her like an equal, like the smart, capable talented woman she was. The one I craved at my side.

I swallowed hard, my eyes on her face, as I waited for Kate to respond. She looked at me, and the pain I saw there would have sent me to my knees if I wasn't there already.

"I need to get down to Austin. To my…" She clenched her jaw, but her mouth still trembled. "I just need to go."

"Are you mad at Daddy, too?"

She blew out a breath, her face softened and she cupped Ike's cheek. He pressed in tighter, his bandages stark against his skin.

"No, sweetie. I'm not angry." She blinked in rapid succession as moisture filled her eyes. Not one tear fell but the tip of her nose reddened as did the skin around her eyes.

Before she said anything further, the doorbell rang.

"You better get that," Kate said.

I wanted to ignore the bell and focus on Kate, on getting her to see that I hadn't intended to lie to her about the vasectomy and I never wanted to hurt her. The bell chimed again, followed by a sultry female voice calling my name.

I groaned out a curse.

CHAPTER FORTY-SEVEN | Kate

Rye went to the door. His second curse drew me from the kitchen. A long-legged brunette in the tiny dress stood on the porch, rocking the newest season of Manolos like a freaking Kardashian.

"Who is that?" I asked, though my twisting stomach pretty much told me.

I hadn't expected an answer, but Ike tucked his hand into mine. He tilted his head, listening to the woman's voice.

"That's my mommy," Ike said, sounding nonplussed.

"Oh," I said gripping the coffee cup I'd snagged off the counter as if it were a talisman that would ward off evil. "Um…I guess I'll just wait in the kitchen, then."

"Who's *she*?" I heard Deirdre ask. She had a slightly raspy voice that set my teeth on edge.

I missed Rye's reply because I was screaming so loudly in my head that I was the woman he was with—the one who loved both Rye and Ike more than she ever could. Tears stung my eyes but I managed to blink them back, thankful for the distance between us and my ability to turn around and walk back into the kitchen.

I needed to go upstairs and close my suitcase. I needed to get to my car and head back to Austin. But I couldn't leave Ike in the kitchen, his face bandaged, unable to see, alone.

So I sat with him and made shapes in the clay, all the while thinking I'd never get this opportunity again. That Rye had taken it from me.

CHAPTER FORTY-EIGHT | Rye

"What are you doing here?" I asked, my voice as tight as my shoulders.

I needed to get Deirdre out of there. The slight tremble of Kate's mouth, the reddening tip of her nose, told me she wasn't okay with Deirdre's presence. I wasn't either. I needed to talk to Kate.

Her face crumpled. "I didn't know if Ike would want to see me. If…" She sniffled. "I wanted to be here yesterday, but I couldn't sit in that hospital, waiting to find out if he was blind or dead or…"

She trailed off, looking lost and small.

"I brought him this."

It was a card. I bit back my retort that his eyes were covered in bandages and he was barely five, so he couldn't read the words.

"Thanks," I managed. "I'll be sure to read it to him. Or," I didn't want to make the offer—not with Kate inside, no doubt still reeling from the bomb I'd dropped on her this morning. "Or you could read it to him yourself."

Her smile was tentative with hope shining from her eyes. She darted her gaze to the house, then touched my wrist—a fleeting gesture that made us both squirm a little. We were long past the stage where touch came naturally between us.

"Daddy told me to tell you that he's sorry about the bribery."

Her lip quivered. "He said I needed to tell you Ike will always be on the company insurance, whether that's primary or secondary, and that Daddy set up Ike a trust fund. He said he's not leaving you a red cent and you still need to learn how to keep your damn paws to yourself."

I snorted. "A direct quote, no doubt."

Deirdre shrugged. "Daddy's not leaving the company to me or to Ike. Well…that's not quite true. I get to keep all the shares but I won't ever run it. Daddy hired a man for that." She hesitated. "One I'm going to marry."

"Congratulations," I said. And I meant it.

Deirdre had been her father's pet more than a child and he hadn't liked me usurping his place. I'd never been able to. I hadn't coddled her enough to fulfill the role. First, I'd been too freaked out by the impending baby, and then too busy with Ike's neonatal needs to focus on Deirdre.

After spending time with Kate, I understood much better what I'd settled for.

"Want to sit for a minute?" I asked.

"Yeah. Okay. I'm not going to stay long. I mainly wanted to tell you all that. And…"

She settled into a chair. "I've never been much of a mother to Ike. I realize now that part of it was my age. I was so young and scared."

"So was I," I said.

She tipped her head so her long dark hair spilled over her shoulder and arm, her eyes wide, searching mine for an elusive answer. "But you've always been so good at parenting."

Deirdre looked down at her hands, her cheeks flaming. "It's just…I want to be involved in his life but not the day-to-day. Randall—that's my fiancé—he's in his forties and doesn't want to have kids. He likes being able to pick up and go on a weekend trip, to eat at fancy restaurants…"

"All the same activities you enjoy," I said without heat. Those hadn't been my favorite activities. I didn't need or crave luxury— not like Deirdre did.

She studied me for a moment.

"I'm not judging," I said, holding out my hands, palms up. "I think it's great you've found someone you can love."

She tossed her hair back over her thin, tanned shoulders. Kate's skin was paler, dotted with freckles. I'd kissed many of them last night. I still had more to map and love. I desperately wanted the chance to do so.

"We're well matched," Deirdre said.

Nothing about love. But then, maybe, that wasn't what drove Deirdre. I shouldn't project my needs onto her. Just because I loved Kate with my whole heart and soul didn't mean Deirdre was cut out to do the same.

She wasn't. She didn't like inconvenience. She adored fancy brands and expensive items. Honestly, if I'd thought before I fucked—and fucked things up—I would have realized quickly Deirdre and I were never suited for more than a short fling— one I'd tried to extend into forever because that was what was expected. That I man up.

But I'd failed to man up when I caved to pressure and married the girl, still more of a child herself. And I'd failed to man up when I allowed Quentin and the judge to take my son.

Her words broke into my reverie.

"He takes care of me, Rye. I know that sounds silly, but I'm not ever going to be a woman who wants a job outside the home. I never wanted to be more than the kind of wife my mother was—a gracious hostess who had a hot meal on the table when my husband came home."

That was true. Deirdre had been raised to be dependent, to dote on her provider. I hadn't provided as well as she needed me to and she hadn't been able to be the partner I needed her to be.

"Nice of you to come all this way and give me the heads-up in person," I said.

She shrugged. "I wanted to come to Dallas to look for a gown. I didn't like any of the ones in Mobile or Knoxville."

I smiled because that was such a Deirdre thing to say.

"So, you're saying I get Ike full time?" I asked.

She nodded. "If you're good with that. I mean, I know I have partial custody, and I love him and I want to see him and talk to him and stuff…"

"But you don't want to raise him."

"I think you're much better at that than I'll ever be," Deirdre said.

"Kate's better," I mumbled.

Deirdre smiled. "That's your lady friend?"

"Yeah."

Deirdre leaned forward like she was going to share a secret. "We really didn't do each other any favors. I'm sorry I screwed you up so bad, Rye."

"I'm sorry I couldn't see past the day he was born and realize that Ike would be my biggest blessing."

"Don't be too hard on yourself. He had lots of issues. Even the NICU staff weren't sure he'd pull through." Deirdre took a long, deep breath. "But we both know what lies and half-truths can do to a relationship. We were much better as a fling than as husband and wife."

I laughed because I'd thought that myself moments before. The air between us felt clearer. I felt lighter knowing she and I were in a healthy place. "You got smart, Dee Dee."

She smirked as she rolled her eyes at my old pet name. "I grew up a bit, Rye Rye." She sobered. "I hope you find your own happy."

I looked at the door behind us, wondering if I'd get the chance to fix my screw up of not telling Kate about my vasectomy sooner. Because I couldn't give up on Kate. She was *my* happy. And my future.

CHAPTER FORTY-NINE | Kate

I stood from the table, the chair scraping back in a rough set of bumps across the oak flooring, as the front door shut. Rye's strident tread was followed by the softer click of heels.

Deirdre hesitated in the doorway as her eyes swept the room. Her eyes widened at the sight of his bandaged face. A faint growl emanated from the back of my throat. I didn't remember moving toward Ike but my hand was on his shoulder before either of Rye or Deirdre managed to blink.

"What's going on?" Ike asked.

"Your mom's here," Rye said.

"Just for a quick hello," Deirdre said. The sensual quality of her voice was less sexy when she was nervous. A large smile slid over her features, lighting up eyes that were similar in shape and color to Ike's.

I felt gut-punched as I noticed more similarities between Ike and Deirdre—like the cowlick at the crown of both their heads and the twitch at the corner of their mouths when they appeared nervous.

"You must be…" she trailed off.

Rye came around and laid his hand on my lower back. "This is Kate. She's my girlfriend."

Deirdre's smile widened further. "I'm so glad for both of you."

Huh. Not the evil queen I'd expected. I needed to recalibrate my response. "A pleasure to meet you, Deirdre. Ike's told me about you."

There, that sounded pleasant.

Deirdre's gaze shot back down to Ike before landing again on my face. She tilted her head as she studied me for a long moment.

"I…er…I brought you a card." She laid it on the table, her cheeks flaming as she stared at his bandaged eyes. "You can, um, look at it…later," Deirdre said. She settled into the chair next to Ike's and moved closer, her arms at awkward angles as she hugged him.

"Your dad said the surgery went well," she said. But her face remained unsure, and my first stirrings of compassion rose. Deirdre had no idea how to connect with Ike. She second-guessed herself and made the entire situation stressful for both of them.

"I'll get to see to climb trees and play catch with Daddy."

Deirdre brushed her fingers over Ike's bandages in a whisper of a movement as tears slid down her cheeks. "I'm so happy for you," she said.

Tears formed in my own eyes because she meant it—she wanted the best for her son, and she'd realized she wasn't it—not as his mother, anyway.

"So, um, I'm going to go." She stood. "Could we…do you have a minute?"

Rye looked pale and on the verge of saying no, but I beat him to it. "Of course."

We stepped back out toward the front entrance, Deirdre

leading the way. I didn't mind trailing behind her—it gave me a moment to smooth out my jumbled emotions and get a handle on my expression.

She opened the door and stepped through, settling in one of the wicker chairs that sat in front of the large living room window.

"He's one of the good ones," Deirdre said.

I closed the door behind me and leaned against it, trying to find my bearings. Rye having a vasectomy…I still didn't know what to do with that information.

"Is he?" I asked.

She frowned for a moment, but smoothed out her features quickly. "Yes, Rye is. He's always taken his responsibilities seriously." She glanced back at the house. "Probably because of his father—man up," she mumbled.

"What?"

Deirdre shook her head. "His father—have you met him? He's…something else. A military man. He was always telling Rye to 'man up'. But his idea of being a man never meshed well with Rye's." Deirdre grimaced. "Don't hold that against Rye—his hang-ups."

For whatever reason, those words galvanized the anger that sat in my chest since he'd told me of his vasectomy. "Making a decision to never have another child at twenty-three isn't a hang-up. It's pretty damn permanent."

Deirdre's lips fell open. Everything about her was perfect, and she made me feel frumpy and…and less-than. My bottom lip quivered.

"Yeah…about that. Did he tell you I made the appointment?"

she said, her voice ragged.

I shook my head.

"And did he tell you that Ike was in NICU and they weren't expecting him to live? And that I wouldn't let Rye touch me because the mere idea of me getting pregnant again caused me to panic? Did he tell you that his doctor tried to talk him out of it but he told the doctor he had to man up and be the husband his wife deserved? That there was no way we could afford another child like Ike? Those were my words, not his, by the way." She bit her lip as tears flowed down her face, mascara puddling under her eyes and drifting down her cheeks.

"No," I said. "I just knew he—"

"That wasn't really his decision." Deirdre straightened in her chair. She clutched the handle of her little purse tightly. "That's on me. He'll tell you this story differently…" She shook her head.

"I seduced him. He was the big music star, taking courses at the college in my hometown. I wanted him because the other girls did. And I got him."

She swiped at her cheeks. "When I found out I was pregnant, I freaked. If he hadn't shown up, I might have…" She shook her head. "I wasn't in a good place. He took me to the doctor, got me on prenatal vitamins and went to talk to my daddy. To say Daddy wasn't happy is an understatement, but Rye said he was marrying me, doing right by the baby and me. And he did. He would have quit music then, for us, but he'd signed his first big record deal right before I found out about Ike. He had obligations. So, he married me, completed his second album, and started planning a six-month tour. I…I went into labor, not really knowing what was happening."

I inched toward the other wicker chair, captivated by her story.

"I hadn't taken the vitamins. I pretended I was still just me." She breathed in deep, held it. "I didn't want to be pregnant, didn't want my life to change."

My heart ached for all of them. They'd been so young.

"We were never going to work—*I* wasn't willing to make the effort."

A newfound respect for this woman settled over me. To be so open about her failures…that took serious guts.

"I'm telling you this because Rye did everything—every single thing right. He did more than that. He's the reason Ike's here today. He even had that vasectomy to salvage our broken marriage."

She met my gaze, her eyes rimmed in makeup and red. "I regret many, many of my decisions from that time, but none as much as pushing him to…I couldn't think past Ike's problems, our problems. I'm so sorry that's going to hurt you now."

"I want kids," I said. I needed to acknowledge that ache left inside from Rye's revelation. "I've always wanted them. To find out he took that option from me…"

Deirdre lunged forward, her slender fingers wrapping around my wrist with surprising force. "He didn't. *I* did. *I* ruined his future. So, if you're mad, be mad at me."

I stared at her hand until she released me. I took a deep, painful breath.

"That doesn't change the fact I can't have the family I always wanted."

CHAPTER FIFTY | Kate

I hesitated after Deirdre left, unsure I wanted to walk back into the house. Eventually, Rye brought out my mug, once again steaming.

"I made you a new cup."

"Thanks," I said. I took it from him. Our fingers touched. My breath caught at the sensation—the connection—we had. I pulled away, taking the cup with me. I sipped, ignoring the passion swirling around us.

"Kate…"

"I don't know how I feel right now," I said.

He ran both hands over his shorn hair and down his face. "It's a shock—"

"That the man I'm dating—who knows how much I want kids—didn't tell me he can't have them?" Sure, he'd said last night, before I basically jumped him that we needed to talk, but… "It's a shock." I took another sip, not wanting to state that this revelation might well be devastating.

"My sister called," Rye said. He looked haggard. I felt old and worn out myself. "My dad's suffering some complications from his MS. Or maybe from epilepsy—the two are tied together. She was driving home at the time, so she took him directly to Parkland."

"I'll watch Ike while you go to the hospital," I said, already heading in the house.

"I can't ask you to—"

"You didn't. I offered. Now, go visit your father. Ike and I will…" I shrugged. "I don't know. I guess we'll read some books together or something."

I didn't want to stay in this house. I needed time to process, but I didn't want Ike back at the hospital if he didn't need to go.

Rye clasped my shoulders and pulled me into a hug that I didn't return because of the cup of coffee. At least, that's what I told myself. Not because I wanted desperately to tell Rye we'd be fine, that everything would work out.

I just wasn't sure it could—or would. He already had a son, so he didn't understand my desire to carry a child in my body, to hold him or her to my breast and nurture the small, sweet life. The pang of loss once more ate at my stomach.

"Would it help if you went home? I mean, to your family ranch?"

"I don't…" But I did know. "Yes."

He pulled back, his eyes sad. "Then go home. Ike and I will be okay. I'll call you, and we'll visit you as soon as I know Dad's stable."

———— ★ ————

My mother might have been surprised when I parked in her driveway later that afternoon, but she made us iced tea and listened to the whole story as we sat in her shabby, sparkling kitchen.

I appreciated that she never tried to sway me. She just let me pour out my feelings and I was caught in the confusion of what

I wanted. After using half of a box of tissues, I rose from the wooden chair.

"I'm going for a drive."

"Katie—"

"To the cemetery," I said. "I have some things to hash out with my father."

Mom continued to look nonplussed, but she nodded.

I pulled up to the cemetery and stalked to my father's grave. I dropped my hands to my hips and glared at his gravestone.

"This is all your fault, you know. You were an absolute ass to Cam. I wish I'd seen the truth earlier—that I couldn't trust you, that your love was conditional, and that just because some people loved you didn't mean you loved them back."

I bent forward and smacked the cold granite. "How could you be so awful to Cam? He's thoughtful, hardworking, so damn talented…"

My words trailed off as a realization choked me. "Good golly." I sounded like Jenna. "You were jealous. Of your stepson. That's why…" I shook my head and pressed my hand to my abdomen. "I think I'm going to be sick."

"You know, I hadn't thought of it like that, but I see your logic," a voice said nearby. Jenna stood a few feet behind me, hands cradling her growing bump. Her face was still thin and her eyes looked too large now. Her elbows appeared like angry nodules through her skin, but her tummy was growing and her eyes lit with an internal hope that seemed to thunder through her.

"Your mom didn't want you going anywhere alone, and I'm sick of my bedroom." She shrugged, but I knew the enforced rest must be driving Jenna toward madness. She stayed busy because it quieted her racing mind.

"How are you feeling?" I asked, moving toward her.

"Like this kid is eating my internal organs. That's not going to change until junior here pops out of me. Now, back to what you were saying. Maybe Cam would feel better if he realized Laurence was jealous."

I shrugged. "If you think it'll help." I wrapped my hand around Jenna's biceps. "Let's get you back in the vehicle."

Jenna swallowed, her lip quivering faintly. "How about a stroll to that bench?" she asked, her tone so hopeful, I couldn't tell her no.

I kept my grip light but firm on her arm as I steered us toward the wooden bench a few hundred yards away.

"I never had a chance to tell you thanks for your help last week with the client from hell and my health issues. And the help the week before. And not being too angry when I said I'd fire you."

I offered her a faint smile. "That's what I'm here to do."

Jenna stopped walking, and for a moment, I worried she was having those fake contractions. Or, worse, real ones. Panic gnawed its way up my throat.

"No, Kate. Just so we're clear about something: I lied about firing you. I could never—I mean *never*—continue the shop without you. I hired you for your ability to fix and maintain the business side, which you do so very, very well. Look at what you've done with the social media campaigns. We're getting nearly as much traffic and likes as Cam and Regan, and they've both seen growth in their fandoms and sales that are correlated to your posts.

You are a genius, and all the artists you showcase are benefitting. The shop's never been more popular or more lucrative."

I snorted. "Well, you're going to be taking a hiatus, so it's not like growth is ideal right now."

She settled on the bench. I chose not to mention her rough breathing. "True. But that just means the work will be there when I'm ready to come back to it. That's because of you, Kate."

She looked so earnest that my cheeks flamed. "And here I thought you hired me to deal with the rock stars."

"Ugh. There are so many snotty man divas." She sighed. "I don't like man divas. Or women divas. I like low-key, easy-going people." She grimaced. "This baby is not one of those. I'm so very ready to have my insides back."

I settled beside her on the bench, taking her hand. "You'll feel better—"

"When the baby finally comes out," Jenna finished. "Which isn't to say that will be a cakewalk either." She shifted her weight. "I spend so much of my time afraid. But, then, I'd be happy to give up my organs as well as sleep and sanity if it meant this little bundle could come out healthy. That we could ensure it."

"No one can guarantee anything," I said.

Jenna nodded, her face grave. "That's the truth. I mean, look at me. I shouldn't be having a kid. I'm too much of a mess."

"You are not," I said, shocked.

Jenna's small smile showed amusement. "Oh, I am. But...you know what? I love this baby like crazy." She cradled the growing mass of her stomach. "Evie tried to explain it to me—loving a child. She said it's no different than the love and joy she feels with each of Paige's milestones versus little Cline's. She and Kai love both those kids something fierce, but, she points out, her stomach was flatter and her hips tighter with Paige."

"Because she didn't give birth to her like she did Cline," I said, a little offended for the munchkin.

"That's my point," Jenna said, tipping her head back toward the sun. "Exactly. I'm going to have this baby just like Regan's going to have hers, and Evie had Cline, and we're going to worry and freak out about everything that could go wrong with the baby and the birth, what we eat and our new post-baby bodies. I'm just saying Evie was correct that you can love any child and not have some of the guilt and discomfort associated with the actual carrying of said child."

Evie was a good friend of ours who lived in Seattle. She and Jenna went back many years to when Jen attended university there. She'd met Evie through Kai, who played in a band with Asher Smith's stepdaughter's boyfriend. Confusing, sure, a little. But Evie was a great person, and I loved her like a sister. Abbi, too.

I shook my head, my lips tilting up in a small smirk. "Laying it on thick again, Jenna."

She blinked at me, all innocence. "Maybe this is just a different perspective."

I fidgeted on the bench. "I do love Ike. More than anything. But I'm not his mother and never will be."

"Biologically? No. But you love him as a mother should. Why can't that be enough? Why can't he be enough for you *to* mother? Why do there have to be more kids that come from your body for you to be fulfilled?"

Why, indeed. And why would I push for more than that when I was so miserable without them both?

"You and Mama worked fast," I muttered.

"When it's important, we are lightning," she said. She grimaced and winced. "I need to lie down again soon."

We began the short trek between the gravestones.

CHAPTER FIFTY-ONE | Rye

Ike remained quiet, lost in thought, as we packed bags for the two of us. Kate had insisted on catching an Uber to get her car, not wanting to bog me down.

She wouldn't have, but I knew she was struggling with my admission, and I didn't want to push her too hard.

Once Kate left, I went to my sister's room and packed her another few days' worth of clothes, though I doubted I'd coordinated the outfits to her satisfaction. Clean, fitting clothes and undergarments would have to do for Aubrey.

The hardest person to pack for was my father. I shuddered as I pulled out his starched, pressed slacks and shirts, hoping I never dressed like him. I even hated his wingtips.

As I yanked another pale blue dress shirt from its spot in the closet, the hanger fell. I bent down to retrieve it and noticed a thick, dark, leather-bound book with my name on it tucked beneath his slacks.

I settled on the floor and pulled it out. Shock detonated through me when I realized Dad had progress reports of my entire life. *Weekly.* The first few years, the notes were in my mother's writing with sweet asides about her missing him. I skimmed through those quickly.

The next few years, the detailed reports—bulleted now, and

less personal—were also in her handwriting.

The last ten years, which would be after my mother moved to Alaska, were from an inkjet printer.

She'd been sending him updates on me this whole time. And he'd *saved* them.

I flipped through some of them, my mouth falling open when I realized my father kept tabs on each of my concerts and album sales. Behind the reports were pictures, also taken weekly, of me. I'd grown from a tiny towheaded tyke into…he even had pictures of me with Kate when I took her to Stubb's.

I rubbed my thumb over her face, wishing I was there with her. As I did so, my gaze slid back to my face—and how utterly in love with her I looked. Not infatuated or in lust. Clearly in love. I closed the book, winded with emotion.

He knew everything quantitative about my life. Yet, he rarely, pretty much never, asked me about my life when we were together.

I stood, grabbing a couple of pairs of his shoes and added them to the suitcase. I zipped it and started from the room. Just before I made it to the doorway, I turned back and went into the closet, grabbing the scrapbook of my life. I hunted through his slacks row until I found another book that detailed Aubrey's life. Hers was a lavender leather embossed in silver.

I shoved them both into my father's suitcase and headed out the door.

———— ★ ————

I called Aubrey and had her come out to the plastic-covered chairs in the waiting room to watch Ike.

I entered the cool, sterilized room with its single bed and

drab walls. The floors were speckled linoleum, and a single, small window overlooked a wall across the narrow expanse of green space below.

"Are you awake?" I asked.

My father lay in the narrow hospital bed, wrinkles billowing out against his pillow, eyes sunken into his cheeks.

"Ryland?" my dad asked, his voice dazed. "You're finally home."

"You're in the hospital, Dad."

"Oh. I don't know what all this fuss is about," he blustered.

"The doctor said you had a stroke," I said. "That's a big deal—worth making a fuss. And before you yell, Aubrey and I care about you. Even if you are still trying to dictate our lives."

Dad slipped into silence. I wasn't sure if he was completely lucid or not, and I held my breath, wondering what the fallout would be from this latest health crisis.

"Aubrey played me some of your songs while we were in the car together this past week. I enjoyed them."

My chest swelled with pride because that was my father's way of telling me he loved me, too.

"Want to tell me why you have detailed biographies on both Aubrey and me?" I asked. "I found them when I was getting your clothes."

Dad swiped at his mouth. His lower lip was stiffer and didn't seem to work as well as the upper.

"I wanted to know how you were, what you were doing." He wouldn't look at me.

"Why didn't you just ask?"

"Because you and your sister hated me," he snapped.

I stared at him in shocked silence.

"You didn't want anything to do with me when I came home from the war," he said.

"That's because we barely remembered you," I told him. "You just showed up one day—"

"And expected life to fall back into the patterns that were comfortable for me. Yes, your mother explained that wasn't going to happen. But I didn't know how to fit into your lives. I was gone so much…"

My father looked so uncomfortable admitting this truth that I walked further into the room and took his hand—the one free of needles. "I would like to build a relationship with you, now."

"Because I'm dying?" Dad barked.

"Because you're my father," I said, my voice even.

"I'll think about it," he said.

Then he closed his eyes and fell asleep. So much for the big Hallmark moment I'd hoped for. But maybe I needed to be aware that this was the best way he knew how to interact—it was terrible, but he'd acknowledged my music career and my interests. That had to mean something.

──────★──────

I stayed in the room, pondering my choices. Aubrey led Ike into the room and shoved a cup of coffee in my hand. Her eyes sparkled.

"I never got to thank you. I actually met Camden Grace," she whispered as we waited for Dad to wake. "He knew I was at his show in Deep Ellum on Saturday and asked me to come on back."

"I know. I told him you'd be there."

"He's *so cool*, Rye."

"I know."

"He seems to think highly of you."

I sighed. "That's not deserved," I said.

"I know," Aubrey said with a smirk. She sipped her drink. "Except it is. You're so talented. You're such a great father. And I know you love Cam's sister something fierce."

Dad blinked his eyes open and turned to face me.

"Look, I know I've been hard on you," Dad said as if no time had passed between this sentence and the previous one. That freaked me out, but I managed to stay quiet.

"*Too* hard. Music's obviously your passion and something you're quite good at. Aubrey told me about the work you did in Austin, singing to those cancer kids." He paused again and Aubrey reached for my hand when Dad's jaw trembled. "That's leadership. Real hutzpah."

I worked hard not to crumple my Styrofoam cup. "I felt like I was making a difference. And I haven't done much of that since I moved to Dallas."

"And I made you quit that work." His voice was quiet.

Aubrey seemed taken aback enough to forget, momentarily, her interest in my relationship with Kate.

The bags under Dad's eyes emphasized his age and ill health, but he seemed alert. Even happier than I'd seen him in ages.

"I wanted to talk to you about your position with the company. I'm giving it to your sister."

The air left my lungs and my eyes burned. "What? No, Dad,

you're on medication. You're not thinking clearly. You can't be serious—"

"While Aubrey's keen to run the company, *you* were willing to drop everything you had going on to ensure it ran smoothly until she got some more experience. I still think she's too young."

He frowned and Aubrey stiffened next to me. "I'm not allowed to say too female—that'll get my ears chewed off."

I raised my eyebrow. "From me first."

"Me second," Aubrey said.

Dad shook his head, his mouth flat. "Well, she *is* too young and too female. Men need a strong leadership style."

"I'd posit your generation needed a strong leadership style." I held up my hand. "And if some of the executives don't want to follow her vision or her leadership, they are more than welcome to leave. Which is what I told them when I moved into your office."

Dad grumbled. His lower lip remained out of place with his upper one. My heart pinched. A stroke. I wasn't ready for this relationship to end, but the MS would continue to adversely impact his health.

"Well, since I don't want you wasting your God-given talent on spreadsheets, I guess I'll have to let Aubrey test out her leadership skills. But I'm awarding you twenty-five percent ownership of the company."

I shook my head. "Dad, I don't—"

"Your sister is starting with twenty-five percent and working her way up to the other twenty-five I intend to hold through incentives and sales targets."

"That doesn't seem fair—"

"She's the one who came up with the plan." Dad's tone was hard, no-nonsense.

I glanced over at Aubrey and she nodded, her eyes pleading. Well, far be it from me to mess up a deal she wanted.

"She's pleased for the opportunity to run the company, and my understanding is that you'll be available to help guide her." Dad's words slurred a little.

"You're not well. This really isn't the time—"

"There won't be a better one, Ryland. I'm not going to get better. But I'm keeping half my company right now so I can continue to veto crazy ideas you two want to try." He blinked, his eyes heavy as he struggled to keep them open. "And so I have good insurance. Christ, getting sick and decrepit is a sad, expensive business."

"We'd never let you go without care," Aubrey said, offended.

I concurred. He was difficult and downright mean sometimes, but he was also scared and sick.

"And now you don't have to worry. I've got Medicare, but I like my private policy. Got me a nice room here."

We all snorted. The brief moment of levity helped me reset my emotions.

"You need time to heal," I said. "To think this over."

"He has been, right, Dad?" Aubrey said.

"I'd already made the decision and talked to my lawyer before my brain tried to do me in. Aubrey in action is something to see." Dad turned quiet, his face softening as he caught her eye. "She reminds me of your mother."

"Aubrey knows more about the business than I do," I said. "She basically walked me through the organizational hierarchy and has a much better grasp on the inventory and sales personnel."

"Which is what Dwight told me." Dwight was the VP of operations. And one of Dad's golfing buddies. "His input swayed my decision. Well, part of the reason I've decided to make this change." He turned to face me. "By the way, I'm stepping off the board and expect you to take my place as chairman. That's a stipulation for those shares. They come with a lot of money, Ryland. You can use it for another surgery if Ike needs it. Whatever you need to ensure his wellbeing."

Being sick obviously gave my father a new perspective. He hadn't said "man up" once.

"I should have offered to pay for it outright instead of trying to force you to step into a job that would never suit you. I was so damnably ignorant. So sure my way was not just the best but right."

Wow. Just…wow. I'd planned to resign, planned to fight with him, even to use those scrapbooks as some sort of leverage… maybe an invasion of privacy or something. But he was letting me off the hook.

He sighed out a thick sound, no doubt a need to cleanse regret he carried.

"What…" I couldn't frame the rest of a question. I was free from the company. Mostly. Except for board meetings. But free enough to pursue my goals. I'd never have to rely on Deirdre, who would attach strings. That was her way. Typically, it was my father's, too, which is why this entire situation made me nervous.

Too many thoughts flitted through my mind. Ike raised his head from the chair he'd curled up in, which reminded me.

"I need to take Ike to the doctor tomorrow morning," I said. "What do you need from me to get started, Aub?"

"Nothing. I've already talked to Dwight. He's got someone cleaning the office, getting it ready for me."

A huge weight lifted from my shoulders. I couldn't wait to tell Kate the good news.

I frowned, wondering if she would consider my new-found joblessness positive.

Before I could change my mind, I pulled out my phone and sent her a long, rambling text.

———— ★ ————

Ike's eye appointment the next morning went better than I'd anticipated. Ike cried when he read some of the words on the posters Dr. Wainwright held up. Ike's gaze roved hungrily around the room.

"It's so pretty," he said. "Daddy...you're..."

I had to wipe away a few tears of my own as Ike put his hands on my cheek and stared up at me, as if seeing me for the first time. I guess he was, clearly.

Afterward, I made a stop at the closest grocery store because I needed to grab something for Kate—something that might show her how serious I was, not just about my love for her but the future I wanted to share with her. I brought in the bag of other items I'd picked up—mainly some decent coffee and muffins for Aubrey, Ike, and me. Ike had insisted on the cut cantaloupe as well, oohing and aahing over the bright color through the plastic.

My father greeted me with a stiff wave. I noted Aubrey's scrapbook in his lap and her damp eyes. She sent me a beaming smile, and my shoulders relaxed.

"We've been looking at these albums," Aubrey said, untangling herself from the side of Dad's narrow bed. She hugged me and whispered in my ear, "He might actually be a softie underneath the asshole."

I wasn't sure I was buying that, but I squeezed my sister before handing her the large coffee and bakery box of muffins. She scuttled away, diving into the food with gusto.

"Hi, Ike," my father said, his voice losing its gruff edge. "I hear your eyes are working pretty good these days."

Ike wrapped his arm around my leg, a clear sign of his growing discomfort. "They're lots better."

"That's great. Just fine. And I hear you learned to ride a bike. Your auntie showed me pictures on your dad's blog."

Before I could answer, Ike, piped up. "Daddy didn't teach me. Kate did. We have fun together."

Dad seemed flummoxed by this—not unlike his reaction to Aubrey being more than capable of running his car dealership business.

"Kate?" my father asked. "Who is this young lady?"

I rubbed the back of my neck. "The one you had your PI take photos of when I took her out to Stubb's." I hesitated for a minute, but then I opted for honesty. "I hurt her badly when I took the job overseeing the dealerships."

Dad frowned. "I had no idea you had a lady friend." He seemed surprised. The doctor had mentioned he might struggle with memories. I'd show him the photo later.

"Would that have changed your decree to come to Dallas in

exchange for health insurance?" I asked, bitterness creeping into my words.

"Hell, yes," my father barked. He shifted in the bed, grumbling. "Bring that woman in here. I want to make sure she's of good enough fiber to be involved in my grandson's life."

"I have to go get her first," I said.

"Well, what the hell are you waiting for?" Dad asked.

CHAPTER FIFTY-TWO | Rye

We drove to Austin with the same suitcases in the trunk we'd left with weeks before, just in a fancier car and with Ike mumbling the names of every item he passed on the road. He still couldn't seem to get over how blue the sky was. That would have caused me to marvel at his pleasure if I wasn't concerned about Kate's reaction to us showing up on her doorstep unannounced.

I pulled over south of Waco to ask her if she'd be home later. *I'd like to talk*, I typed.

I'm in the middle of something with my mother and Jenna. I'll be at the ranch until seven, she texted back. *Can you call me this evening?*

I glanced at the clock. No, I wasn't going to call her. But I wasn't ready to tell her I was already most of the way to Austin either.

"What do you think about grabbing some ice cream cones from Amy's?"

"Yes!" Ike bellowed.

We stopped at the cute shop on Pecan Street and stood in line. Ike and I enjoyed trying a few flavors before settling on chocolate raspberry for him and decadent apple cinnamon for me. We settled into the spindly metal chairs and made serious work of our treat.

"Is Kate mad at you?" Ike asked.

I startled to find his eyes fixed on me. The new glasses he wore were thinner and his eyes seemed brighter, more engaged behind the lenses.

"I'm not sure she's mad, but I think...." How to explain the details to a five-year-old?

I took a bite of my cone, trying to collect my thoughts. "She's upset. I didn't tell her about me not being able to have kids as soon as I should have."

Ike licked a long drip just before it slipped onto his fingers. "Why?"

Kids always slammed straight into the heart of the matter. "I was afraid I'd lose her."

"But if she loves you enough, then she'll forgive you."

I smiled at him but it felt bittersweet. I wasn't sure how to tell my son that some dreams couldn't be reworked or forgotten. For Kate, one of those was her own child.

I pulled my sleek sedan in behind Kate's sporty red car after four that afternoon. I couldn't wait to see her any longer. Heat shimmered across the meadow as I looked up at the modest home where Kate and her brothers grew up. With a short mental pep talk, I grabbed the sack, hoping it was enough.

Ike's hand came down on my shoulder, his small face appearing between the two front seats. "She loves us," he said, as if the world were really that simple.

I tried to smile at him, but this time Ike was the one to pat me again, offering reassurance.

He flung open the car door and ran toward the porch. He

didn't trip once. My heart turned over at the apparent ease Ike now had in his own body.

I eased out of the car more slowly.

Ike knocked while practically dancing. When Kate opened the door, he barreled out into the hall, his arms wrapped tight around her, his face pressed into her belly.

She embraced him. Jasmine peered around the corner and smiled when she saw Kate and Ike.

"Want to help me bake a pie, Ike?" she called.

His whole body straightened and he zipped around Kate toward her mother. That left Kate and me alone. I stood just outside the open door, the cool waft of air conditioning unable to slow the prickles of heat from the late summer afternoon. Sweat bloomed across my skin and my heart thundered.

Before I could change my mind, I leaned in and kissed Kate. Well, it was more of a claiming of her mouth—me telling her just how much she mattered to me.

"Will you come outside?" I asked, stepping back.

"Um, sure."

She closed the door and stared up at me, two fingers touching her lips.

I lifted a wrapped box from a brown bag and thrust it into her hands.

"Anything you need. I'm all in. I'll show you just how much I love you forever. Please. Give me this shot."

———— ★ ————

She opened the box with a shaking hand.

"A turkey baster?" She wrinkled her nose. "Um."

My stomach dropped to my feet. "Crap. No, this is not a knock on your cooking. I thought…well, I thought it was a bit better than putting the appointment card in there."

Her brow furrowed. "I don't understand."

"I'm going to try to reverse the vasectomy. It may not work, but the amount and quality of the sperm should improve, so if nothing else, eventually we could try artificial insemination. I mean, that is if you still want to have a kid. I mean. With me." The words poured out in a rush, tripping over each other in my haste to explain.

Her lips parted and her eyes rounded. "Oh. *Oh*."

Then she turned quiet, staring down at the turkey baster. That had been a bad idea. I needed a big gesture. Something that proved how committed I was. Maybe the ring would have been smarter, even if it was bought in haste.

I sucked in a deep breath and resettled my weight. The porch boards creaked under my feet.

"I made a rash choice at twenty-one. I regret it now, not so much for me. I'm still terrified about having another kid, but I shouldn't have expected you to fall in line with my choices. I should have been honest with you."

"Yes," she murmured. "You should have." She raised her head and met my gaze. "Would you still love me, would you still want me, if I were pregnant?"

"Right now?" I asked. My heart kicked into my ribs and I gulped. "I mean…are you?"

She gripped the turkey baster in both hands, her knuckles white. "I asked you a question. I want your honest answer."

I looked into her eyes. They were gray with flecks of blue. Stormy from worry and a bit defiant. Because Kate was defiant. She had to be in her life, to get ahead, to prove her worth. And I loved that about her, just as I always would.

"Yeah. I would. I'll *always* love you."

She seemed to deflate a little. Then, her lower lip quivered and she dropped her head into her hands, the turkey baster clattering to the floorboards.

CHAPTER FIFTY-THREE | Kate

He loved me. *Rye really loved me.*

"Are you?" he asked.

I lifted my face from my hands, blinking back tears of relief.

"Am I what?" I asked.

"Pregnant?"

I tilted my head to the side as I considered both Rye's question and what I wanted from my future.

"I'd like to be," I said, my voice soft with the longing I'd felt from the moment my brothers both announced they'd be fathers. "Someday. Maybe even soon. But, no, I'm not pregnant."

"Does that mean you'll give me the chance to knock you up?" He blinked, his cheeks turning red. "Um, I mean, are you willing to date me?"

My heart raced, making me giddy. I had to smile at him. He wanted the chance to have a baby with me—even after all he'd been through with Ike.

How did this man make me feel this way *still*? Maybe the answer was he always would.

"I know this sounds silly, but you're all I've seen, all I've wanted since I heard you sing." My lips curved into a rueful smile. "I would have done it—taken you to my bed that first night we met. I don't even kiss on the first date, and within an hour or two of meeting you, I wanted to be in yours in every way."

"Ah, Kate." He pressed his lips to mine, his large hands cupped my cheeks, cradling me with his palms. "You are so special to me. Beautiful inside and out."

I clasped his sturdy wrists in my hands. "I'm not perfect."

His lip twitched in that slight smirk that told me he was still nervous. "Neither am I. But I love you, and I'll do my best to make you happy. Even if it means going back to the urologist and letting him cut into my balls."

I choked a little. "Umm."

His eyes burned into mine as he settled over me. "I'm serious. I'll go."

"Not, like, *right* now. But…yeah. I mean, eventually. When we're ready…" I trailed off as a new concern bubbled up. "Is it that bad?"

Rye's lip curled in distaste. "It's not pleasant. But…" He shook his head, eyes downcast. "I couldn't see past Ike's problems and feeling like I caused them."

He looked up and his eyes swirled with emotion.

"I couldn't see the possibilities of someone like you breathing life and joy and so much sunshine into our lives."

"I don't know what the future will hold—kids we have biologically or that we adopt or what," I said. "But I do know I don't want to put limits on our family, on what it could look like or the love we'll feel for each other."

His expression warmed me like a much-needed hug. "I agree."

I grinned as I leaned in closer. "You're just saying that to get in my panties."

His answering smile turned mischievous and his eyes lit up. "Nope."

He paused, brows lowering into a sultry smolder that caused my belly to tumble in anticipation.

"Well, maybe," he murmured, inching closer to me. "Is it working?"

"Yes." I pressed my lips to his and the kiss spiraled out, lush and brimming with possibilities. I pulled back, a little off-kilter and breathless.

He pressed his forehead to mine. "You deserve romance and flowers and big, huge gestures of love."

"I liked this one. I'm going to frame that turkey baster, put it in my living room."

"Can we stay with you tonight?" Rye asked, eyes still burning with passion.

"You better," I replied.

Ike flung open the door. "Are you fixed now? Can I go into the yard and look for Sergeant Pepper?"

I laughed as I took Rye's hand. He gave my fingers a gentle squeeze. "Absolutely."

We followed Ike into the house. Rye stopped to talk to my mother while I trailed Ike out the back door and into the yard. He darted around like a sparrow while I leaned my arms against the porch rail.

Rye stepped out and wrapped an arm around my waist. The day was too hot for us to touch, but I wasn't complaining.

"You handed me my music career when I was sure it was dying," he said.

I turned to face him, but he continued to squint into the afternoon sun, watching Ike grapple with a low tree branch.

"I did not," I said hotly. "You deserve the recognition. And I'm serious, Rye. If you're too concerned about other preemies, we don't have to get pregnant. I've watched Jenna suffer through her pregnancy, and I saw how much my friend Evie loves her daughter, Paige, even though someone else gave birth to that beautiful little girl. It's what I feel for Ike. He's mine."

Ike dropped the branch and began to turn circles in the middle of the meadow, arms stretched out. This was what childhood should be, I thought, with a widening grin.

Rye rubbed the pad of his thumb over my cheek, and that simple caress meant so much. "Much more so than he's ever been Deirdre's."

The expression on my face felt as soft and warm as my heart. "I'm not threatened by her anymore. She's his mother."

"No," Rye said, his tone adamant. "She birthed him. You're the only *real* mom Ike's ever had."

And that's when I realized that I'd met the man who would fight for me and with me—no matter the cause or the foe. And I knew, somehow, we'd be okay. Not that we'd have the perfect fairy tale or even get along all the time, but that we'd find a way back to each other. Because we'd recognized how important we were to each other's happiness, and just how bleak our worlds would be if we had to traverse the years alone.

"I love you, Kate," he said, staring into my eyes.

"I love you, too."

"No take-backsies," he said with a wink.

CHAPTER FIFTY-FOUR | Kate

It had taken a month of planning, and now Operation Day of Fun was a go. I'd enjoyed having Rye and Ike in my condo these past few weeks.

Especially Rye after Ike fell asleep.

I tried to keep my butt in my chair and not wiggle from both excitement and nerves. Every child needed to play, and Ike was no exception. Today, the first official day of summer, seemed like a good time to show them both how glad I was to get to spend time with them.

Rye came into the living room and looked me up and down. Lust burned hot in his eyes as he took in my sundress and sparkly sandals.

"Who's ready for some fun?" I asked.

Rye scrubbed his hand over clean-shaven cheeks. I wasn't used yet to *this* version of Rye. His cheekbones were more pronounced, and I'd never considered I had a thing for bone structure until I caught myself staring.

Rye's lips quirked up. "Definitely me. Again," he said, with the rasp of lust that seemed to slide over me. I shivered. Much as I enjoyed spending the days with Ike, the nights with Rye scorched my memory.

"What are we doing?" Ike asked from his spot at my small

wooden breakfast table, pulling me out of the sensual haze Rye had spun.

"It's a surprise," I said.

"Aw. I wanna know," Ike said.

Rye shook his head, his eyes lit with pleasure. "Kate's got a surprise for us, son. I'm sure we're going to love it."

I hoped so. Now, I was nervous. I ushered them both toward my car, which held a multitude of towels, sunscreen, a floppy hat for both Ike and me, and a pair of prescription goggles that had been the hardest to come by. Once again, having rich, well-placed brothers proved handy. I'd thanked Carter profusely when he came through on the eyewear, but he'd protested, more than happy to help out a child, especially one he knew and liked.

And it was hard not to be charmed by Ike. I smiled as he settled into the booster seat I'd bought him, enjoying his constant chatter.

"These are for you," I said to Ike. "A glad-you're-seeing-better present from Carter and Regan."

Rye folded himself into the passenger seat. I could feel the weight of his gaze on me even from behind his sunglasses.

"That was nice of them."

"I maybe asked Carter to pull a few strings," I said with a shrug. "The perks of being related to the one percent."

Rye's lips twisted up. "You have a rich boyfriend, you know."

I patted his knee. "Nope. You're my sugar daddy."

Rye laughed.

I headed toward Lake Travis. The parking lot was half-filled by the time we arrived, and I chose a spot under the dubious shade of a live oak.

"We have ten minutes until we're up," I said, as I bent into the trunk of the car, pulling out the various items I'd brought. I held up the life vest and asked Ike to slip it on.

"Too big," I muttered, grabbing the one a size smaller. Rye shoved his hands into his pockets and watched, his lips tempting me, something I wasn't used to yet. I couldn't believe how much I really missed his beard. This much Rye Lawson was too potent for my concentration.

Once I was sure the flotation device's size was correct, I pulled out a long-sleeve rash guard and tugged it over Ike's head. "I got one for me and your dad, too," I said, showing Ike mine before he could do more than frown at the nylon covering him from wrist to neck to knee. I tossed Rye his, which he put on without comment. I tried, and failed, not to drool as his muscles rippled with his movements.

"You, too," I said, my nerves back full force.

Without a word, he slipped into the life vest. I removed my cover-up and pulled on my rash guard before tugging on my life vest. "Sunscreen and hats," I said.

Rye applied Ike's sunscreen while I massaged the thick, white, paste into my exposed skin.

Then, I settled my hat on my head and offered Ike the smaller version.

"What about Daddy?" Ike asked.

"Well, I wasn't sure what he'd want…" I opened the bag with the hats. Rye dug around until he found the Texas Rangers ball cap and tugged it down to his ears.

I closed the trunk, locked the car, and placed my keys in my voluminous bag that held the rest of our necessities.

"This way," I said, trotting off toward the boat dock. Rye slid up beside me and took my hand in his. He kissed my knuckles but didn't make a comment about our activity.

I stopped at the slip and gave the worker my receipt. I heard Rye's breath swoosh from his mouth in a long hiss.

"A pontoon?" he asked.

I turned toward him. "You said Ike hadn't been on the lake. This was such a big part of my growing up in Austin, and I wanted to share the fun with you."

"A boat?" Ike cried. "I get to go out in the boat? Can I drive it, Daddy? Can we fish? Look, there are poles. I'm going to catch a big one."

Rye bent down to Ike's level. "You want to fish, buddy?"

Ike nodded, eyes wide and filled with excitement behind the plastic lenses of his glasses.

"Then, let's do that," Rye said. He helped Ike onto the boat, then turned back to offer me a hand. As I stepped onto the deck, he pulled me close and pressed a kiss to my temple, with a soft thank you.

I glanced up at him, glad to see his eyes through the reflective lenses of his glasses. They were a little glassy and brimming with emotion.

"You're welcome," I said in a soft voice.

He brushed my hair back from my cheek and placed a gentle, chaste kiss on my lips. "This is amazing. But there's one problem."

My stomach clenched. "Oh?" I squeaked.

"You're going to have to man the wheel. I'm not sure I can handle it."

My eyebrows raised before my lips split in a wide grin. I saluted him sharply. "Aye, aye."

"What's that mean?" Ike asked. He was sitting on one of the benches in the middle of the boat, not quite brave enough to view the water lapping at the sides. No matter. This was about the experience—as much or as little as Ike was comfortable with.

Rye helped me untie the loops holding the boat to the dock and then I went and started the motor. I'd never been the person in charge of driving before—that task fell first to my father, then my brothers. But I smiled as I began to maneuver us from the dock and out into the lake.

My smile grew as I piloted us toward one of the coves I'd read about and studied.

Ike squealed with joy as I eased on the throttle, moving forward with just enough speed to make us bump gently on the waves.

Once we were settled in the spot, Rye dropped the anchor and double-checked the reading.

I gasped. "You have *totally* driven a boat before," I said, my voice accusatory.

"Grandpa has a boat in Lake Lewisville," Ike said as he lowered his line into the water. His tongue moved between his teeth in concentration.

I spun toward Rye with my hands on my hips, ready to demand an explanation. But he met my opening mouth with his, covering my lips with a kiss that caused my toes to curl and my head to float.

He pulled back after a moment, no doubt as aware as I was of how quickly the passion flared between us—and the fact that Ike was watching us with interest.

"You said it was a day of firsts," Rye said, his voice a bit deeper and rougher than usual. I thrilled at the hope that this was due to my kisses.

He traced his thumb along my jaw. "And I'm going to bet your brothers never let you drive."

"They didn't," I said.

"Which means you just had your first experience as the boat captain." He glanced over at Ike, who was slowly and carefully reeling in his line. Rye leaned in and pressed his lips to my ear and his hips to my bottom.

"I want to give you as many firsts as possible, Kate." He bit my ear with gentle pressure before he said, almost as if the words pulled themselves from his thoughts, "And I wish to all that is holy and real in this world, I can give you all your lasts."

CHAPTER FIFTY-FIVE | Rye

Kate looked up at me, eyes wide—like she couldn't believe her luck. I tucked a strand of her flame-bright hair behind her ear. I was the lucky one. Kate was smart, driven, and a hella good brand manager—my social media following had quadrupled since she began her first campaign featuring my work. My music downloads were up over twenty percent and the label had asked me to please, pretty please, finish my album.

Jenna had confided in Kate a couple of weeks ago that she'd never gotten around to talking to Asher—she'd been too sick, thanks to her pregnancy, so she'd never passed along my rejection. I'd called the man myself, so nervous I'd had to hold Kate's hand through the conversation.

She said I did great, but I knew she was laughing at me when I stuttered over how much I loved his early work. Asher, being the superstar that he was, took my fawning in stride and got down to the business of what I wanted out of the album.

Now that I was free to make music—and had enough cred-ibility with the record execs to make the music I really wanted, I decided to push my creativity. Asher and I talked for nearly an hour, discussing possibilities. I only let go of Kate's hand long enough to play him "Kissing Kate Goodbye"—the anchor song I envisioned for essentially a new EP.

"Hell to the yes!" Asher said. "I'm really digging the melody. And the lyrics brought a tear to my eye, man. Let's punch in that direction."

So, we worked out a schedule. It meant me traveling to Seattle, but Kate was excited to visit with Abbi, Evie, and Nessa, Jenna's friends she'd become close with over the past couple of years. We were planning our first trip for next week. I needed to take advantage before Ike started kindergarten full-time.

"Thank you for giving me my dreams," I said.

I fingered the ring in my swimsuit pocket, but before I could say something else, she darted forward, an exclamation on her lips as Ike struggled to maintain his grasp on the fishing rod.

She gripped it tightly in one hand while she showed him how to reel in his fish.

"Oof," she said when the rod's end caught her in the belly. "This is a big fish."

I sent the text I'd written earlier before I grabbed the net I'd found with the fishing gear and bent over the side. It took another few minutes before Ike and Kate managed to reel in the fish enough for me to see it.

"Holy…that *is* a big one!" I exclaimed.

"Tell me about it," Kate panted. She was doing most of the work now with Ike standing next to her, jumping up and down.

I netted the fish and pulled it out of the water. We all gaped at its size.

"That's got to be the biggest catfish I've ever seen," Kate said, awed.

Ike wanted to throw it right back but Kate talked him into

one picture with it. She then put on a pair of gloves and worked the hook from its mouth before letting the fish splash back into the lake.

And if I hadn't already been in love with her before that moment, I would have fallen hard because the look on Ike's face was total adoration. And Kate looked back at my son with the same expression on her face.

That clinched my decision and a sense of rightness settled over me.

I turned my head at the sound of a motor, lifting my chin in hello to Cam, Jenna, Carter, Regan, Jasmine, Aubrey, and my father, who all waved in response. I placed my finger to my lips and they grinned.

When Kate told me she had a surprise planned, I'd coaxed Jenna to give me the details. I knew Kate would want to celebrate with our families—and that she'd be shocked I'd managed to out-surprise her.

Jasmine, Jenna, Regan, and Aubrey all had their phones out, not willing to miss a single moment.

CHAPTER FIFTY-SIX | Kate

The gray-green water smacked the side of the boat as we rocked gently in the wake of another speedboat passing us. The thick white trail of water caused ripples that made Ike giggle. The splash of the fish caught us both in the face, and I sputtered.

"Rye, would you hand me a towel?" I asked.

I removed my sunglasses, shaking the lake water from the lenses, keeping my eyes closed. A soft, fluffy piece of terry cloth gently wiped my eyelids and cheeks.

I silently thanked my lucky stars Ike had lost interest in fishing because I did not enjoy touching their scaly bodies, even through the thick protective gloves. But I would have kept it up just to see the smile on his face.

This small boy with his too-large eyes, millions of questions, and megawatt smile made me do things I'd never thought possible. Like pilot a boat and put a worm on a hook.

Rye pulled away the towel, and I opened my eyes. My family and Rye's all smiled at us from a boat bobbing less than five feet away.

"What—"

They waved at me and I waved back, confused.

"Hey, Kate," Rye said.

His voice was low and I looked to him. I gasped, my fingers flying to my mouth.

Rye was on one knee. He took my hands, pulling them from my face.

"Thanks for noticing me down here," he said, a smile growing and warming his eyes. He'd removed his sunglasses, too. Ike stood behind him, dancing from foot to foot.

"Wh—"

"Katherine Rose, I love you," Rye said. His voice was strong and sure. My lower lip trembled.

"Ohmygod. I have to have mascara streaks on my face," I moaned.

He chuckled. "I made sure to wipe them away."

My breath hitched. "Thank you."

He winked. "I'd do anything for you. Your happiness is my happiness. Your smile lights up my day and makes me smile. I want nothing more than to wipe away your tears and love you all night."

His eyes smoldered. My cheeks bloomed with color and I cursed my pale complexion, sure my family could see the blush from their vantage point.

"He wants to marry you," Ike shouted. "And I do, too, so you can be my mommy."

I laughed, as did Rye and the rest of the crew on the other boat.

"Way to steal his thunder!" Carter called.

Rye shook his head, his mouth quirking in that sardonic way that caused my heart to flutter.

"I want to marry you and love you forever," Rye affirmed.

I glanced from Ike to Rye and back. "Come here," I said to Ike.

He maneuvered around Rye and I gave him one of my hands. I squeezed both his and Rye's.

"I would love to marry you, Ryland, and I want to be your mom, Ike. Yes! All the yeses!"

Rye stood, grimacing, and I realized he'd been on that knee for too long. But I didn't care because I threw myself into his arms and tugged his head down so I could kiss him.

"I want to see the ring!" Jenna called.

"You helped pick it out," Ike called back.

"I want to see it on her finger," Jenna shouted back. "See if it looks as good as I thought."

"Stop kissing my sister and give her the ring," Carter yelled.

I heard my mother shush him and Cam grumble about too much PDA. I pulled back, laughing.

Rye rested his forehead against mine. "It's always going to be like this, isn't it?" he asked.

I shook my head, eyes dancing. "Nope. It'll be worse when the babies are born."

He groaned as Ike hugged my waist. I pressed my cheek to his buzz cut and squeezed him back.

"I love you, Ike."

"I love you, too, Kate."

Rye slipped the ring on my finger to cheers and hoots.

I smiled as I saw the band. Tears filled my eyes. I loved haute couture and he'd come through big with the ring.

"Do you like it?" he asked.

I nodded, unable to speak.

"It's a vintage floral solitaire," Jenna called, answering my question on the diamond shape—it was unique and beautiful. So sparkly. I grinned.

"Marquis diamonds surround the central stone with pink diamond inserts all set in platinum. Now, lemme see it." Jenna's tone turned commanding. I stepped out of Ike's and Rye's embrace and climbed onto the cushioned seat on the edge of the boat. I hung over the edge and shoved my hand toward Jenna's waiting hand. She, my mother, Regan, and Aubrey all oohed and sighed.

"Rye picked it out," Jenna said. "I just went along for moral support."

Regan squinted as the diamonds caught the sunlight and burst into prisms of color. "He's got mighty fine taste," she said.

My mother leaned up on her cushion and cupped my cheek, kissing my forehead. "I'm so very happy for you, Katie."

I let the name slide because I was so deliriously happy.

Rye pulled me back into the middle of our pontoon boat, belting out "When I'm Sixty-Four." Regan and Cam joined in, harmonizing beautifully.

Our lives together wouldn't be a perfect fairy tale, but it was going to be pretty damn special. Especially when I saw Ike's face.

"I'm starving," he yelled over the final chorus.

I laughed until tears fell from my eyes.

Yup. Damn special.

EPILOGUE | Two years later

Rye rested his hand on the small of my back, leaning over my shoulder as I cradled our daughter, Lyric.

"She's so sweet sleeping."

I snorted. "It won't last long."

Rye turned so I met his eyes. "Not a chance. They should have named her Piper. The girl's got lungs."

She was loud. And sassy. And absolutely precious. I leaned back against Rye and he slid his arms around my waist.

"That baby looks damn good on you," he said, nuzzling into my neck. "I should have gotten you one months ago."

I pressed a soft kiss to his lips, then another to Lyric's chubby baby cheek. "And you didn't want any more kids."

He pressed my flat tummy back so my bottom was flush against his hips. "Oh, I wanted kids. A passel of them, just like you. But I like the way we did this."

We'd adopted Lyric two weeks before—along with her older brother, three-year-old Jeremy. We'd known she was to be ours as soon as we saw her, but hearing her name sealed the deal. The fact that Jeremy would be part of our family was a wonderful bonus.

Ike was over the moon to get not one, but two siblings. Now, at seven-and-a-half, no one would know Ike was a preemie with serious eye issues. He was gregarious, happy, and *big*. My prediction for Ike taking after his father in height and body mass might have been an underestimate.

Ike loved Lyric, but he was thrilled one of his siblings could talk and walk and do more interesting things other than sleep, cry, and poop. And Jeremy adored his big brother and followed Ike everywhere, striving to match Ike's gait and other mannerisms.

"We did good with our family," I said, laying my head against Rye's shoulder. Like Ike, Lyric had been a preemie with some serious health issues. Most of those were correcting, just as Ike's had, though they'd kept her in the NICU until her withdrawal symptoms dissipated enough to make it safe for her to come home with us.

At five months, Lyric was a pudgy cherub with big blue eyes a shade or two darker than her daddy's and strawberry blond fuzz. Yes, she could well have been our biological child, but she was *our daughter* in every way that mattered. Just as Jeremy was our son.

Rye's experience with Ike had made us the best family to care for Lyric, and I loved every moment of this new role I'd taken on—even if I was sleep-deprived and harried as I tried to get out the door to work most mornings.

Yes, I still worked for Jenna. After the birth of her son, Jameson, she'd sat me down to see if I minded reducing the shop's hours. Jenna still took on clients, but she refused to work more than three days a week. That dovetailed well into Rye's and my schedule. Rye went into the studio or to the hospital on the days I was home and he made sure to be home for Ike, and now Jeremy and Lyric, on the days I needed to be at the shop.

Asher held true to his word and produced Rye's album. He

also offered some of the complicated guitar melodies that Rye
had to work to reproduce. But he did, and his six-month tour's
success drove his next album to even greater heights. Rye didn't
add as many dates on his calendar as the execs wanted, something
he'd talked over with Cam and Asher.

Instead, he spent his time at the hospital, helping to set up a
program that had already been replicated in Seattle, Dallas, and
Nashville, with more locations for the Music for Life program
in the works.

"When are we supposed to be at the ranch?" Rye asked,
glancing over at the clock.

"In an hour," I said on a sigh. While Jeremy and Ike loved
visiting Nana Jaz, as my mom was now called, Lyric hated her car
seat and let everyone know it.

"Did Regan and Carter make it back from the Bay Area?" Rye
asked.

"Yep. They're here for a while, Regan said. So my guess is she's
got a big announcement to make," I said with a smile.

"Already?" Rye said, a smirk playing on his mouth. "Harrison
isn't quite eighteen months old."

I giggled. I still found it hilarious Carter and Cam had
named their sons—born mere days apart—twin-sounding
names. Granted, we called them James and Harry, but still.
Their twinness was a deep bond, one I'd reconciled once I came
to terms with my place in my family: right smack in the center,
where every baby sister belongs.

I kissed Lyric's tiny forehead, hopeful she, too, found that
closeness with her brothers.

Ike tore around the corner and tumbled into the room, Jeremy on his heels. Rye tensed, ready to catch either boy, but they straightened, huge grins on their faces, cars clutched in both of Jeremy's fists.

"You guys ready? Nana Jaz said Sergeant Pepper's in the lawn. I want to see her nest."

"Let me get the diaper bag and then we can try to wrangle Lyric into her seat."

"I'll talk to her, Mama," Ike said, straightening his spine.

Ike heard my brothers refer to my mother as "mama" and dubbed me with the same moniker, not to be confused with Mom D., as he called Deirdre. I think half the reason he called her that was to watch her cringe—not that she called often. Birthdays and holidays were the extent of Mom D.'s parenting forays, and that worked best for everyone involved.

"I help, too," Jeremy bellowed, causing Lyric to shudder, wake and start crying.

I glanced at Rye, who met my gaze with a resigned look and a smile.

"This ought to be fun," he said.

"Yes, it will," I said, over Lyric's cries.

Ike brought the car seat and Jeremy trotted off to use the bathroom and grab his shoes.

We met at the garage door and bundled into our minivan— safest vehicle for a family, Rye said when he brought it home the same day his last album went platinum.

I clasped his hand in mine as he pressed the start button. Ike began to sing to Lyric—one of Regan's songs, because Lyric seemed to like those best—as we rolled down the driveway.

Lyric quieted, and we made the drive in relative peace.

Yes, this was exactly what I'd hoped for.

Especially my mama opening her front door and waving from the porch as we pulled in, the boys spilling out, whooping as they headed toward the backyard.

Rye popped out Lyric's seat and we walked up to greet the rest of my family, hand-in-hand.

We'd never been a perfect fairy tale, but what we'd built together was, indeed, damn special.

ACKNOWLEDGMENTS

Daqri Bernardo of Covers by Combs created the delightful cover for this book and this series. You made something special, Daqri, and I thank you!

Thank you, Sarah Allan, for your detailed comments in the manuscript. I LOLed a couple of times. I really enjoy working with you.

Thanks to Charity Chimni for her time, understanding of AWS, and amazing proofreading skills.

And, as always, to Chris. You help me in so many ways. Thank you for all that you do (and for putting up with my crazy all these years).

ABOUT THE AUTHOR

USA TODAY Best-Selling Author Alexa Padgett's books have garnered recognition from Kirkus Reviews, The Romance Reviews, Publishers Weekly's The BookLife Prize, National Indie Excellence Awards, and Readers' Favorites. Her novel, Deep in the Heart, has been added to myriad Goodreads "Best" lists and her mystery, A Pilgrimage to Death, which she writes under the pen name J. J. Cagney, topped international Amazon bestseller lists.

Alexa spent a good part of her youth traveling. From Budapest to Belize, Calgary to Coober Pedy, she soaked in the myriad smells, sounds, and feels of these gorgeous places, wishing she could live in them all--at least for a while. And she does in her books.

She lives in New Mexico with her husband, children, and Great Pyrenees pup, Ash. When not writing, schlepping, or volunteering, she can be found in her tiny kitchen, channeling her inner Barefoot Contessa.